Born for Death

Born for Death

Society of Immortals

Book 2

Geralyn Wichers

Synecdoche Publishing

For information contact:
Synecdoche Publishing
synecdochepublishing.wordpress.com

Edited by Emily Burkey
Cover design by Tiffany Schank
Book design by Amanda Hovseth

ISBN: 978-1-945018-07-7

Library of Congress Control Number: 2017944721

First Edition: August 2017

Also By Geralyn Wichers

CHAPTER 1

London, 1921

All was quiet on the landing of the little tenement flat. Alexander laid his hand on the rough wood door and strained for any noise within, until the bells sung out from the Christ Church tower and obscured all he might have heard.

Daniel reached around him and tried the latch. It rattled, and the door opened a crack.

Alexander nodded and pushed his shoulder into the door. It opened, smoothly and quietly as the church bells fell silent. He beckoned for Daniel to follow him.

"Mr. Oswald?" Alexander called softly.

He entered into a small, cave-like room. Four walls, straight back. There was only one window, at the back, and a closed door off to the side. Alexander could hardly make out the interior, but he could make out the outline of a table, piled high.

His boot crunched onto something. Alexander glanced down. A thin glass cylinder lay in shards under his sole. Pieces skittered away, across the floorboards. A deep black stain seeped into the wood.

Alexander blew out his breath. "Mr. Oswald, are you here?"

"Oh!" Daniel's boot smashed into a wooden crate. He kicked it aside and waded into the room. "Good Lord, what a mess. What a smell!"

They surveyed the table, strewn with papers, books, boxes, and vials spilling onto the floor. Light spilled through a window about the size of a handkerchief, thick with dust motes. Prominently, in the midst of the crowded table, sat a jar.

"That is a heart." Daniel stooped and peered into the vessel, filled with blood-laced liquid. "Alexander, that's a heart!"

"Mr. Oswald?" Alexander called. He turned his face away from the heart in the jar and opened the already half-open door beyond the table. "Oswald? Oh, dear God!"

Daniel's boots clumped behind him. "Shit."

The emaciated form of Joseph Nils Oswald slumped, face down, in a claw-foot bathtub. He wore no shirt. His spine protruded, a parade of little bumps trailing down into his trousers. His kneeling legs were so thin they made wet pant legs appear empty. His hair floated in the water.

"Alas," Alexander muttered. Alexander wrestled his way out of his stiff topcoat, and then his suit coat. He tossed them over a wooden chair to remain dry. Daniel did the same, rolling his sleeves up over his muscled forearms. Alexander stepped forward, gripped Oswald by the hair and pulled his face from the water. The man's face was pale and spongy up to his ears, his nose bulbous and soft.

Daniel grabbed Oswald's legs and helped Alexander ease him, dripping, from the bathtub. They lay him on the floor, among bits of paper and some sort of fine, salt-like grit.

"He won't be long now," Daniel said. "He's been in the water quite a while."

"Indeed." He knelt over the unfortunate immortal, pressed his ear to the cold, wet chest, then felt the water-distorted neck for a pulse. "But he is not yet rebounded from death, poor soul. Does he have a bed in this pig sty?" Alexander glanced around the room.

His eyes found a pallet bed. It was soaked brown with dried blood. He swallowed hard.

"He'll be comfortable enough here," Daniel said gently, for a red stain had risen in Alexander's cheeks—anger and grief stirring within him. "Turn him on his side, for when he wakes he'll likely expel water from his lungs. Meanwhile, let us examine his quarters. We'll see to his earthly comforts once he returns to the living."

Alexander exerted titanic effort, pushed aside his feelings, and rose to his feet. They poked through the squalor of the tiny apartment, unearthing among the scattered papers detailed, neat, logical records of umpteen attempts to deny immortality. A whole portfolio was dedicated to poisons, pages about freezing, hanging, and every manner of wound.

Alexander glanced at a few of them and rushed to the window. He yanked at the latch, bile rising up in his throat. The window swung open abruptly. Alexander hung his head out and sucked in deep breaths of the damp, grimy London air. He heard a tinkle of glass and a creak behind him. Daniel cursed to himself.

"How could this have gone on for so long without Ardovinni's knowledge, on his property?" Alexander said with his head still out the window, his voice rough.

"Ardovinni's only just returned from business—no pulse in the poor devil yet—he's got a landlady here, but God knows where she was."

Alexander turned around slowly. He left the window open.

They sat on the floor beside the inert Joseph Oswald, reading through his notes, every line explaining how he'd tried to kill himself, what he'd experienced, and how long it had taken him to rebound.

Joseph lay still and silent. Alexander pressed his fingers to the man's neck every few minutes, but there was nothing to feel.

"He must have had an accomplice. There are two sets of handwriting in the notes," Daniel said, his nose in one of the fat, dog-eared notebooks. "Where's the bastard now?"

"Perhaps he knew that Ardovinni had summoned us." Alexander felt for Joseph's pulse again. "Good heavens, how long will he remain this way?"

Daniel unfolded his sturdy limbs and stood. "I'll find the landlady."

When Daniel had gone, Alexander rubbed his face with both hands and sat staring at Joseph's distorted visage, his thin chicken-like neck, his prominent ribs. They would need to bring the poor soul to the little hospice they'd created in Stuttgart. Maybe he'd recover; maybe he'd find a reason to live again.

"If only..." his words trailed into a sigh. How many immortal corpses had he sat beside over the centuries? Every time he did, it broke his heart.

Daniel returned a few minutes later. "She says there was another young man who would come and go out quite regularly, but she never spoke to him."

Alexander didn't reply. He leaned over Joseph and listened for his heart beat.

"Nothing?" Daniel shifted in the doorway.

"Nothing." Alexander got up slowly. "We'll wrap him up and carry him out. Call a cab."

They brought Joseph Oswald to Alexander's rented rooms in South Kensington and laid him out in the spare room. Daniel cooked supper, but Alexander couldn't eat. He sat beside Oswald, reading through a book of Oswald's notes by lamplight. The glow of the lamp cast weird shadows across the man's still face. Alexander kept glancing at him every time he heard Daniel move in the other room, only to see Oswald as motionless as before.

Alexander went to bed at his usual time but kept waking every hour, getting up, going to Oswald, feeling for a pulse and feeling nothing.

Each time, he returned to his bed with a sick feeling in his stomach. Finally he slept.

In the morning, Daniel shook Alexander awake. "He's not rebounded yet."

"What?" Alexander swung his legs off the bed, scrubbing his eyes. He staggered into the other room. In the bed the grey face of Joseph Oswald protruded from the sheet he'd been swathed in. Alexander pulled back the fabric. The man's skin was purple-grey, green in places. He touched the man's hand. The skin was pliable, but the fingers were stiff.

"Good Lord," Alexander said, "he is in rigor mortis, Daniel. This man is dead."

Daniel's face contorted. "I know, but that isn't possible."

"Leave him be. We'll wait."

But twelve hours later, Joseph Oswald was still dead. By the next morning, he'd begun to stink.

∞

Joseph Oswald's coffin, a flimsy wooden box, landed hard at the bottom of the grave. Alexander winced and turned away as the two gravediggers stepped back from the gaping hole, as if he, or the other immortals standing around the grave, might want to say a few words. Daniel, beside him, kicked at the clumps of dirt at his feet. The Scottish woman, Idina McCullough, stood across the grave from him, peering down into the depth of the earthen hole from under the velvet brim of her straw hat. A man stood behind her, just far enough to appear at a respectful distance, but close enough to be able to hold Idina's gloved fingertips, behind her back. He was Cyrus Fontaine, an ebony-skinned son of an African woman and an Englishman who must have carried the immortal seed.

Giovanni Ardovinni stood on the other side of Alexander. The Italian had his chin resting on one gloved hand, his lips pressed tightly together. Alexander could see his dark eyes darting back and forth, distant. It had been Ardovinni's rooming house Oswald had died in, and somehow he'd found out that the man was dead before Alexander or his lawkeepers could tell him.

It seemed Ardovinni had known the man at least a little—enough to show genuine, but brief distress at his death. It was more than Alexander could say for himself.

Alexander sighed, and nodded to the workmen. As the first shovel of earth fell, he cleared his throat and turned away. Ardovinni and Daniel followed along behind him. Idina and Cyrus lingered for a moment, then followed.

"But what if—" Ardovinni began.

"He won't," Daniel said without looking over. "Putrefaction had set in. He was good and dead."

Ardovinni ran his fingers through his dark curls before replacing his top hat. Alexander thought the stiff English clothes still looked strange on him, though he had been wearing them for just over a year.

They passed by the dark, stone church and paused on the street.

"Until we can determine what has happened, there will be no speaking of this," Alexander said to Ardovinni, quietly. "With your permission, we'll retain Oswald's rooms while we investigate. Miss McCullough and Mr. Fontaine will assist us."

"Certainly." Ardovinni's eyes fixed upon the muddy road at his boots. Alexander could practically see his mind spinning, as his had been since they'd found Joseph Oswald dead, churning like the English rain clouds above them.

Thunder crackled.

Ardovinni lifted his head, looked down the street. "If I'd been here...if I hadn't spent so much time on business, or if I'd paid more attention to what was happening on my own property...I should have, at the very least, known he was unwell!"

Alexander sighed. "Good heavens, we were right here in this city."

"There are a lot of people in this city," Daniel growled, "and a great many streets between Whitechapel and the immortals in

South Kensington. You can't blame yourself when the man cut himself off from us. Blaming won't change the fact that he is dead, and we haven't the faintest idea why. Ardovinni, we'll keep the apartment."

"It's yours as long as you need it." Ardovinni paused. An automobile rattled by. Alexander realized they were standing before the door of the rooming house. Ardovinni stared up at the door. "The landlady said there was another man she saw coming and going. Did you determine who that was?"

"Not yet," Daniel said, "but we haven't read all of Oswald's notes yet."

Ardovinni turned on his heel to go. "I will look into it myself."

"Do you think he'll find anything?" Daniel's forehead wrinkled as he squinted after the receding Italian.

Alexander turned and trudged up the stairs toward the rooms where Joseph died. Daniel followed. "It wouldn't surprise me at all. He has an uncanny way of knowing things that I envy. He'll take care of his own."

"Who are his own?" Cyrus asked quietly, behind them.

"A good question, love." Idina unpinned her hat, and slipped past him, up the steps.

Daniel said to Alexander behind his hand, "Would it be too soon to begin investigating?"

"Go to it," Alexander said as he paused in the doorway of Oswald's flat. Idina already stood in the center of the room, picking at the things on the table with one hand, and lifting her narrow, black skirt off the dusty floor with the other.

"Where to start?" Daniel rubbed at his jaw.

"Oh, Mr. Fontaine! You don't have to do that." Idina brushed her hand across Cyrus's shoulder as he scrubbed furiously at the one intact chair in the room.

Daniel already sat, cross-legged, on the floor, reading one of Oswald's journals.

"Pfah, it won't come clean," Cyrus said. His handkerchief was grey with dirt.

"Pfah!" Idina parroted. "I wish I could have my tartan and my wool back and stop going about like a mincing lady. Then perhaps the man I love would let me sit on a dirty seat."

"Even then it might be very difficult." Cyrus straightened, and smiled. His teeth were brilliantly white in his dark face. He struggled out of his coat and laid it across the grimy plush seat. "Your chair, Miss McCullough."

"Thank you," Idina sat primly on the edge of the chair and gave him a tight little smile. "Hand me a journal, Mr. Gunther, there's a dear."

Daniel handed her a leather-bound book.

Alexander turned his back on them and began sifting through the detritus on the wooden kitchen table. He picked up the canning jar with the heart in it. "Daniel," he said, "is this a human heart?" He held it out to the side, and Daniel took it.

"Yes, human," he said.

"It's his," Idina said in a remarkably cool voice. "He says it right here. His accomplice cut his heart out. He rebounded within four hours."

"Good Lord!" Cyrus peered over her shoulder at the book, then at the jar in Daniel's hands. "Someone cut out his heart?"

"His beating heart." Idina frowned, but light gleamed in her eyes. "Whoever we search for, we know one thing;" a vague grimace of a smile crossed her lips, "he's a sick, sick bastard."

CHAPTER 2

Dresden, Germany. Present Day

Jack's head lolled in time to the potholes on the road up to Schwalenburg. His body was limp, curled up in the back seat, but his mind could not relax. He forced his eyes shut, but instantly saw Lia's raised hands and the winking, whining blade of the circular saw. Just before it bit into his skin, his eyes popped open and his lungs heaved.

"You alright, Jack?" Idina asked from the front seat.

"I feel like shit, thank you," Jack said. His head flopped against the back of the seat.

She glanced back. Her green eyes glinted. "A stupid question. I apologize."

Jack's breath shuddered out. He just wanted to sleep, to see the vision of Mary Rose again, see her blue eyes and gossamer skin, feel that peace one more time.

The car stopped and turned off. His eyes flickered shut, but he forced them open. The door opened by his feet, and cold air whisked under the wool coat covering him, across his bare chest.

"Jack," Idina said softly, "can you get up? We're here."

He brushed her hand off his arm as he stood. His shaky knees galvanized and he staggered toward the high wooden doors of Schwalenburg.

It was Alexander who swung the door open. His face went pale.

"That bad, eh?" Jack looked up at him.

A hoarse laugh burst from Alexander. He grabbed Jack and hugged him hard. "Yes, that bad Jack. That bad. Oh God!"

Jack looked down. Beyond Cy's wool coat, his jeans were brown and patchy with blood, and so were his shoes. The white laces were mottled burgundy. Jack reached up and touched his face. Something flaked off under his fingers. He pulled his hand away and saw dried bits of blood on his fingertips.

Jack swallowed hard.

"Daniel is still processing the scene. Uh..." Idina glanced at Jack and pressed her lips together. "Let's get this man inside and call the doctor. I'll fill you in."

"You didn't... you didn't catch them?" Jack's chest clamped up. He pressed his hand to the scar seam. His fingers were icy on his bare skin.

"No," Idina said softly, "but Cyrus is sending Marcus Koenig here with one of Hardwin's guys."

"But Lia, she…" Jack swayed against the door.

Alexander grabbed his shoulders and forced him into the lobby of Schwalenburg's keep. "You need to get cleaned up and you need to sleep. The lawmen know how to find people. You just rest. I'm going to have the doctor look you over."

"I'm fine." Jack tried to keep his voice steady, and stand straight.

"I'm sure you're whole," Alexander supported him across the lobby, into a corridor opposite the offices. Idina followed behind. "But fine, you are not. Idina, can you please ask Anastasie to find Jack some clothes?" Alexander said over his shoulder. He ushered Jack through a door, into a hall that unfolded into an apartment, lit by the bright white light of the winter sun. Jack looked past the kitchenette to the open bedroom door.

Alexander pushed him gently toward the bathroom. "I'll have clothes for you by the time you get out. Doctor den Hollander will be here by then."

Jack shut the bathroom door. It took him a moment before he moved again. His pants were stiff with dried blood. His underwear was soaked by it. He undressed and stood naked, staring at his gore-streaked body in the little bathroom mirror. The lines Lia's knife made were completely gone now.

Jack began to shiver. He shoved the hot water faucet open. As steam began to fill the little washroom, Jack stepped under the scalding water, but even the hot water couldn't stop him from shaking. The bar of soap slipped out of his hand and skittered across the bottom of the tub, obscured by the warm fog. Jack slumped forward and leaned his head against the tiles. His eyelids sagged.

"I will kill you! I will cut out your heart!"

Jack's head jerked up, ears ringing with the scream of the rotary saw. His heart hammered painfully in his chest.

"Get it together," he groaned. Really, what had Lia done that he'd never done to himself? He got out of the shower and sat on the closed lid of the toilet with his head in his hands and water streaming down his back. He tried to collect his thoughts. As he did, he heard movement outside his door, and a soft, feminine voice said over the still-running shower, "Jack, here are clothes. I'll leave them outside the door."

Jack raised his head and flipped off the faucet.

He stuck his head out the door and found a pair of sweats, a little short for his six-foot two-inch frame, sitting beside the door on top of a white t-shirt. Jack snaked his arm out and pulled them into the bathroom. When he'd dressed, he left his bloody clothes piled in the brown-ringed bathtub and wandered out rubbing at his temples, which had begun to pound.

Alexander sat on a chair by the little kitchenette. His head drooped nearly to his chest, but he lifted it when Jack came out. "How are you feeling?"

"Why the fuck do people ask me that?" Jack lifted his head. "Can't you just give me a bottle of whiskey and a handful of painkillers?"

Alexander got up stiffly. "Doctor den Hollander will likely help you with that. I'll tell him you're out. Why don't you lie down?"

Jack eyed him, and walked into the small bedroom. The cold sunlight fell across a double bed with a simple, modern headboard. He threw himself down on it. Damn the doctor. If he couldn't have a drink, couldn't he sleep? There wasn't anything wrong with him.

A soft cough by the door brought Jack's head up.

A thin, blond-haired man gazed at him from behind tortoise-shell glasses. "Mr. Krause, I'm Doctor den Hollander." He had a stethoscope around his neck, hanging out of the collar of his grey sport coat.

"I'm fine." Jack sat up. His head emptied and he nearly fell back on the bed.

"I'm just doing my due diligence. Sir Alexander's order." The slim doctor set down a leather bag beside the bed. He put his stethoscope in his ears. "May I?"

"Knock yourself out." Jack tugged up his shirt.

The metal circle was icy against his clammy skin.

"I'm sure you'll find a heartbeat," Jack said, shivering. "It's a b-b-brand new—" His throat clamped up tight. Damn it! He was not breaking down on this chump.

Doctor den Hollander pressed his lips together. If he'd noticed Jack's hitch of breath, he ignored it. Silently, he took Jack's vitals. As he released the blood pressure cuff he said, "You're dehydrated. Otherwise, you need food and rest." He snapped his bag shut and straightened. "I'll bring you water now, and have Anastasie bring a sports drink."

He narrowed his eyes at Jack. "I'll see you again in two or three days. I want to assess your mental state."

"I'm sure you will." Jack just wanted to put his pounding head back on the pillow. "Is Marcus okay?"

The doctor, halfway to the door, turned back, "Mr. Koenig is catatonic."

"Shit," Jack said, taken aback.

"I'll see you in two days." The doctor withdrew from the room without another word. Jack lay back and wrestled the covers around himself.

He lay, staring up at the bare, oaken beams on the ceiling. His head throbbed like a bass drum.

Catatonic wouldn't be so bad right now, if it meant he could sleep without nightmares. Still, Jack's eyes flickered shut. He was too tired to resist.

"I will cut out your heart!"

The saw screamed down toward him.

Jack jerked, half awake.

"Ahh," a woman's voice said, as if she were rocking a small child to sleep, "poor soul."

Jack opened his eyes. In the half-dark, all he saw was a halo of blonde hair. He let out a strangled cry.

"Oh!" Anastasie drew back. "I'm sorry, Jack."

Jack groaned and sat up. "I guess I was out cold," he said roughly.

"I'm so sorry to wake you." Anastasie set a bottle of sports drink down on the bedside table. "Drink some of this before you go back to sleep. Dr. den Hollander asked me to bring it to you." She slipped out of the room.

Jack leaned against the headboard and pressed the heels of his hands to his eyes. If he was going to get any sleep he'd have to take something, or drink something—and not the cherry sports drink sitting in the ring of lamplight. Still, he picked up the bottle and cracked it open. The salty-sweet, watery fruit drink moistened his dry lips. He drank half, and set it down again. As he did, he noticed the small, old-fashioned alarm clock on the bedside table. It was five past eight. It had been mid-afternoon when they'd brought him in. He had slept after all.

Jack tipped his head back against the wall. So it had been about ten hours since Lia sliced him open.

The images flickered in front of his eyes in random order: Lia screaming with the saw in her hands, a red hole punched through his chest, running through a concrete meat cooler with a phone clutched in his hand, the phone, Alannah's sleepy voice squeaking with panic.

"Shit," Jack breathed. He straightened up in bed, imagining Alannah back in Winnipeg, paralyzed with anxiety. He glanced around. Had his phone stayed in Alexander's house? That was such a long time ago.

With a sigh, Jack slung his legs over the side of the bed and got up. The blankets dropped onto the hardwood floor beside the bed. He took a glance at his sweatpants and his baggy t-shirt as he padded across the room to the door. Decent enough, he figured, as he opened the door a crack.

Soft voices filtered in: a quiet feminine tone, and a slightly hoarse baritone, both in French. Jack swung the door just wide enough to stick his head out, and met the icy-blue eyes of a man sitting at the little kitchenette table outside. He had buzzed short blond hair, and a neat beard that was about the same length. Underneath his black, leather jacket, he had a serious set of shoulders on him. His face drooped with fatigue.

Anastasie sat on the man's knee, cuddled against him, but she straightened up and stood when she saw Jack. "Jack! I'm sorry, were we disturbing you?"

"Um," Jack said, "I was just wondering if anyone had called Alannah." His eyes strayed to the stranger again. He'd seen the guy before in Alannah's photo album. He forgot the name.

"Alexander called her." The stranger stood and laid one hand on Anastasie's shoulder, "She knows I found you."

"But she's okay?"

The man paused. "She's had some other excitement today, but as best I know she's alright."

That didn't sound particularly reassuring. "I want to call her," Jack said, taking a step forward.

"I doubt you'll be able to right now."

"Why? What time is it?" Alannah's ex-boyfriend, that's who that was. Jack still couldn't remember his name.

The man rubbed at one eye. "Listen, I'll explain. Take a seat. Would you like something to eat?"

"No, uh..." Actually, his belly was gnawing at him. "Yeah, yeah I guess so."

The other man gave Anastasie's shoulder a little squeeze and shot her a questioning look. She slipped out of the room without a word. "I'm Daniel Gunther," he said.

"Yeah?" Jack dropped into the flimsy metal chair across the little round table from him. "So you found me?"

"Yeah." Daniel dropped into his seat again and sighed heavily. "Thanks to your description we were able to find you. It was an out-of-business abattoir."

"But did you find Lia?" his voice squeaked as he asked. Jack cringed.

Daniel shook his head.

"Then what are you doing here?" Jack jerked one hand toward the door. "I'm fine! Go chase her."

A hint of red flushed Daniel's cheeks. He poked his finger toward a laptop, sitting open on the square foot of counter beside the two-burner kitchenette stove. The screen was split between a scrolling list of unintelligible letters and numbers, and a plain search box with a blinking cursor. "I was. I am."

"And?"

"Cyrus and Idina are pursuing a possibility. A couple of Hardwin's guys are on it. And when you're ready, you're going to give me as much information as you can." He paused. "We found her phone where you dropped it."

"So you know what I look like when I've been shot in the head," Jack said.

Daniel flinched. "And straight out of the freezer. I'll get your formal statement tomorrow."

"You can ask me now."

Daniel looked sharply. "You need to rest."

Jack shook his head. "I can't rest. Ask me now."

"That's probably not a good idea." Daniel set his palms down flat on the table, shoulder's set.

Jack rose halfway out of his chair. "How the fuck am I supposed to rest while those psychopaths are out there? Just take my goddamn statement. When I rest is my own problem."

"Actually, it is my problem," Daniel retorted. "You're one of us. You are my problem."

Jack sat down.

For a long moment, Daniel didn't say anything further. Finally he rubbed his eyes and said, "Listen, I don't want Anastasie to hear this."

"No." For once, Jack was glad Mary Rose was gone. She could never hear about what had happened to him.

"I'll send her out when she comes back." Daniel got up and bent over the laptop. Occasionally he made a few keystrokes. His phone buzzed. He glanced at it, then sent a text.

A few minutes later the door creaked open, and Anastasie walked in carrying a tray. She smiled tightly at him. Her pale face was rigidly composed. She set the tray in the center of the table and began opening containers of food: a basket of soft, white rolls, cold sausage, pickles, and some sort of pale orange cheese. She leaned on Daniel's shoulder again and opened her mouth to say something.

"Mon Coeur," Daniel cut her off gently, "will you go? I need to interview Jack."

Her lips pressed together again. She nodded and slipped back out of the apartment.

"Eat something." Daniel gestured to the food with one hand as he pulled a phone from his pocket.

Jack picked up a roll and began to butter it.

Daniel set the phone between then on the table and tapped the screen. "I'm going to record this, alright?"

"Fine," Jack said thickly, through a mouthful of bread.

An hour later, the food sat mostly untouched between them and Daniel and Jack sat slumped, without looking at each other. Jack had told the whole story, starting with meeting Lia at the club.

"God, I'm such an ass." Jack laughed ruefully under his breath. "The one time I slip up. I never—"

Daniel's lips twitched but he did not smile. He tapped the pause on the phone screen. "I'm fairly certain that's how she got Koenig too. Don't beat yourself up."

"Koenig's talking?"

"No, I found texts on her phone between them. They were of a romantic nature." He tapped the resume button on the recording app, and indicated for Jack to continue.

Jack went through what he could remember of his deaths, breaking his arm, goading Lia into shooting him so his arm would heal, to escaping from the abattoir only to be shot again.

He stumbled over the details he'd relived so often: the whining saw, Lia screaming, white hot agony and the plunge into death. When Jack looked up, Daniel's lips were pressed together so tightly they were white rimmed.

"Is that all?" Daniel said softly.

Jack licked his parched lips. "Yes, that's all." He wasn't about to let Daniel record for all posterity how he'd dreamed of Mary Rose as he lay dying.

Daniel turned the phone off, and sat flipping it over and over in his hands. He rocked slowly back and forth, as if searching for more words. Finally he just shook his head and slapped the phone down on the table. "You should get some more rest, Jack. I'll give you something if you need it."

"Yeah," Jack muttered, "I'll take whatever you've got."

Daniel gazed down at his hands. "I'm sorry. This is our fault. I'm sorry."

Jack staggered to his feet. "Well, sorry doesn't fix shit does it?"

Daniel grimaced. "Indeed not." He stood stiffly. "I'll get you a sleeping pill."

Ten minutes later Jack wandered back into the bedroom. His arms and legs had begun to feel like dead weight, and he didn't think it was the sleeping pill kicking in. He flopped down on the bed and rolled up in the covers.

As his eyes slid shut, the images of the day began to flicker in front of him. This time, however, he fell into a dreamless sleep.

∞

"London? Why?"

A haggard Cyrus slumped across the little dinner table from him, shoveling scrambled eggs into his mouth with one hand, and leaning on the other. He paused and swallowed before saying, "Giovanni Ardovinni paid Alannah a visit yesterday with an unknown guest who was rather threatening."

Jack's fists balled up on top of the table. "Is she okay?"

"Shaken up. Tired. She landed at Heathrow about an hour and a half ago."

Jack sat staring at his plate of eggs for a minute before asking, "Yeah, but London?"

"Idina-a-a—" Cyrus's jaws cracked in a yawn, "—and I own a flat there."

"Can I call her or something?"

"Cy?" Idina burst into the little apartment, bringing a cool draft from the castle hall. "Daniel got into the laptop!"

Cyrus jumped up. The little metal chair tottered before falling onto all four feet again. "I'm coming."

"Me too." Jack pushed away from the table.

"No," Cyrus said with a glance toward Idina, "you can't."

Jack jerked one hand in the air. "Stop treating me like a goddamn invalid and help me catch—"

"No," Idina held up her hand. "This is an official investigation and we won't have you running willy-nilly through it."

Jack opened his mouth.

"No." Idina pierced him with a gaze that both forbade him to question, and begged him to challenge her one more time so she'd have an excuse to hit him.

"Can I call Alannah?" he asked meekly as he dropped back into his chair. "My phone is at Alexander's place."

Cyrus pulled a smart phone from his pocket and slid it across the counter. "It's not locked. She's in the contacts, but she might not be in her hotel yet."

"Okay."

Idina and Cyrus slipped out. Jack harrumphed and stabbed his fork into his eggs. Belatedly he asked the empty room, "Where is the old guy anyway?" He hadn't seen Alexander since he'd arrived at Schwalenburg. He shrugged and shoved the bite of eggs into his mouth. As he chewed he flipped through Cyrus's phone until he found Alannah's number. He texted her: "Hey, this is Jack on Cyrus's phone. Are you okay?"

About a minute later the phone buzzed with her text: "Jack! Are you okay?"

"Fine. Can I call?"

"I'm in a taxi," she texted. "Give me an hour. I'll call you."

Fine? Was that what he'd tell her? He was fine?

He was fine, wasn't he?

Jack dropped the phone onto the table, rattling his fork and knife. He leaned back limp in the chair. He didn't know. It was the most bizarre feeling, sitting here, knowing that twenty-four hours before he'd been running from the killing plant in bare feet, dodging bullets. He didn't feel any different, but he didn't feel the same either.

About an hour later, Jack lay flat on his back on the bed with Cyrus's phone beside his head on the pillow. The phone began to buzz, long and sustained vibrations. Jack rolled over to swipe the screen. As he sat up, Alannah's face appeared on the phone screen framed by her coffee-colored curls.

"Jack!" Her face distorted and her eyes grew huge as she leaned in. "What happened to your hair?"

"What?" Jack palmed his head and felt the patchy stubble where curls had been. "Oh that." He had the briefest flashback, the whine of the razor in his ear, the bite as it nicked his scalp.

"Alexander wouldn't tell me anything." Her face focused again. "He implied that you had a... traumatic time."

Jack barked a laugh. "Yeah, that sounds about as detailed as what they told me about you."

Alannah's nose wrinkled. "I'm sorry, but really, Alexander told me nothing and when he tells me nothing I know it's bad, and I sat through that whole stupid flight thinking about it."

"It, uh, kind of was bad..." Jack fought to keep his face very straight while he worked out which bits to leave out—the near sex with Lia for instance. "Well... I went to a club a few nights ago, and I met this immortal bitch who ended up being a psychopath intent on finding a way to kill me and some guy named Marcus. Daniel found me, and Idina and Cyrus whisked me back to Schwalenburg," he ended lamely.

Her face was so still that Jack thought the phone had frozen.

"I'm fine," Jack said quickly. "Really."

Her dark eyes peered anxiously into his. "Are you?" She bit her lip. "You really do look bad, Jack. You can tell me about it—you can."

"I just told Daniel everything. I don't want to rehash it." A tightness began to grow in his throat, the verge of tears. He pressed his lips tightly together.

"Jack," Alannah said softly. Her face wobbled on the small screen, and Jack caught a glimpse of two generic, hotel beds behind her.

Jack's throat clenched so tight he felt like he was strangling. "When she, uh, when Lia tried to kill me the last time..."

Alannah waited, her eyes soft and earnest.

"I—" he swallowed hard against the lump in his throat. "Forget it. You don't need any more trouble on your plate."

"Oh Jack." Even on the tiny screen, he could see tears filling Alannah's eyes.

Jack swiped at his nose. "You okay?"

"Yeah, I'm okay," Alannah said in a small voice. She glanced around like she was surveying her hotel room. "I'm pretty calm. It's weird. I guess I'm too tired to be upset anymore. It was a long flight."

"What the heck happened?" Jack asked gruffly. "Cy said something about some cat named Ardovinni showing up and getting rowdy."

"Rowdy?" Her lips formed a faint smile. "His friend was a little threatening. I shoved your gun in his face."

Jack stared at her a moment.

"I'm not a complete ninny," Alannah said.

Jack raised an eyebrow. "Indeed," he muttered. He leaned back against the pillows. "But really, who is Ardovinni? Why did he chase you out of Winnipeg?"

"No, it's not Ardovinni, it's..." she ran her teeth over her bottom lip, "it has to do with Zoran. I thought the man with Ardovinni might be... might be his son."

Jack just looked at her.

"It's complicated, alright?" she said, her forehead furrowing. "I was probably wrong, but it got me out of Winnipeg. Are you happy?"

"No, I'd like to find Ardovinni and Zoran's kid and smash their teeth in. Why the heck were they knocking on your door?"

"I don't really know."

Nearly a minute passed in silence, with Alannah staring off to the side where Jack imagined the window was.

"Are you going to be okay?" Jack asked softly. He leaned forward, toward the screen.

"Yeah." Alannah shifted in her seat. "I don't know if I'll leave my hotel room at all. I just feel like curling up in the center on the bed and sleeping until Wednesday. I-I think Idina will come soon."

"She's going through Lia's stuff right now."

Her voice was nearly inaudible, "She'll come when she can. She told me. I can survive until then." She smiled weakly and said as an afterthought, "After all, there is a Starbucks in the lobby."

Jack clutched the phone and rocked slowly back and forth. It seemed there was nothing left to say but he didn't want to hang up and leave her alone, or to be alone.

Alannah straightened. "What are you going to do now?"

Jack glanced around the room. All that filled it was the bed he lounged on, a wardrobe, and a bookshelf. All the titles were in German. "Well, I dunno. I don't even have a TV."

"Well," she shrugged, "I really need a nap, okay? I'll talk to you later."

"Okay." Jack sighed.

Her image abruptly froze and then 'Call Disconnected' appeared on the screen. Jack sighed and dropped Cyrus's phone on the bed beside him. He slid down so his head could rest on the pillow. What was he going to do?

Heck, even if he found something to do today, what would he do the day after? What was he going to do in Germany? Be a goddamned immortal castle janitor? He didn't speak a word of German.

Jack curled up and wrapped his arms across his chest. Maybe he'd go to London. At least they spoke English over there. Of course, he had a feeling his babysitters wouldn't be letting him out of their sight.

Jack's head drooped on the covers. "Hmmf," he grunted to the empty bedroom, "do you suppose that since Cy gave me his phone he minds if I use it for other things?"

It didn't even have a password.

In the end, Jack passed the next hour by watching videos, and then on a whim, googled Clarissa's name. Her social media profiles popped up. He lay the phone on the bed beside him and stared at her profile picture: Clarissa, backlit by a bright winter sun, with a few blond tendrils peeking from under a chunky-knit cap and cheeks pink with cold. She was snuggled up against a smiling young man in a khaki green jacket.

Deep sorrow sunk into his chest, right where his new heart was beating.

∞

"Jack... Jack." A gruff voice woke Jack up and made him lift his head. Cyrus's phone still lay beside him. It was Cyrus in the doorway, smiling a little sheepishly.

"Oh." Jack sat up. He picked up the phone and tossed it at the man in the doorway.

Cy caught it easily and slid it into his pocket. "There is lunch."

"Okay, I'm coming."

Cyrus withdrew from the room and closed the door. A waft of savory aroma breezed into the room with the gust from the closing door.

Jack flung himself off the bed. On his way to the door he passed by the mirror and caught a glimpse of himself. "Geez." He paused, rubbing his shorn head and gazed at his haggard face, the dark circles under his eyes. "I look like a concentration camp survivor." He went to the bathroom and washed his face with freezing cold water, brushed some water over his stubble-covered head. He was so glad Mary Rose couldn't see him.

In the little kitchen, Daniel sat in one of the flimsy chairs, tipped back on two legs. He punctuated his words with jabs from his hand. In the background, Idina and Cy were dishing up food onto plates. Anastasie had gone. Alexander sat across from Daniel. Both of their faces were pale and weary.

"I'm so tired of this," Daniel said. He dragged his hand across his eyes, "I'm more than four hundred years old. I should be settled down somewhere, working at a desk job. Not this. Not folding a man's chest back together and praying that he'll rebound, hoping for his sake that he doesn't. Dear God."

Jack remained, frozen, in the doorway. No one had seen him yet.

"Just when I think I've seen every way an immortal can attempt suicide. Dear God, Alexander. How many sons of bitches have I scraped up and sat beside until they rebounded and tried to do it again?" Daniel shook his head. "How long before I go stark, raving mad?"

"I've said it before, and I'll say it again." Alexander leaned forward. "You don't have to stay in my forces just to please me. You're your own man, Daniel, just please wait until we have this sewn up."

"Or you can train a replacement," Cyrus said. He set a plate in front of Daniel. Jack caught a whiff of marinara sauce.

"Perhaps if you and Anastasie marry—" Alexander began.

Jack spoke up then. "How did they get you into the law force in the first place, Daniel?"

The airborne feet of Daniel's chair hit the tile floor. He fixed Jack with bloodshot blue eyes. "They get you while you're young."

Alexander snorted.

"Train me." Jack blinked as the words came from his mouth. "I want to help you catch Lia."

"Did you hear what I just said?" Daniel stared at him.

Jack plopped into an empty chair. "Every word."

A hint of red crept up Daniel's neck. "I'm sorry. It wasn't as if you did it to yourself."

"Well, wait around a little longer..." Jack said snidely.

Alexander fixed him with a tired stare. "Given your past few days, we won't even consider inducting you into the service right now."

"Well, I've got to do something," Jack said weakly.

"We will," Daniel growled. "Don't listen to me. A bit of lunch and I'm back to work."

No, I said I have to do something. Jack slumped in the chair, but his eyes wandered to the plate that Idina carried toward him. He picked up the fork and dug it into the pasta, twirling it around on the fork without inserting it into his mouth.

"The truth is," Alexander said, matter-of-factly, "they've gotten away. We have Lia's phone, and one of their computers. We have a lot of information to process, and for the time being, things won't be exciting."

"Don't patronize me," Jack snapped around a mouthful of pasta. "It's not excitement I'm looking for."

"Forgive me," Alexander breathed. "What I meant was—"

"There is a real chance that we will need more information from you," Daniel said firmly. "Unfortunately right now there is nothing else you can do."

"That's great." Jack laid his fork down. "Well, I'll be here when you need me. If you have a second, maybe I could get a TV or something. Heck, a book."

Daniel's mouth twitched. "I'm sure we can set you up."

"You're not officially one of us," Alexander said slowly, "so we can't lawfully force you to stay, but for the sake of the investigation..."

"What about Alannah?" Jack asked.

"I'm flying out tomorrow morning," Idina said.

"Let me come."

Idina glanced at Alexander and Daniel. "I, uh..."

Jack sagged back against the chair. "Okay, never mind. I just..."

If he was to do nothing, to go nowhere, what was there to shield him from the ghost of Lia and her saw?

CHAPTER 3

London, Present Day

"Here you go: Home sweet flat." Idina swung the door wide and stepped back so Alannah could pass by.

"This is nice." Alannah dropped her suitcase and her coat beside the little pub-style table and unbuttoned the top button on her coat as Idina flicked the light on. Anything would be nice after the endless orbit between the standard four walls of the hotel room, and the Starbucks downstairs. The flat was a cozy, cottagey sort of place with roughed up wood cabinets and mismatched chairs at the tall, narrow table. A small flat screen TV was mounted over the little fireplace, opposite a stuffed bookcase. Idina flung back the burgundy velvet curtains, and bright London sunlight infiltrated every corner of the flat.

Idina dropped into the brown leather couch. "Hmm, I'd forgotten how nice it was. I haven't been here for a year at least. Last time I was in London, I stayed with a friend—a friend I'll put you in touch with here. Her name is Louisa."

"How do I know I can trust your friends?" Alannah asked softly.

"I can vouch for Louisa." Idina fingered the end of her red braid. "They're all quiet, upstanding immortal citizens as far as I know." She looked up at Alannah. "You can't guarantee everyone, Alannah, and you will not hide in here. I forbid it. There's a nice little immortal society here, far better than what you had in Winnipeg."

Alannah blew out her breath and balanced on the arm of the Queen Anne chair. "I know. I just... I just..." Her eyes began to well up. She gritted her teeth. "I hate this. I hate being scared. I don't even want to be here!"

Idina gazed at her with limpid green eyes. "Jack wanted so badly to come visit you. He's having a rough go of it."

She could only imagine.

Idina stuck her hands into the pockets of her leather jacket and sighed. "So, there are definitely no groceries worth eating in this house. Do you want to get something to eat?"

"I suppose." Alannah wrapped her arms around herself. If she went out to eat with Idina, maybe she could find a grocery store on the block, and maybe she'd get enough food to last a few days—in case she couldn't work up the courage to leave.

"Well, I haven't eaten much of anything yet today, so I guess just humor me." Idina stood up.

In spite of herself, Alannah soon found herself across from Idina in a little cafe with coffee and a huge cob salad in front of her. They both shoveled it in at less than lady-like rates.

"So," Idina said after she'd wiped her mouth on one of the burgundy cloth napkins, "I'll also be collecting your statement about your *visitors*."

Alannah wrinkled her nose and pushed the last few leaves of lettuce around in the dressing. Her phone, in the pocket of her coat, drew her like a magnet, like a guilty secret. She'd never sent the picture of the blond stranger to Alexander—she just couldn't work up the courage.

Idina pulled out a tablet computer and unfolded a keyboard from the case. "I'm ready to take notes whenever you're ready to talk."

"Well, one of them was obviously Giovanni Ardovinni..."

Idina nodded as she tapped the screen of her tablet. "I talked to Hardwin's keepers. They thought Ardovinni was in Los Angeles, and they have no idea who he might be travelling with. But I was a bit sparse on the details; I didn't tell them what you told Alexander, that Ardovinni claimed his friend was the immortal son of two immortals."

"About that," Alannah recalled Alexei's haunting ebony eyes and gnawed at her bottom lip. She pulled out her phone. "I have a picture of him."

"Oh!" Idina reached for the phone. "Why didn't you send this to me?"

Alannah held out the phone to her, Alexei's picture on the screen. Idina took it, started a little, then pressed her lips together tightly. For a full minute she didn't say anything.

"Alannah, you never met Cosima did you?" Idina asked. Her forehead pinched together in tight vertical lines. She put the phone down on the table. "Because the resemblance is quite remarkable."

Alannah swallowed. "I thought he looked like Alexander."

"He does," Idina said quietly. "I only thought of Cosima first because of the—"

"Eyes," Alannah said, "the eyes. This man, h-his name was Alexei."

"You didn't send this to Alexander, did you?"

Alannah stared at her hands. "I was afraid, and I didn't want to jump to conclusions. It could be a distant descendant. But since Alexander *did* sleep with her..."

"Oh," Idina breathed. "Oh."

"You didn't know...?" Guilt pricked at her. Alannah realized Idina hadn't known this. Daniel knew, she knew that, but perhaps Alexander hadn't told any other member of his inner circle.

A long silence passed.

"Ohhh." Idina leaned back against the booth and rubbed her eyes. "That could explain so many things."

"I didn't know you didn't know." Alannah waved one hand helplessly. "I just kind of thought..."

"I feel awful," Idina groaned as if Alannah hadn't even spoken. "No wonder he hunted for her like that after she disappeared. And I criticized him so much. He was just trying to do the right thing." She pressed her palms to her face. "Cyrus and I both said unkind things. I feel so bad!"

Alannah let her go on, bewildered. She'd known of Cosima and Alexander's affair, but Alexander had been tight-lipped about everything following Cosima's disappearance. She'd never pried. Cosima's loss had ruined his health for many years. She knew he had his reasons for silence.

Idina wiped at her eyes and pulled Alannah's phone toward herself again. Alannah tapped the screen and unlocked the phone again. "We certainly shouldn't jump to conclusions, but it would explain why Cosima would feel the need to vanish. She wouldn't be the first pregnant immortal woman to hide, though certainly the most successful." Idina bit her lip. "Email me this picture."

"I just don't want to make a mess out of nothing. I don't want to send you on a wild goose chase. I don't want to—"

"It's alright," Idina said gently. "I'll look into it quietly. Alexander has enough on his mind."

The waitress arrived and cleared their plates. Idina and Alannah leaned back against their respective sides of the booth.

"And you?" Idina asked softly. "What are you going to do?"

Alannah leaned her head back. "I don't know. I-I just don't know. I suppose I have to find a job." How she would work herself up to that she didn't know. She clapped her hands down on the table. "I had dreams before all this—" she meant before her breakdown, before she'd moved to Winnipeg "—Daniel and I wanted to travel. I wanted to get married. I'd just gotten my history degree. I wanted my doctorate. That's gone now. It's all gone!"

Idina looked up at Alannah, serious, conflicted, as if there was something she wanted to say but couldn't. She didn't understand.

Idina was securely planted in a career, a marriage, and a place in society. Alannah could imagine Idina telling her to get a grip and move on.

But Idina let out a long, slow breath. "It won't be easy to start over," she said softly, "but you don't need to worry about time or money, alright? Alexander said he'd take care of the money and let you have some time to settle before you start looking for a job."

Relief washed over Alannah. Dear Alexander.

"I'm going to give Louisa a call and ask her to contact you. Once you're a little more comfortable perhaps the two of you can connect. Alright?"

"Alright," Alannah said meekly.

Idina touched Alannah's hand. "I'm sorry I can't stay, I really am. Call me, or call Alexander if you need anything. Alright?"

"Alright," Alannah said again, her voice very small.

It took every bit of white-knuckled energy for Alannah not to beg Idina to stay, to not return to Dresden. Without her, even the little flat seemed like a howling wilderness. When Idina said goodbye and left the flat for the airport, Alannah stood staring at the door for a full five minutes, with her chest winding into an ever-tightening knot.

Move.

Alannah pulled her suitcase from the door to the single bedroom and hoisted it onto the unmade bed. She forced her hands into the motions of opening it, and took each individual item from the bag to the dresser. Her worldly goods filled two drawers of the five in the upright chest of drawers.

She returned to the entrance and brought over her carry on, with the photo collection, and Papa Krueger's Bible, and the few good memories she had left.

What are you going to do?

Tears sprang into Alannah's eyes. She parked the suitcase by the bedside table and sat down on the mattress. Alannah stretched across the bed and opened the curtains. The window viewed the narrow side street. Directly across from her, a sign over a doorway said 'John Lin Academy of the Martial Arts.' As she watched, a man emerged from a doorway and crossed the street. Looking straight down, she could see the top of his blond head as he straddled his motorcycle and put on his helmet. In a moment, the motorcycle revved and peeled away from the curb.

It sent up a wave of longing in her. The anonymous biker reminded her of Daniel, because Daniel was a fighter, and an adventurer, everything she wanted when she was younger.

∞   ∞   ∞

They had met in March of 1945, when both Dresden and her life were in ruins. Alexander spent every day in the smoldering city, cleaning up rubble and corpses, and assisting the suffering citizens wherever he could. Daniel came back to Schwalenburg with him one day, covered in soot from head to toe, but with his blue eyes clear and sparkling in his grimy face.

"This is Daniel Gunther," Alexander said as he struggled out of his filthy coat. Alannah plucked a piece of debris out of his blond hair. "Daniel, this is Miss Alannah Krueger. I told you about her."

Daniel's teeth flashed in his blackened face. "I'd shake your hand, Miss Krueger, but I'm not fit to touch you." His hand reached out slightly toward her anyway, and she realized he was missing three fingers from his right hand.

Those fingers eventually grew back.

∞   ∞   ∞

It was only when she'd seen him two hours later, washed and in clean clothes, that she'd thought him handsome, and it was only in the early seventies when both she and Daniel returned to Germany again, that she fell for him. He was so strong, such an adventurer. They'd climbed mountains together, driven on motorcycles across Europe, swam in the ocean.

She thought they were going to get married. But Daniel was someone else's now. She didn't really want him back, just the person she'd been when she was with him.

Alannah turned away from the window.

CHAPTER 4
London, 1921

"Sir, I didn't expect you—"

Giovanni Ardovinni held up his hand as Stevens, the skeletal, bushy-eyebrowed butler barreled out of the drawing room. Stevens skidded to an undignified halt and quickly intercepted Giovanni's hat and dripping umbrella as he made to hang it on the rack.

Giovanni pushed past him, saying over his shoulder, "I'll dine in the library tonight. Send Burke up, will you?"

"Sir?" Stevens made a tentative step in his direction.

Giovanni paused.

"In regards to Miss Ardovinni's arrival tomorrow, were you hoping for anything in particular for dinner?"

Giovanni's shoulder's sagged. He'd meant to invite guests to greet Cosima, and he'd told the butler as much, but he'd never given Stevens a list of guests. He'd never gotten as far as to invite them. "Forgive me," he said with a sigh. Invite Sir Alexander? God, no. Miss McCullough and her fiancé. Would they come? "It will only be the two of us."

"Very good, Sir."

With Stevens appeased, Giovanni ascended the stairs. He caught a glimpse of the housemaids dashing out of sight, and then he slipped into his bedroom and went straight to the oak desk under the window. He threw back the curtain, letting the grey light wash over the shiny desktop, and yanked open the top drawer. From the files within, labeled by month and year, he withdrew the month of February. He'd just pulled out a sheaf of three letters, bundled together by string, when a quiet baritone said behind him, "Let me take your coat at least, Sir."

Giovanni glanced over his shoulder. Burke's erect figure had appeared in the doorway. With his hands clasped behind his back, Burke regarded him for a moment with somber blue eyes. His dark hair was slightly askew across his high forehead and there was a hint of wind-redness in his thin cheeks and aquiline nose.

Giovanni laid down the letters and complied by crossing the room and allowing the valet to remove his damp overcoat. "Where did I make you rush from?" he asked.

"Just a walk, Sir." Burke eased the sack coat from Giovanni's shoulders. "But I'd already laid out evening wear in case you had need of it."

"Just something dry." Giovanni swiped his hand across his damp brow. "Tomorrow I'll need a case packed. I need to go to France. I—" He sighed. "Oh God, and I'm already so tired."

A soft laugh escaped Burke, the breath from it brushed the back of Giovanni's neck. Burke crossed the room, dropping Giovanni's coat on the bed as he passed, and yanked the drapes shut again. Burke returned to his former spot behind Giovanni. He slid one arm around Giovanni's waist, the other across his shoulders, and pulled him gently against his thin frame. "Is something wrong?"

The last vestige of formality slipped away. Giovanni sagged and tipped his head back against Burke's shoulder. "I was at a funeral this morning, John. The man died under uncertain circumstances."

"A friend?" Burke's voice rumbled low in his ear.

Giovanni sighed and rubbed his burning eyes. "One of my society. " Burke didn't know all, but he knew a great deal more than he ought to.

Burke's body, pressed against him, stiffened. "I thought that was impossible."

"Yes." Giovanni stared at the sliver of light between the drapes, which fell across the packet of letters. "That's why I need to go to France. I need to visit a man there, a man who I suspect knows what happened."

"And then?"

"Whether he swears innocence or not, I have a quarrel with him. He owes me money."

Burke laughed, a low vibration in Giovanni's ear. "You're taking your ruffians then."

Giovanni smiled and did not answer. He would take a strong-arm with him. He would also take Burke. If there were any benefits to this hasty trip, it was that it would garner him some privacy with his lover.

Finally he spoke again, "In the meantime, Cosima is arriving and she has no connections here. I was to plan a dinner to introduce her to all the ladies in my acquaintance, but I've failed to do it."

"It can't be too late."

Giovanni leaned against Burke thoughtfully. "Perhaps not. No, I should at least make the attempt. If I pen a few invitations, will you have them sent?"

"Of course."

When Giovanni had written invitations to Miss McCullough and her fiancé, and one immortal Miss Louisa Spencer, John slipped back into the formality of Burke the valet, and left with the notes in hand.

Giovanni watched the door close, then slid the drapes back open and resumed his papers. In a moment, he held a letter in his hand: a note from Zoran requesting a loan to buy a house in France.

∞

Idina would hardly have appreciated Alexander comparing her to a schoolmarm, so he smiled to himself and held his peace as she jotted notes on the little blackboard propped on Joseph Oswald's dilapidated kitchen table. Her red hair was gathered into a severe knot at the back of her head. But unlike any school teacher Alexander had seen, she had a fierce gleam in her eye. Her rolled up shirt-sleeves exposed strong, lean wrists and hands that had once wielded a claymore with the same skill as any man.

"Of twenty-two experiments, the notes are written in the second person's handwriting in three instances. He cut out his heart, he bled him to death, and he drowned him."

"Drowned him?" Daniel shifted in his seat, one of the two new, wooden chairs they'd procured for the apartment.

"He rebounded in—" Idina referred to the journal in his hand, "and I quote, 'As long as it took me to boil the tea, and drink it'."

"Good heavens," Alexander muttered.

"He has a strange way of phrasing things." Idina frowned and flipped the page, "Perhaps English isn't his native language." She noted on the blackboard "*Not an Englishman?*"

"But we only have three native Englishmen," Daniel observed. His eyes followed the piece of chalk as she wrote, "And one native English—pardon me, Scotswoman, that being you. I wouldn't put it past you to cut out a man's heart, but certainly not for sport or science."

Idina laughed and set the journal on the table with a bang. "Good lord, Mr. Gunther! Thank you for that observation. There is only one heart I plan to steal, and that being one of the Englishmen on your list. Speaking of which, Alexander, did Ardovinni tell you that Cosima is coming to London in time for the wedding?"

Alexander's heart thumped. "Sh-she is?"

"She's arriving in London today. I got Ardovinni's note yesterday."

"B-but wasn't she in India?" Alexander hadn't seen Cosima Di Gaspare in many years, not since one fateful evening at Ardovinni's house in Lisbon. Her letters since then had been sporadic, and decidedly neutral.

Idina eyed him.

"She hasn't written in more than two years," Alexander said in a choked-off voice.

"Ardovinni didn't tell you then." Idina's freckled nose wrinkled. "I don't understand that man at all."

Alexander took a deep, steadying breath and turned around. *Cosima here?* He surveyed the little room, tidy now yet still a far cry from clean and attractive. There was dirt in the lines on his hands from cleaning it, since they'd refused Ardovinni's offer of hired help. Dirt, mixed with flakes of Oswald's blood, which the Persian rug on the bedroom floor had been crusted with.

He could remember her words to him that evening: *"Why do you break yourself in wars that don't concern you when there are things to fight for at home? Where are your Scriptures and theologies?"* If she'd been disappointed in him then, with his body scarred from fighting for nearly a century, she wouldn't be pleased with him now: arms muscled, hands hardened from a little manual labor, extensive travel, and fighting in the Great War. The soft-handed scholar was a ghost now, the books in Schwalenburg many miles from London. At the very least, she could not complain that he wasn't fighting for his own.

"Alexander," Idina said in a voice uncharacteristically soft. She circled the table and laid a hand on his arm. "I'll send for some food, if you'd like."

He nodded, still in reverie.

"I'm sorry," she said, closer to his ear. "I thought you knew she was coming. Is it alright?"

Alexander turned toward her. "Yes," he said, "of course. Of course I want to see her."

Idina patted his shoulder and slipped out of the room.

Daniel turned in his chair and glanced at Alexander. "May I continue?"

"Sorry?" Alexander wiped at his eyes and felt dirt smear.

Daniel's eyes narrowed for a moment before he turned and gazed at the blackboard. "There are what, now, one hundred and nineteen immortals?"

"One hundred and eighteen." Alexander pulled himself erect and tugged the other chair toward him. "Nine live here—twelve if you count the three of us."

"Ardovinni makes thirteen. Would you rule out Ardovinni? I certainly wouldn't."

"I would," Alexander said flatly. "And we can rule out the women, which puts us at ten souls."

"What's more important, anyway?" Daniel threw up a hand, "Is it more important to know who helped Mr. Oswald kill himself, or how he did it?"

"What if the helper knows how he did it?"

"There is no indication he was here at the time." Daniel poked one finger at the journals. "The last entry in the other hand was six weeks ago."

Alexander held out his hand. Daniel gave him the book.

He examined the page explaining, in clinical detail, the first and unsuccessful drowning of Joseph Oswald. "After four minutes and twenty seven seconds of emersion, Joseph appeared to be dead," he read in a rapid undertone. "He remained submerged for two more minutes, and then was removed." Alexander lowered the book. "Of course, we can't know how long Mr. Oswald was in the water in this instance because no one was here to time him."

"But the details are likely the same otherwise," Daniel said. "The use of a mild sedative to dampen the reflex to fight death, and then his head and shoulders were immersed in the bathtub. The recorder notes that Mr. Oswald voluntarily drew water into his lungs to hasten death. I suppose we cannot know that this time."

He grimaced. "We need a medical examiner in our number, Alexander. What about that Dutch doctor?"

"I agree with Mr. Gunther," Idina said from the doorway. She crossed the room and sat down beside Cyrus. "But it's rather late for poor Mr. Oswald. He probably does have water in his lungs now, and water in his bowels, and his stomach, and—"

"Dear," Cyrus cut her off with a hand on her arm.

Idina smiled impishly. "Ardovinni is leaving for France tomorrow, I hear. Do you want Mr. Fontaine and I to question him when we dine at his house tonight?"

"Not at a dinner party," Cyrus said. His dark skin creased with worry around his eyes. "It will be awkward enough, even if his servants don't flinch when they're forced to serve a black man."

Alexander and Daniel glanced at each other.

"After dinner?" Idina asked, oblivious to her fiancé's discomfort.

"If you have an opportunity, Cyrus," Alexander began slowly, "Ardovinni did say he was looking into Oswald's unidentified visitor. Will you ask him if he has further information?"

Cyrus nodded.

"Likely I need not say this," Alexander said then set down the journal and folded his arms tight across his chest, "but do so privately. Thus far no one knows that Oswald is dead, permanently or otherwise. No one really knew him. No one has noticed his absence."

"But we have to tell the society eventually," Idina said. "Don't they have a right to know?"

"We cannot lie to them," Alexander said slowly. He palmed his forehead, imagining the wave of fear and turmoil that would wash over the tiny society. "But we must ask our questions carefully. I want to wait for the right moment."

What the right moment would look like, Alexander could not tell, and his mind was only half on the matter. His thoughts were already returning to Cosima.

∞

As the car halted outside Zoran's rambling farmhouse, Giovanni peered out the fogged window. He turned to the burly young man who was driving and observed, "Well, Mr. Robin. I see my money has been spent well."

His companion adjusted his bowler hat and glanced past Giovanni at the house. "I dunno, guv. A bit of a fixer-upper."

"It looks like it just managed to survive the war," Giovanni said.

"I imagine it did, guv."

Giovanni smiled wryly. An entirely new roof would just about set it to rights, but it was private, set well back in a grove of trees. There were no other immortals for miles. That was what Zoran wanted, surely.

Robin rapped on the oaken front door with one large fist. No one answered. Robin knocked thunderously. A moment later a stout middle-aged woman, with frizzled salt-and-pepper-curls poking out of a mobcap, appeared at the door.

"Good day," Giovanni greeted her in French. "Is Mr. Kosar in?"

The housekeeper glanced at the burly Robin, then back to Giovanni's own slender, well-dressed form. "Yes, Sir." She held the door for them to enter and left them in the little drawing room off the entry.

Robin planted himself behind the delicate, brocade settee, and Giovanni took a seat. He glanced around at the pianoforte in the corner, and the droopy flowers in the vase on the mantle over the smoldering hearth.

It took about five minutes for Zoran to appear. He burst into the doorway, his jacket askew and inky-black hair disheveled. He surveyed Giovanni, then Robin, then Giovanni again. "Ah," he said in German, "I see by your choice of companion that you aren't here on a pleasure trip."

"I see by your choice of housing that my loan wasn't nearly sufficient," Giovanni said dryly. "Collecting money, however, is secondary."

Zoran raised an eyebrow and crossed to the armchair across from Giovanni. "Well, Ardovinni. What can I do for you?"

Giovanni turned and said over his shoulder, "Mr. Robin, will you step into the entry?"

When he returned his gaze to Zoran, Zoran had slouched down in the chair.

"Mr. Kosar," Giovanni began slowly, "I know that you visited Mr. Joseph Oswald about six weeks ago."

Zoran's eyebrows rose slightly.

"Were you aware that he was attempting to find a way to kill himself?"

"Certainly." Zoran leaned back and folded his hands. "I've never been secretive about my scientific endeavors. Oswald asked me—"

"Oswald is dead," Giovanni said.

Zoran froze. His face drained of color, while simultaneously his obsidian eyes lit up from within. "How?"

"He drowned in a bathtub." Giovanni watched Zoran. His eyes were distant, over Giovanni's shoulder. His hand went to his collar, to a glass vial hanging on a chain around his neck, dangling between his lapels. The hair on the back of Giovanni's neck stood up. He didn't know why.

After about a minute, Zoran asked, "How has the community received the news of Oswald's death?"

"They don't know," Giovanni said.

"Oh," Zoran breathed. He licked his lips then, with a jerk, sat up straight and alert. "Very well, I'll return to England with you. That is what you wanted, right?"

"It is." Giovanni said, boggled by Zoran's sudden turn of mood.

"Good," Zoran said. "I can be ready to go in short order."

Giovanni eyed him. "Very well. I don't suppose you shall acquiesce to my second demand with the same alacrity?"

Zoran's lips twitched. "Money?"

"Yes. You know what you owe me. You know when you agreed to pay."

Zoran laughed and leaned back in his chair. "I can't give it to you. I need it."

"Do you?" Giovanni felt a tinge of nausea, mingled with anger as he gazed at Zoran's arrogant, handsome face. "I can't imagine what for. Perhaps for a new roof?"

"And what do you need it for? Are you paying a kept woman... oh, pardon me, a kept man?"

Giovanni felt as if his head and shoulders had been plunged into cold water. He could feel control slipping from his grasp. He was tired. He didn't want to listen to this. "Very well, Zoran. Come with me to England, and we will negotiate." He turned toward the door. "Mr. Robin, if you please?"

Robin slouched into the room and leaned against the door casually.

Zoran sneered at him and opened his mouth to speak.

Giovanni cut him off. "I simply want an item of collateral, Zoran. I'll have your necklace."

"No," Zoran said.

"Robin." Giovanni lifted his chin toward Zoran.

Robin grasped Zoran's arm with his ham-like fist, and snapped the silver chain and vial from his neck.

"Give it back!" For the first time since they'd arrived, a hint of panic skittered through Zoran's voice. He reached for the necklace, but Robin held it up out of the way. "Ardovinni, not that! Give it back!"

"Zoran?" A soft, female voice cut through the brief silence.

Giovanni turned to the doorway Robin had come from a moment before. A woman stood in the doorway, one hand poised mid-gesture. She had curls the color of coffee, tumbling from a knot on top of her head. Her slim tea-gown showed off the curves of her hips, and also, the distinct swell of her belly.

Pregnant.

The instant Zoran saw her, he dropped his hands. "Marie, forgive us for disturbing you," he said in French. He held out his hands to her, crossing the room toward her as if to herd her out of sight.

Robin took the opportunity to hand the chain and vial to Giovanni. Giovanni stuffed them in the pocket of his coat. He pressed his lips together, caught between revulsion and an odd sense of amusement.

With soft reassurances, Zoran succeeded in shooing his mistress into the interior of the house. He turned, his face hesitant.

"I see what you need a house for, then," Giovanni said dryly. "Do you intend this to be public knowledge, or..."

Zoran sighed. His lip curled. "I'll come with you quietly tomorrow, Ardovinni. Today I will go to a friend and he will get you the money, only give me the vial back."

Giovanni closed his hand around the vial in his pocket. "Tomorrow, when you give me the money, I'll give it back."

∞

"Now that the woman is pregnant, surely they can't take the child from them." Burke lounged on the bed, gazing languidly up at him.

"They've done it before." Giovanni turned away from the window. A sharp draft of cool night air blew across his back, through the thin fabric of his unbuttoned shirt. He shivered and wrapped his arms across his chest. "Zoran caused a tremendous uproar that time, the little bastard. It wasn't even his child. Good Lord, I cannot imagine what will..." He sat down on the bed and didn't finish.

Burke reached over and tapped the vial, hanging by its chain around Giovanni's neck. "What is this?"

Giovanni held it up between them. "I don't know. Zoran was remarkably anxious to recover it." He shook it gently. Clear fluid splashed up against the cloudy glass. Burke leaned near, his face only inches from Giovanni's, and took the vial in his fingers. The chain tugged at Giovanni's neck as Burke examined it, pulling their heads together.

"I can only surmise," Giovanni said, allowing his forehead to lean against Burke's, "that it contains something significant." He surmised more than that, but he'd never told Burke about the Immortal Fountain, which was deep beneath Schwalenburg Castle and buried by tons of rock. He didn't know how Zoran could have acquired it, but Zoran had been close to Lord Alexander at one time. "I'll give it back when he gives me a portion of the money."

Burke's blue eyes sparkled. "If he wants it so bad, leverage it until you know what's in it."

Giovanni extricated it from Burke's fingers and sat back. "No, I gave him my word. I'll return it when he gives me the money."

As it was, it took Zoran three days to get together the money he owed. He arrived at the inn, where Giovanni and his entourage were staying, on the morning of the fourth day.

In Giovanni's little sitting room, Zoran held out an envelope to him. "You'll say nothing to Alexander about Marie," he said tersely.

Giovanni pulled the petal-shaped vial from his pocket and held it, just out of Zoran's reach. "You intend to hide her and the child from the immortals forever?"

"Long enough to test a theory. Give me the vial, Ardovinni." Zoran's fingers grasped for it.

Giovanni took the envelope and put the necklace into Zoran's hands. "Very well then, but I'd hate to be in your circumstances when the Lords find out."

"The Lords can go to hell," Zoran said calmly.

CHAPTER 5

Dresden, Present Day

Jack woke at about ten in the morning, like he had for the last week. He lay in bed. A crack of sunlight shone between the blackout drapes across his bare chest. He glanced at his phone, which was completely devoid of messages, and flopped back on the pillow again. The house was silent.

His eyes drifted shut, he drew up a memory of Mary Rose like a summoned ghost. Her face rose up before him, a little smile on her pink lips, her golden hair falling around him spreading the scent of roses. He touched her skin—

"Oy!" The bedroom door rattled.

Jack gasped and half sat up in bed. "Fuck!"

"It's ten bloody thirty," Idina's strident voice pierced the wooden door. "Get up!"

Jack groaned and propped himself up on his hands. "What the hell?" he shouted. Since when was she home from England?

She laughed and slapped the door again. "Good morning, sunshine." Her footsteps receded.

So, today they weren't leaving him alone? They'd left him in the house by himself for a week straight. Now he had company? Jack rolled over and flopped off the mattress onto his feet. He pulled a pair of Cy's castoff jeans over his ratty boxers. They hung loose on his hips. He glanced in the mirror as he pulled on a t-shirt. In a short week his face had become thin and haggard. He looked like shit with his stubbly hair about the same length as his scruffy beard. Anger turned his stomach. He didn't know why.

Jack took a couple of minutes to compose himself.

He padded from the room in his bare feet, then down the stairs. Idina stood in the kitchen in a loose t-shirt, and her long, thin legs clad in black tights. Her cheeks were pink and her hair was smashed down like she'd just pulled off a hat. Jack smelled coffee.

"Breakfast?" she said, her lips quirked in amusement.

"Yeah, sure," he said quietly. He plopped down at the table, and a moment later Idina put a cup of coffee in front of him, along with a little, cut-glass sugar bowl and a carton of cream. "So," she said with a little smile, "Where are my menfolk?"

"Huh?" Jack looked up from stirring his coffee.

"Cy and Alexander took off to Schwalenburg and left you to fend for yourself?"

Jack blinked. "Um, pretty much."

"They do that every day while I was gone?"

"Uh..." Geez, company would have been nice but he didn't need babysitting. He wasn't about to go off with another strange woman.

"I need to talk to my husband," Idina muttered under her breath. She turned toward the stove. A frying pan clanked onto the element.

"How is Alannah?" Jack asked hesitantly. He twisted around in the chair to face her.

"She's okay," Idina said toward the stove. "Not sure she'll manage to leave that flat. I'm going to try to get a couple of the immortal women to go see her." She turned, rapped an egg sharply against the enamel stovetop. A moment later it sizzled in the pan. She turned around again. "I wish I could've stayed there with her for a while, but I really can't. The guys are still pegging away at your case, and we also have to track Ardovinni and ask him what the bloody hell he was doing in Winnipeg, harassing Alannah."

"Is he dangerous?" Jack asked quietly.

Idina turned around. "Ardovinni?" She sighed. "No, he's just a loner. He belongs to us only as far as he has to." She paused. "And that's a shame. He's a very decent fellow."

Idina turned to the frying pan and cracked a couple of eggs into the pan. They sizzled, sending up a delicious aroma. "Anyway, it's a beautiful day."

"Yeah...?"

"You wanna take the motorcycles up to Schwalenburg?" The spatula scraped against the skillet.

Jack considered this for a moment. "Yeah, I guess."

"Frederick von Schwalenburg flew in from Brazil yesterday. The Lords are convening—"

"Holy shit," Jack said. "That sounds ominous."

"—for council about your attack but they can also swear you in."

"Swear me... What?"

Idina set a plate of eggs down in front of him. "Make you one of us: officially. You want that, right?"

"Umm..." Jack blew out his breath. "Yeah. Maybe? I think so?"

"Well then, you better make your mind up right quick." Idina plunked down across from him. "Eat and we'll go. Do you have any decent clothes?"

He had a suit, and he ended up wearing it under Cyrus's motorcycle gear, speeding along behind Idina on the road to Schwalenburg. She darted fearlessly through traffic, dodging back and forth through the little German cars like a pinball. When they'd emerged from Dresden onto the highway, she cracked the throttle wide and screamed down the wet road with Jack hot on her tail. In his gloves, his knuckles were white on the handlebars.

In the courtyard inside Schwalenburg's walls, Jack swung off the motorcycle and undid his helmet with fingers that shook. He was shot through with adrenaline.

Idina's frizzy red hair emerged from her helmet. She glanced over her shoulder, grinned at him and shrugged. "Don't tell Cy I did that."

Jack grinned back. "Holy smokes, Idina, I thought you were trying to kill me."

They sauntered into the castle with their helmets dangling by their sides. Thirty minutes later, they were in the council room with the three immortal Lords standing in a semi-circle in front of him.

"It is your right as an immortal to protection from lawkeepers of your clan, and others. It is your right as an immortal to fair trial before the court of Lords," Daniel read from his position at the end of the line of lords. "It is your right as an immortal..."

Was he supposed to remember all of this? Jack tried not to fidget despite the chokehold his suit collar had on him. A yawn was stuck somewhere in his gut. He'd be damned if he let it out. The sweat that had accumulated during the jaunt out to the castle was drying, making him cold. Alexander grinned like he was a proud father, or umpteenth great grandfather, or whatever he was. The other two gazed solemnly at him like they were conducting a funeral.

"It is your duty as an immortal to keep the secrecy of the immortal society..."

They looked so comfortable in suits. The one guy even had a high collar with one of those old-fashioned wrapped neckerchiefs; made him look like damn George Washington.

Jack imagined Daniel, who today wore a navy three-piece with apparent ease, saying 'it is your duty as an immortal to wear a suit.'

"Jakob Gerhardt Krause," Alexander said.

Jack snapped to reality and stood straight and tall. He met Alexander's eyes.

"Do you accept these rights and responsibilities, take them upon yourself, and declare yourself a member of this immortal society? Do you take upon yourself the authority of your Lord, Alexander Leopold Karlstan Von Katlenburg, and his deputies? If you accept, say 'I do'."

"I do." It came out of Jack's mouth hoarse, nearly inaudible. He cleared his throat. "I do."

Daniel glanced at him. His mouth twitched. Jack thought he heard a snort behind him—either Cyrus or Idina.

"Then I hereby accept you into the society of immortals, and extend the hand of friendship." Alexander held out his hand, and Jack grasped it firmly. Alexander clasped his shoulder. "Welcome, Jack."

"Thanks," Jack said. Well, that was that. He was one of them.

"I do," Idina mimicked his strangled voice as everyone gathered around with congratulations and handshakes in the antechamber outside the council room. "I—" she cleared her throat loudly "—do."

"That's how Cyrus said it when he married you, 'dina." Alexander sidled up next to Jack. "Welcome, Jack."

"Thanks," Jack held out his hand, but Alexander pulled him into a rough embrace. Jack stood stiff until he was released.

Alexander grinned. "We'll have dinner later to celebrate. I have to return to the council." He clapped Jack on the shoulder and pushed open the council room door.

"Cy, I have to talk to you," Jack heard Idina say to Cyrus.

"Come have lunch," Daniel said at his elbow.

About forty-five minutes later, Jack had finished his lunch with Anastasie and Daniel and was, once again, alone. He set out in the general direction of the library and ended up wandering past the offices. As he passed by Cyrus's door, he thought he heard his name. He paused.

"Alexander is going to Berlin. Jack will be alone in the house," Idina's voice said.

"Yes..." Cyrus's tone was distracted.

Idina's reply was hissed, "Cyrus, you can't leave an arguably depressed, arguably traumatized man with a history of self-harm alone in a house. It's not responsible."

Jack bristled. "Well, shit!"

Inside the room, a chair scraped.

Jack hurried away from the door.

"Eavesdropping, are we?" Idina said behind him.

Jack stopped and turned around slowly. "I heard my name."

She narrowed her eyes at him. "Oh yeah? Well, come in here. You might as well weigh in."

"Idina," Cyrus protested within the room.

"I, uh..." Jack glanced down the hall toward freedom.

"C'mon, Jack." Idina slipped back into the office.

"Shit," Jack muttered. He was getting dragged into a marital spat wasn't he? A spat over him, no less. He opened the office door and saw Cyrus, sitting in the office chair behind a wide, oak desk. Stacks of books and papers surrounded him. Idina perched across from him on the edge of the desktop.

"Have a seat." Cyrus pointed to a flimsy wooden chair across from him. His expression was resigned. "Idina and I were just discussing how best to host you while we are both travelling."

"Where are you going?" Jack asked, somewhat begrudgingly sitting down in the offered chair. He glanced around at the high-piled bookshelves, the framed photo of Cyrus and Idina together hanging behind Cyrus, and the electric kettle on a TV tray behind the desk.

"Italy," Cyrus said.

"Austria." Idina crossed one long leg over the other and picked at the heel of her boot. "Looking into a possible friend of Lia's. Alexander is going to Berlin."

"And you don't want to leave me alone because I'll drink all of Alexander's liquor and spend the rest of the time in a pool of blood on the kitchen floor?" Jack said in run-on monotone. He eyed Cyrus, then Idina.

Idina raised both brows and gave a succinct nod. "Pretty much."

Cyrus coughed softly.

"No, she's probably right," Jack said sarcastically. "I've been known to do that, as you may recall."

Idina's foot bobbed in the air between Jack and the desk. She pursed her lips and rested her chin on her hand. "Don't suppose you fancy a trip to Italy?" she asked.

Jack blinked.

Cyrus eyes drooped at the corners. "He could probably go to Berlin."

"Alexander will be in seminars all day. Jack doesn't understand German," Idina said gently. Her eyes softened as she gazed at her husband.

Cyrus leaned forward and folded his hands on the table. "I'm going to Italy to look into Alannah's visitors."

"This Ardovinni chump?"

"His unidentified friend is our concern, right now." He dropped his voice before continuing, "Ardovinni's home base is in Florence. His business is there. If Ardovinni won't answer any correspondences, perhaps his employees can tell us where he's gone. If not we'll look around. It should be fairly... routine."

"Well," Jack said wryly, "if I'll be in your way..."

Cyrus shook his head, "No, I'm trying to say that I can't show you around. We'll be there for a day. I'll gladly take you."

"Oh." A grin crept onto Jack's face. "Okay. When do we leave?"

Cyrus slid his chair over to the computer. "Well, let's see when we can get a flight."

CHAPTER 6

London, Present Day

"Italy? Lucky you." Alannah sank down on the bed with the phone to her ear, and gazed down at the street and the door of John Lin Academy across the street.

"Well, I dunno," Jack said, "doesn't sound like we'll be having much fun."

"You never know," Alannah said. "Cy is pretty serious, but I've heard a few wild stories about him." She smiled to herself, recalling a few evenings in a Dresden beer hall, perched on Daniel's knee, listening to Cyrus and Idina telling tales of the old days.

"What are you doing?" Jack asked softly. "Have you left the flat yet? Aren't you running out of food?"

It was two days after Idina had let her into the flat, and Alannah had subsisted on delivered Chinese food, pizza and tea. From the window that faced the front street, she had a view of a trendy little coffee shop. The idea of a large, dark roast coffee taunted her. Yet every time she put on her shoes and coat, she ended up taking them back off.

"No, not yet," she said. "I, um, I'm next to a martial arts school. I've been-been thinking about taking lessons."

"Really?" Jack laughed. "That's awesome. You should."

She'd already punched the number into her phone three times, and each time, locked the screen again and set it down. "Yeah, maybe I should start by going to the coffee shop."

"C'mon, do the martial arts thing. It'll be badass."

Alannah craned her neck and caught a glimpse of the black motorcycle. "Yeah, maybe."

There was a long pause.

"Well," Alannah said lamely, "have fun in Italy."

"Yeah." Jack sighed. "I guess."

After Jack hung up, Alannah slapped the phone down on the bed and padded into the bathroom. She stared at her bedraggled hair, tied in a messy knot, and the baggy t-shirt she'd found in the closet. It was probably Cy's. It covered up the fact that she was pretty sure she'd gain a couple pounds, or at least was bloated.

"I can't go to Jiu Jitsu," she said to her dull-eyed reflection. "What the heck would I wear?" Did she have to wear one of those white suits? What was it called, a gi? Whatever she was supposed to wear, it wasn't jeans and a man's faded black t-shirt.

She boiled the kettle and took her cup of tea back to the bedroom and sat on the edge of the bed sipping it. She picked up the phone and dialed John Lin's number again. Her chest tightened. Tears welled up in her eyes, and she tossed the phone down again.

"Damn it!" she cried. "I'm so sick of this!"

That should be her out there on the motorcycle. Heck, it wasn't as if she didn't know how to drive one.

∞ ∞ ∞

"Miss Krueger." Daniel's blond head poked into Alexander's office.

Alannah straightened from behind a stack of papers she'd been reorganizing. She swiped at her disheveled hair. Faint heat came into her cheeks. "Yes?"

A little smiled quirked on his lips. "Alexander has gone home. He asked me to take you back to Dresden."

"Oh," Alannah said slowly.

"Shall I..." he glanced around the room, "shall I go get my car, or is my motorcycle acceptable to you?"

A little jolt went through her belly. "Oh no, that's fine."

"Excellent." He winked and ducked back out of the room.

An hour later, they were flying down the highway toward Dresden. Alannah clung to Daniel's waist, exhilarated by the wind whistling by her open helmet and by his taut frame so close to hers.

When they stopped outside Alexander's house, the same one he still owned, Alannah climbed off the motorcycle with shaky legs.

Daniel laughed. "Did I scare you?"

"No!" Alannah said. She paused, a bold thought germinating in her mind. "You should teach me to drive that thing."

His blue eyes sparkled. "See if I don't."

∞   ∞   ∞

Alannah opened her eyes and sipped her tea. Across the road the door of the John Lin Academy opened, but instead of the blond motorcycle driver, a slight girl bounced out. She wore a bright blue coat, her long blond braid dangling from a stocking cap.

Alannah set the teacup down on the windowsill as the young girl skipped around the corner. She picked up the phone and took a deep breath. "I don't want to be scared anymore. I'm better than this."

Alannah punched the John Lin's number into the phone.

"I'm better than this."

She turned away from the phone, and pressed the call button. Within five minutes, she was signed up for a beginner Jiu Jitsu class.

CHAPTER 7
London, 1921

"This is useless," Alexander said as Idina arranged herself in the chair across the desk from him and Cyrus seated himself beside her. "None of our immortals even spoke to Oswald in the last six months. He isolated himself completely."

"We have to reach out to the immortal community. It surely seems he did not have friends, but he may have had contact with at least one of them," Cyrus paused and frowned, "besides Mr. Ardovinni."

"The matter is how to contain it," Alexander muttered, "and how to ask questions without being asked too many. I don't want anyone panicking if we have no idea what we are dealing with."

"Given," Cyrus said. His eyebrows drew close together.

"We will have to do it," Idina stated, "because there is nothing to suggest in that whole goddamned series of diaries who his partner was."

Cyrus's eyebrows rose, but he said nothing to this ungentle speech.

"Meanwhile, Ardovinni has yet to return from his trip to France, and he was rather cryptic about what that was about."

Idina's nose wrinkled, half sneer, half an expression of bemusement.

"He was going to see Zoran," Cyrus said quietly, "to collect money, he said, but he implied that he had other interests."

"With Zoran?" Alexander stared at him. "He hasn't been in London in the last year!"

Cyrus and Idina glanced at each other. "Well," Cyrus began, "after dinner, when I spoke to Ardovinni in private, he asked me if I was aware that Zoran had been in town about six weeks ago."

Alexander blinked.

Cyrus opened his hands. "Of course, I was not."

"You're sure Zoran was here?" Idina said in a skeptical tone. She picked at a thread on her cuff.

"If Ardovinni says Zoran was here, I believe him." Alexander dug his hands into his hair. "I only wish he'd told me. God knows what Zoran was doing here, whether he visited Oswald or not. Did Ardovinni say?"

"No, he didn't say, because we were interrupted by the ladies, and none of the other immortals had seen Zoran when I interviewed them later," Cyrus said. "I don't know how Ardovinni knew he was there."

"Who knows how Ardovinni knows anything?" Idina muttered.

Alexander got up and began to pace in the little space behind Cyrus and Idina's chairs. The floorboards creaked beneath him. "When does he return?"

Cyrus twisted around in his chair to watch Alexander. "Not for some days. He was concerned he might not return in time for the wedding, and offered his most sincere apologies, as well as his home for the reception."

Alexander stopped in place and smiled in spite of himself. "That was good of him."

"One has to admit it's a far cry from hosting at Miss McCullough's—our home, I mean." Cyrus smiled sheepishly at Idina before repeating, "Our home."

She smiled and reached for his hand.

Alexander turned away.

"Miss di Gaspare will host," Cyrus said softly. "Have you seen her yet?"

"No," Alexander said and turned around slowly, "when would I have seen her?" Good heavens, he could hardly march over to Ardovinni's house and let himself in. She hadn't written him for so long, by mortal terms they could be strangers.

"I suppose both of you are waiting for the other to move?" Idina's lips twitched.

Her amusement irritated Alexander. He looked away. "Call it childish if you wish, Idina," he said, "but we didn't part on good terms. Surely you can understand how this might be awkward."

"Now that I've met her in person, I can also understand why your usual good judgment is impaired whenever she's around," Idina said sharply. "You should just get it over with."

Heat suffused Alexander's face before he realized what Idina meant—that he should visit Cosima and break the ice. He heard Daniel snigger.

"You're probably right," Alexander muttered, "but it's only three days until the wedding, and now that I've stayed away so long..."

Idina made a disgusted sound in the back of her throat.

∞

"Alexander, is this how you tie this neckerchief? Alexander? Alexander?"

Daniel's hand came down heavily on Alexander's shoulder.

"Oh, good Lord, Daniel!" Alexander sucked in a deep breath as he snapped out of his daze. He stood in front of his mirror with his own bowtie hanging in his limp hand. He turned around and saw Daniel, his shoulders scrunched uncomfortably in his stiff tailcoat, picking at his cockeyed bowtie, backlit by the fading sunlight shining through the bedroom door.

Alexander shook his head and wiped at his bleary eyes. "No, Daniel."

"Gah!" Daniel whipped the offending accessory off. "I had only figured out the last one, then they went and changed the styles again."

"Give it." Alexander held out his hand and felt a smile creep across his face for the first time that day. "You need a valet, Daniel." He straightened Daniel's starched shirt, and wrapped the bowtie around Daniel's muscled neck.

"By rights I should *be* a valet," Daniel muttered. "Isn't Ardovinni's valet a veteran of the war? So am I."

"So am I," Alexander said wryly. "Anyway, you look presentable now. I'd get a valet, but a mortal servant so close?"

Daniel opened his mouth, narrowed his eyes, and simply said, "Curious, isn't it?" He leaned against the post of Alexander's bed. "Well good, we are two presentable gentlemen, but you look as nervous as if it were your wedding, not Cyrus's."

"Pathetic, I know."

"Not at all." Daniel picked at one fingernail and added, "but you'll have to see her today. What will you do?"

Alexander smiled ruefully and glanced again in the mirror. "I will do exactly what I always do—fall for her."

"But now you can marry her."

Alexander didn't reply.

"You know you've thought it. Damn sure she's thought it."

Idina and Cyrus were the fourth immortal couple to marry that year, after many, many years in which no immortals had been given in marriage. They were all those of the group Zoran had mockingly called 'the virgins,' fastidiously celibate so as to not spread immortality to their heirs. Alexander had watched them struggle mightily with loneliness, which he knew only too well.

Then, nearly ten years ago now, Adolf Hardwin had written that he and Sophia were using a contraceptive. Would he... could he... allow them to suggest it to the others?

And they had. Alexander had wanted to throw it in Zoran's face, but Zoran was nowhere to be seen. So he had celebrated quietly, danced at the weddings of those in his care, and thought about Cosima.

He *hoped* she'd thought about it.

At the church, Alexander paused in the doorway, and scanned the little cluster of humanity in the front pews. He would know her if he saw her, wouldn't he?

There were only two women seated, their gorgeously plumed hats rising above the somber black and grey shoulders of the men. The little woman with a blond coif, that was Miss Louisa Spencer, and beside her, leaning in confidentially, that was Benjamin Turner's wife Anna.

Alexander closed his sweaty palms.

"Sir Alexander," a voice, sweet like honey, rich like merlot wine, said behind him. Fingers brushed his elbow.

Alexander felt like a fist had closed around his heart. He turned.

She stood, smiling up at him from under the straw brim and piled flowers of her hat. Her eyes sparkled. She held out her hand. "Hello, dear Sir."

He took her warm fingers. Instinctively, he bent his head and pressed his lips to her knuckles. Her warm, olive skin glowed bronze against his England-pale skin. "It's good to see you," he choked as he released her hand.

"And you."

Their eyes met. Cosima smiled at him, and appraised him frankly. He allowed himself only a short survey of her person. She seemed a little thinner, but perhaps it was her modern dress—a subdued cut and hue of airy beige. She'd tucked a bright silk scarf around her neck and into her bosom, of an ornate oriental pattern with bright reds, purples, and vermilions that brought out the coppery strands in her dark hair and ebony eyes. How beautiful she was. In comparison to all he'd seen in fifty years, looking at her felt like his first true sight.

"You look so well..." she trailed off. Her eyes turned down just a little. Her hands twisted together. "Are you well?"

"I think so," he said as close to a neutral tone as he could manage. He wanted to take back those wringing hands. "It's a cold country after India, is it not?"

Her lips quirked a little. "So it is."

Alexander glanced back toward the door of the church. "Where is Ardovinni?"

"He hasn't returned from France."

"Oh."

"But," she smiled, more easily, "I am here, and everything is all well in hand."

"I'm—" Alexander looked down at his feet "—I'm sure."

Cosima laughed suddenly, and bent down to peer into Alexander's face. "Let's not be strangers, dear Alexander. At least let us catch up on all that has passed."

"It's good to have you in England," he said in a low, choked voice, held by her deep brown eyes. "I wish we could bypass the wedding so I could begin asking you everything about India, and these past years."

Her mouth quirked into a little smile. "Give me your arm, Sir Alexander. I am unescorted."

Alexander quickly bent his arm to offer his elbow.

Her hand closed firmly on his arm. "In a few hours we shall dance together."

Oh dear God! Alexander cried inwardly as he seated her and took his spot beside her. *Let me not hope in vain!*

He neither heard, nor saw much of the wedding.

The instant Cyrus and Idina were pronounced man and wife, Idina let out a whoop and tossed her bouquet in the air. "There!"

she said, "now no one can take you away. You are mine for eternity."

Cyrus laughed as he swept her up into his arms and dashed down the aisle and out of the church.

The immortals burst into laughter and happy chatter. Everyone stood up at once. Cosima seized Alexander's arm and nearly lifted him bodily to his feet. They joined the small swell of immortal life and exited the church.

"I will see you at the house," Cosima said in his ear. She squeezed his arm and released him. As Alexander turned away, he caught Daniel's eye. Daniel raised his eyebrows. Alexander nodded and blew out his breath. A faint tremor went through him.

The ice was broken between them. More than broken. He felt like a spring thaw had come upon his heart.

Alexander and Daniel were the last to arrive at Ardovinni's house. Cosima was nowhere to be seen in the knot of immortals clustered in the drawing room, so Alexander drew his shoulders up, shoved aside his nerves, and smiled as he moved in among them. Someone put a glass of wine in his hands.

"No Ardovinni?" Benjamin Turner appeared at his elbow.

"He is in France on business," Alexander said, busying himself with his wine.

"Oswald?"

"He's not coming." The words tasted bitter in Alexander's mouth. Turner moved on. Not long after, they were summoned into the dining room.

Alexander was seated beside Cosima, but Louisa Spencer immediately engaged her in conversation. Cosima kept glancing over at him as the footmen brought in the soup course. Her hand rested on the table next to his spoons, her fingers inviting him. She turned to speak but was pulled into conversation again. On his other side, Daniel's hand jabbed at the air as he talked to Benjamin Turner.

Alexander sighed softly and tasted his soup, all the while his ears were tuned to the conversation between the ladies next to him.

Again, Cosima glanced over but Louisa spoke before she could.

Finally he could take it no longer. Louisa paused, and Alexander blurted, "How long will you be in London, Miss di Gaspare?"

Cosima turned toward him. A little smiled curved her mouth before she said, "I haven't yet decided. Perhaps until Giovanni decides to return to Italy, but I don't know when that might be."

"Ahh," Alexander said.

They both opened their mouth to speak, glanced aside, then back.

"What brought you back from India?" Alexander asked softly. "When last I wrote you seemed happy there."

"I was," she said. Her mouth puckered and her eyes turned down, vaguely sad. "I was lonely there. I missed Giovanni. I missed... I missed those who could understand me."

Alexander's throat tightened.

Cosima's fingers closed the last few inches and touched his fingertips. "Have you been well, Alexander? All Giovanni could tell me was he had seen you better."

A chuckle burst from Alexander's mouth. "Ardovinni said that?"

Cosima smiled.

"I..." Alexander's brow bent. He could feel long-dormant emotion welling up in his belly, feelings that he could not release in such a time or place.

Cosima seemed to sense this. She took his hand, squeezed his fingers for a moment, and released him. "Let us be merry today. Another day I will scold."

Alexander laughed softly. An odd sensation of relief filled him, not because she didn't insist on plumbing the depths of his soul right there and then, but because he knew eventually she would. She would understand.

The footmen began to clear the dishes in preparation for the next course. Alexander's soup bowl disappeared, still full.

Cosima peered at him, her eyes twinkling. "You eat, Alexander, or I will scold. You'll need strength to dance with me."

"Miss di Gaspare," Miss Spencer said from her other side, "when is Mr. Ardovinni returning?"

Alexander sighed. Cosima's attention was pulled away again, but as she turned to answer Louisa her hand reached out for his.

Cosima's fingertips brushed his thumb as she spoke. An ache settled deep inside of Alexander. Alexander gently withdrew his hand and turned away. Just that small touch, he was drowning already.

Beside him, Daniel coughed softly.

Alexander glanced over.

Daniel raised an eyebrow.

Alexander only smiled.

It was late before he and Cosima were able to be together, only the two of them, again. Cosima danced with Alexander for the first dance, then circulated among the other men. As the night drew to a close, she returned to his arms for the final number. The violins lolled into a slow, sensuous waltz and Alexander and Cosima danced face to face, closer than they'd been all evening. At the center of the small dance floor, Cyrus and Idina danced in small circles, cheek to cheek. Cyrus's dark face was nearly hidden by Idina's disheveled, fiery hair. They murmured to each other, as if completely unaware of the other couples.

"Do you remember the last immortal wedding we were at?" Cosima said in his ear, "It was Adolf and Sophia's."

"I remember," Alexander whispered. "We did not dance."

She inclined her head in agreement. They completed another slow turn, but Alexander's mind spun faster. He was warm, flushed with wine, heated by her nearness and her scent.

"Your mind was in darkness," she said. "You know, with every letter you sent I searched for that encroaching darkness. I never quite found it in your words, but I never saw true happiness either. Did it stay away? The darkness, I mean?"

"I—" Alexander lifted his head, away from hers. She'd cut him to the quick—bone and marrow—without warning.

"Ardovinni!" someone called—Daniel's voice, bright with drink. "The master of the house!"

The music ebbed away in a graceful diminuendo. The dancers stood still.

Alexander dropped his hands from Cosima's waist and turned. Ardovinni stood in the doorway to the little ballroom, hat in his hands and a grim expression on his face. Beside him, looking tired and beleaguered, stood Zoran.

CHAPTER 8
London, 1921

Alexander felt the gentle pressure of Cosima's hand on his arm, before she slipped past him, hands outstretched. "Giovanni, you've returned. Welcome, Mr. Kosar."

Zoran's black eyes met his across the room and narrowed briefly before moving on. Alexander caught a glimpse of the erect figure of Ardovinni's valet, John Burke, gazing suspiciously across the dancers, who still lingered in the pattern of the dance.

Ardovinni's face was solemn, pale with weariness as he took Cosima's hands and kissed her on both cheeks. He looked up, caught Alexander's eye, and glanced around the room. He smiled, "Friends," he said, "it does me good to see you so merry. A belated welcome to my house, and many congratulations to the happy couple."

Light applause rippled through the immortals.

"Please," Ardovinni said, gesturing toward the musicians, "carry on."

He turned, said something to Burke, and tugged Zoran away from the doorway. Zoran followed him meekly.

"Why has he brought Zoran here?" Daniel's voice was at his elbow. "That's why he went to France? Zoran?"

Fragments were connecting into a semblance of a picture in Alexander's mind: Ardovinni's offer to investigate, his question about seeing Zoran. Alexander hadn't known Zoran was in France. How had Ardovinni gained that intelligence?

"Alexander?" Idina strode toward him, her eyes bright, white dress trailing behind her.

"No, no." Alexander held up his hand. "This is your wedding, Idina. I won't allow Ardovinni's schemes to ruin your celebration."

"But Zoran!" she hissed. "Admit it, this is something he might do!"

"I do admit it," Alexander said with a sigh, "but Daniel and I will see to it."

She made a little huffy sound. Cyrus slipped behind her and took her elbow. "Sweetheart..."

"We won't interrogate him today," Alexander said. "Enjoy your wedding, enjoy each other. I'll deal with whatever Ardovinni and Zoran have in store for us."

Idina's mouth opened, shut, then opened again. "Very well." She spun around. "Strike up the band, if you will!"

∞

"Send coffee up if you will, Stevens. Burke, come with me." Giovanni stumbled on the first step, then plunged up the staircase toward his bedroom. "I'll play good host and put on evening wear for a few hours," he said over his shoulder.

"Oh God," Burke laughed under his breath. "Plenty of coffee then, I should think."

"Fifteen hours of travel and another two of dancing." Giovanni sighed as he pushed the bedroom door open. "How quickly can you get me out of this and into tails?"

Burke closed the door behind them. "Out? Very quickly."

Giovanni smiled wryly. "And in?"

"Fear not," Burke said, reaching to help him from his coat. "Your evening wear is in good condition."

Twenty minutes later, Giovanni was out of his damp and dirty travelling clothes and had washed a day's worth of travelling grime from his face and hands. Muffled strains of music seeped through the floor as Burke held his evening coat for Giovanni to shrug into. Giovanni gulped down the last of his coffee. "Am I presentable?"

Burke leaned in. He adjusted Giovanni's white bowtie, then touched his cheek. "Quite."

"You are going to help Zoran after this?" Giovanni asked.

Burke grimaced. "You are a good host to offer to him, but he was lying when he said he was accustomed to having a valet. He declined."

"Did he decline yesterday?"

"Yes, he did." The valet smirked.

Giovanni shook his head. "You didn't say."

"I was amused."

"Listen, John." Giovanni caught his hand and pressed it. "Keep watch on Zoran's door for me. I don't think he'll escape, I just—"

"I'll watch the bastard." Burke disentangled their hands and smiled wryly at him. "Go dance."

With a last look back at Burke, Giovanni slipped into the hall.

Alexander was at the foot of the stairs before Giovanni's shoes hit the ground floor. "Ardovinni!" he whispered. "Zoran?" His handsome face was taut, blue eyes wide. Giovanni glanced past him to the bandleader flourishing his baton and the violins, now skirling out a Scottish tune. Cyrus and Idina whirled around the little dance floor with bright eyes, laughing. Cosima dragged Daniel through the steps, giggling at his fumbles.

So this was what it took to separate Alexander from Cosima. It didn't take much imagination to know that before he'd arrived the two of them were drawing together like the north and south poles of magnets.

It wasn't that he didn't sympathize.

68

"Zoran," Giovanni said slowly, "I am delivering on my promise to investigate."

Alexander leaned in. "You believe..."

"He knows about it, at the very least," Giovanni said in an undertone. "Go back to the wedding. Come first thing in the morning and question him."

Alexander met his gaze and nodded.

CHAPTER 9

Dresden, Present Day

"How convenient that there were only first class seats left." Jack stretched his long legs out in front of him and stretched his arms.

Cyrus didn't look up from his tablet. "It's a short flight."

"You're a short flight," Jack muttered under his breath, "short legged."

Cyrus ignored this and turned the tablet toward him. "When we land, we'll go to Ardovinni's offices in Rifredi. His manager is an immortal. She'll be able to answer our questions in the vein we need."

"They manage all his property?"

"Just his Italian property," Cyrus swiped the screen. "That failing, we'll have a poke about his house."

"He's not home?"

"No."

Jack smiled. "B and E?"

"If you mean 'bacon and eggs,' then no." A tiny smile crossed Cyrus's mouth.

Three hours later they were loading their bags into a tiny rental Fiat. Cyrus laughed as he slid into the driver's seat. "I had to make up for the first class tickets."

"Can't you expense all of this?" Jack jerked the passenger seat as far back as he could.

"Eventually," Cyrus said as they pulled out of the parking spot. "Alexander doesn't know about this little expedition yet."

"Right," Jack muttered.

Cyrus's brow furrowed. "Hopefully by the end of the day we'll have enough answers to explain everything to Alexander in simple fashion. But, I fear that will not be the case."

"Are you going to explain everything to me too?" Jack eyed him.

"Probably," Cyrus said with a sigh.

Ardovinni's offices were in the upper story of a yellow brick building, where it wasn't covered by crinkling, dead ivy. The ground level was a cafe, with a few little tables outside.

Cyrus glanced at the sign hanging over the door and shut off the car. "Excellent. I'm hungry. I'll text Ms. Santorini. Perhaps she'll join us downstairs."

A wind chime jingled over them as Jack pushed open the door. The deep aroma of coffee washed out, mingled with boisterous flamenco guitar. Jack paused in the entry, as Cyrus had instructed him, and swept his gaze across the room. A petite young woman, her dark hair bound back under a brightly patterned scarf, leaned over the counter. Her chin rested on her hands as she gazed at the source of the music—two young men seated on stools in the opposite corner. They strummed furiously at their guitars and grinned at each other, eyes gleaming with fun.

Cyrus glanced at his phone and said over the music, "Let's get coffee and sit down. Ms. Santorini is coming down."

They carried their foamy cappuccinos to a table. As they sat down, the guitars struck a final chord and stopped, and a dark-haired woman in a pantsuit came through a door at the end of the cafe.

Cyrus stood. "Ms. Santorini?"

"Marlena." Marlena's eyes went from Cyrus to Jack.

"Vi presento Jack Krause," Cyrus said.

Jack pushed back his chair and extended his hand awkwardly. "Uh... pleased to meet you?"

"Pleased to meet you, Jack," Marlena said in thickly accented English. She caught the eye of the barista and called out, "Mio solito, prega." She pulled a cell phone out of her pocket and dropped it into the empty chair next to her. She appraised Jack frankly. "You must be young yet."

"I, uh, yeah. I guess." Geez, what gave it away? She looked about twenty-five. Jack blinked. Maybe. Or forty. He wasn't sure.

"But to the point," she said, turning to Cyrus, "how can I help you?"

"Ardovinni," Cyrus said and leaned forward. "We understand he's been abroad for quite some time."

"Yes."

The barista sidled over and set a little porcelain cup of espresso in front of Marlena. In the interim, Cyrus pulled out his tablet and prepared to take notes.

Marlena took a gulp, wiped her lip, and continued. "Giovanni has been travelling with his partner. When we last spoke, he was in Los Angeles."

"When was that?" Cyrus's fingers were poised above the slick surface of the tablet screen.

"About two weeks ago?" She tilted her head to the side and lifted her coffee again.

"Did he, at any time, mention going to Canada?"

Marlena shook her head.

"He never said anything about visiting Lord Alexander or Alannah Krueger in Winnipeg?" Cyrus asked.

Her brow furrowed. "No, why?"

"He visited Miss Krueger a few days ago, along with a man named Alexei." Cyrus stared at her. "Do you know who he is?"

Marlena's eyes brightened. "Oh yes, yes. Not to worry. That is Giovanni's boyfriend."

Jack's eyebrows shot up. He quickly hid his surprise behind his cappuccino.

"But," Marlena whispered as she leaned closer, "he's mortal. A very nice young man, but mortal."

Cyrus glanced at Jack, his expression inscrutable. "What else do you know about him? Where is he from?"

"Oh…" Marlena leaned back and rubbed her chin. "Well, not very much. His mother is Italian, I believe, but he is not from here. Giovanni met him in America, or at least I think so. Giovanni brings him back after a trip to America. Honestly, there is not much else I can say."

"Do you know his surname?" Cyrus asked.

She shook her head. "No, he didn't mention it. I meet him maybe twice, three times. He only lives here part of the time."

"Where if not here?"

"London. He works there, the boyfriend."

Cyrus pursed his lips and nodded. "I see. Has Ardovinni mentioned returning?"

"Soon," she said, "but not precisely, no."

Cyrus picked up his untouched cappuccino. "Then I have very little else to ask you, Ms. Santorini."

Back in the Fiat, Cyrus pulled out his phone. "I need to make a call to Idina."

Jack leaned back in the leather seat, digesting all the mostly meaningless information he'd absorbed. "You said you were hungry," he muttered, "but we didn't eat nothing."

"'dina," Cyrus said into the phone.

Jack could hear Idina's voice, unintelligible but still strident through the phone speaker.

"She gave us a bit," Cyrus answered. "Listen, I need the order to go into his house." He paused, listening, "Take it to Hardwin. He won't even ask. 'kay. Alright. Alright, text it to me."

Cyrus hung up and grimaced. "Goodness. Let's find food. We'll be waiting for a while."

"What's that about?" Jack lifted his head off the headrest.

"We'll have our B and E," Cyrus said wryly. "If Alexei is Ardovinni's boyfriend, maybe he left some things around his house."

"Okay man," Jack said as he twisted around in his seat as Cyrus pulled the Fiat away from the curb, "I didn't understand too much of what you guys were talking about, but I feel like there's a little more going on than I think."

"Yeah, there is." Cyrus said, staring straight ahead. "But it's pretty damn complicated, Jack. I probably can't tell you too much without violating Alexander's privacy."

"So this is about him," Jack said.

"Yeah, sort of." Cyrus's mouth twisted. "What I can tell you is that Ardovinni claimed that his companion was immortal, despite what Ms. Santorini said. Immortal child of two immortal parents."

Jack blinked. "That happens?"

Cyrus shook his head. "Yes and no. Alannah is one, but that didn't just 'happen'. It was quite deliberate."

Jack shivered. Clarissa's blond curls swam in front of his eyes, and the picture of her snuggled up to some young punk. "You've got to explain that."

"Water from the fountain." Cyrus's jaw tightened. His eyes were fixed far distant. "Her father gave her mother water while she was pregnant with Alannah. She is the only immortal child of immortal parents that we know of. I suppose theoretically it could happen, but..."

Jack wasn't paying attention any more. His mind was stuck on the words 'water from the fountain'. How could he have forgotten? There was this fountain that could make anyone immortal—his wife, his child. A sick feeling formed in the pit of his stomach.

It was stupid just thinking of it. Mary Rose wouldn't have wanted immortality even if he could have offered it. Clarissa probably wouldn't either.

"...anyway," Cyrus continued. Jack came to. "It's not a small claim to make, and Ardovinni owes us an explanation. So we'll start with looking around his house."

"You're going to break in?" He tried to shove Clarissa's face aside. He couldn't quite do it. "What if he has an alarm?"

"That's possible." Cyrus smirked. "Some people you can just tell. Like you, you wouldn't have an alarm, would you?"

"Nah." Jack gazed at him, skeptical.

"Idina?"

"Uh... no. I don't think so."

"Right. But I would, so we do. Daniel, he has an alarm and monitors his door from his phone. He might even have laser tripwire traps. Ardovinni... Ardovinni I just don't know about."

Jack continued to stare, bemused.

Cyrus shrugged. "But you'll drive the getaway car for me."

"Alannah was right," Jack said. "You're a little more crazy than I give you credit for." He tipped his head back against the headrest again. The Fiat swung around a sharp corner. Clarissa swam in front of Jack's eyes again.

∞

It was eight-thirty at night. Cyrus pulled up in front of a two-story, yellow brick house, illuminated by the last golden rays of sunlight. The streetlights weren't on yet. Purple climbing flowers wound up the columns of the entrance and bobbed over the edge of the terra cotta roof. The heavy wooden door opened nearly onto the street.

"Nice shack," Jack said under his breath. "What does Ardovinni do, exactly? Besides own properties, that is."

"Do?" Cyrus said as he reached into the back of the car, "Anything he likes. He comes from old money."

"Lucky him." Jack smirked.

Cyrus straightened, holding a flashlight. "It's his old money. Ardovinni is more than four hundred years old."

"Right."

"Good," Cyrus said. "Get in the driver's seat. I'm going in."

"What are you looking for?" Jack undid his seatbelt and glanced at the dark house, and the house beside it. There was a light on behind the curtains.

Cyrus shrugged. "Not an alarm and not Ardovinni. Otherwise, anything that might tell me who Ardovinni's boyfriend is." He opened the driver's door and slid out. "If all goes well, I'll be fifteen minutes."

"Alrighty then." Jack watched Cyrus, who wore a dark leather jacket, walk toward the side of the house. As soon as he was outside the circle of the streetlight, his dark skin faded into the shadows. A moment later, Jack couldn't see him at all.

Jack sighed and leaned back in the seat. The only sound in the car was his breathing. He was alone for the first time that day.

Unbidden, the idea of the Immortal Fountain came back along with the concept of immortal children. How many memories did he really have of Clarissa? By the time she was in kindergarten he was just seeing pictures of Clarissa that Mary Rose sent to him— her first day of school, piano in second grade, ballet in grade four: a chubby little dancer in a pink tutu.

Jack's heart ached.

A weird scenario began to play out in his mind. He had enough pictures of Clarissa, pictures of Mary Rose, pictures of his younger self. Heck, he had two years' worth of text messages on his phone between him and Mary Rose. He could prove to Clarissa that he was her father.

Jack bit his lip. He could even explain to her where the healthy trust fund in Mary Rose's will had come from.

If Clarissa knew him, would she want to live with him forever?

A soft thump made Jack raise his head. A glow of warm light shone from behind him. He glanced in the rear-view mirror and saw an older woman bent over the flowerpots on her front step with a watering can. Jack's eyes followed her as she stepped down onto ground level and straightened up. She peered at the rental car.

Jack fought the urge to slide down in his seat. "C'mon Cy," he whispered. There must not have been an alarm. Jack glanced at his phone. It had been five minutes.

The woman went back inside. The door closed, and the glow vanished.

Jack's thoughts immediately went back to Clarissa. Who was he kidding? He didn't have any water from the Immortal Fountain. He couldn't exactly fly back to Winnipeg and pour her a glass of eternal life.

"Ahh, shit," he said under his breath as he slid down in the Fiat's bucket seat. He was in Florence, Italy. He was so far from his little girl's life. Did he ever cross her mind?

Jack was in such a stupor that Cyrus's rap on the window made his head hit the ceiling of the tiny car.

"Holy shit!" he gasped.

"I got what I need. Let's go." Cyrus shooed him out of the driver's seat and into the passenger side. He started the car.

"What did you get?"

Cyrus glanced in the rearview. Jack cranked his head around and saw a gap of light in the drapes next door. He released the clutch and the car rolled slowly down the street. "I'll show you at the hotel."

For being an Italian hotel, it still had two plain twin beds with uncomfortable shiny bedspreads and wallpaper that peeled beside the shower in the postage-stamp bathroom. Jack dropped onto the squeaky mattress and watched Cyrus methodically unpack his day bag, plug in his phone, put his toothbrush in the bathroom. Cyrus's forehead was deeply furrowed the whole time.

Finally he sat down opposite Jack and sighed. "Well." He picked up his tablet off the nightstand and tapped on the screen.

"Yeah, what's going on?" Jack said wearily.

Cyrus gazed at the screen. "I found a few things. First of all, Alannah's picture of the man matches photos in the house of Ardovinni and his boyfriend." He held up the tablet to show Jack a picture of a framed photograph of two men, one with dark curly hair and a wry smile, and the other with short blond hair and brooding dark eyes. Cyrus tapped the dark haired man. "This is Ardovinni. The other is Alexei, and according to documents I found in the house, his surname is di Gaspare."

Cyrus's lips pressed tightly together for a moment. He leaned forward, making the hotel bed creak. "This is what requires explanation," he said slowly, "because Ardovinni was very close with a woman by the name of Cosima di Gaspare. Cosima was also Alexander's lover—"

"Oh, so he's Alexander's and this Cosima's kid? Or this is Ardovinni's kid? No, wait—" Jack rubbed his chin and squinted at Cyrus.

"I guess you've about connected the dots, then," Cyrus said wearily.

"But that's illegal, yeah?"

Cyrus held up his hand. "We haven't proven anything, but yes. It is definitely illegal. The fact that Alexander would never have intentionally fathered a child—"

"No?"

"No, definitely not!" Cyrus rubbed his forehead with the back of his hand. "This is a man who didn't marry the woman that he loved because he didn't want to have children. He *put* the law in place."

"Oh." Jack raised an eyebrow. "Whoops."

Cyrus gripped his tablet for a moment and stared toward the window with his lips pressed tightly together. His eyes were sad. "Alexander doesn't want a child, Jack."

There was a burn of irritation starting in the back of Jack's throat. "Well, what if he's got one? And an immortal one, maybe?"

He got up and began to pace with his arms crossed tightly across his chest. "Most of us don't have the luxury of keeping our kids."

"Some never have children at all," Cyrus said under his breath. "The idea that Alexander may have a child isn't as concerning as the idea that he may be immortal."

"Because of the water?" Jack asked.

Cyrus nodded. "Exactly. Where would Cosima get water from?"

"Alexander could get it, right?" Jack said slowly, "He was the one who... you know."

"That wouldn't make any sense, though." Cyrus gnawed his bottom lip. "All we've done is open a larger can of worms, Jack. We have to talk to Ardovinni."

Jack's phone dinged. Cyrus glanced reflexively at his own phone as Jack dug his out of his pocket.

It was Alannah: *Getting ready for first Jiu Jitsu lesson. Tell me I can do this.*

A little smile came to Jack's mouth in spite of himself. He texted back, *You're a badass.*

"I'm going to call Idina," Cyrus said. The bed groaned as he got up.

Jack picked up his phone to text Alannah again but couldn't summon words. He was suddenly tired beyond belief. He crossed the room toward his backpack, but ended up staring out the window at the blowing cypress tree, illuminated in the hotel lights. He wanted a drink. He wanted a drink so bad.

Actually, that wasn't what he really wanted. For the first time since Daniel had pulled him out of the slaughterhouse, he wished for a bullet in his brain.

Jack glanced furtively around the room. Cyrus was engrossed in a quiet conversation with Alexander.

I've got no gun, no knife, and a lawman in the room.

"I'm gonna..." Jack looked over his shoulder at Cyrus, but Cyrus wasn't facing his direction "...I'm gonna go take a shower."

He carried clean clothes into the bathroom and locked the door behind him. He planted his hands on the counter and stared at the little one-cup coffee maker and the two glass cups, wrapped in plastic. An image flickered in his head, of smashing the glass, using the sharp edge to slash his throat.

Maybe if I just cut myself a little... Jack fumbled at the buttons of his of his oxford shirt.

You think Cyrus won't hear you smash the glass?

I can say it was an accident. Jack picked up the glass in one trembling hand. He pulled off the plastic bag that covered it.

No, I can't.

Jack groaned and set the cup down. He scrubbed at his eyes. He didn't even know what he was thinking. Maybe he was just tired and overwrought. He knelt beside the bathtub and turned on the cold water. He was about to thrust his head under when something vibrated in his pocket. The phone vibrated again, and Jack straightened and fished out his phone from his pocket. Alannah's picture signaled her desire to video chat.

Jack slapped the faucet off and swiped the screen. Alannah's blurry image popped up. "Hey Jack. Oh... are you in the bathroom?" She laughed nervously.

Jack clapped his free hand to his chest. "Oh, uh, I was going to take a shower." He grabbed his shirt off the top of the toilet and slipped it on. He set the phone down and started to do up his buttons. "Aren't you going to Jiu Jitsu class?"

"I..." Alannah's voice came small and quavering from the phone, "It's not for fifteen minutes. I'm trying to work myself up to it."

His shirt done up, Jack sat down on the toilet and picked up the phone. He ran his free hand through his short hair.

"It's growing back," Alannah said softly. "Your hair."

Jack looked down. "Yeah, I look a little less like a POW now."

"You okay? You look..."

"Tired." Jack forced a smile. "Seriously, aren't you going to Jiu Jitsu?"

"I'm scared." After a long pause, she said, "You must think I'm ridiculous."

"No," Jack said softly, "you're talking to the man who made a habit of killing himself. I don't think you're ridiculous."

"In Winnipeg I had my routines, you know? I felt safe. It's not logical, and I'm a logical person. I just need to walk across the street and I can't... I can't logic myself into it, Jack!" Her face scrunched like she might cry. "What was I thinking?"

Jack shifted on the toilet seat.

There was a thump on the bathroom door. "Jack, are you talking to Alannah while sitting on the toilet?"

Jack jumped off the seat. "No!"

"Well, kind of," Alannah said from the phone in his hand. She smiled just a little.

"Umm..." Cyrus's muffled voice continued, just on the other side of the door, "I'm going to find us some food, I guess."

"You can do this, Alannah," Jack said in a low voice. "Are you ready to go? I'll walk you across the street."

The screen swirled as Alannah stood up. Jack caught a glimpse of a nylon duffle bag as she picked it up. She squared the camera on her face. "No," she said resolutely, "I'm going to do it. I'll text you when I get there."

"Do it."

Alannah's eyes were still uncertain but she nodded. "Okay, here I go." Her finger hovered over the screen for a second, and the call disconnected.

Jack blew out his breath and set the phone down. He was still tired, but the urge to die had dissipated.

CHAPTER 10

London, Present Day

Alannah only stood staring at the brown-brick exterior of John Lin's Martial Arts Academy for about two minutes. Her chest was tight. She didn't want to go in, but she didn't want to stand in the street either. In the end, a teenage boy came swaggering out and stared at her, for standing and staring. So Alannah walked in and paused just inside the door, in front of a tiny front desk where a busty young woman in a black, John Lin t-shirt sat on a stool, laughing with a dark-haired young man who perched on the edge of the counter. The wall behind them was a backdrop of posters, mostly of shirtless men posing with fists up, advertising MMA fights. Above the patchwork of posters, two samurai swords glinted in the bluish fluorescent lights.

She pulled out her phone and texted Jack with shaking hands: *I made it.*

"Hey," the young man said as he dropped from the counter, "are you here for the beginner classes?"

"Umm..." Alannah fumbled with the plastic shopping bag holding her gym clothes, clothes that had arrived by mail the day before. She'd ordered them online, of course. "Yes, yes I am." Why hadn't she just worn the clothes? She'd just walked across the street, for goodness' sake.

"If you need to change, the women's room is to the left." He nodded in that general direction. Alannah glanced left and saw a set of doors, across the red mat floor. "I'm Lewis, the instructor. We'll meet right..." he leaned forward and pointed to the corner opposite the ladies' room, "...there in ten minutes."

"Thanks," Alannah said, breathlessly.

"Cheers," Lewis said, and turned back to the woman behind the counter.

She opened the locker room door into bright sunlight, shining through a barred, textured-glass window to the outside street. Two young women stood in their sports bras, talking casually as they swept their hair up into ponytails. Alannah picked a locker that was hanging slightly open, and glanced around for a stall or partition— why hadn't she at least put on her sports bra at home?

In the end, she made do in the two-stall bathroom, emerging in calf-length tights and a t-shirt to stand in front of the now vacant mirror to wrestle her curls into a French-braid. When was the last time she'd worn sports wear? Twenty-five, thirty years had changed fashions considerably, but truth was she had no idea what to wear to a Jiu Jitsu class. She might never wear this new suit again.

Alannah glanced at the black, skin-tight pants she wore, which emphasized her more than adequate thighs. Perhaps she was alright with never wearing them again.

She drew a deep breath, and walked out to join the two other women in the corner Lewis had indicated. They were both twisting this way and that and stretching. Alannah looked around and bit her lip. She wanted to puke.

"Oh my god," someone groaned nearby, "I can't believe I signed up for this."

Alannah glanced behind her as she wiped her sweaty hands on her tights. A tiny girl in a gi, probably college age, with a long blond ponytail, bounced from foot to foot, simultaneously tugging on the ends of her white belt. Her green eyes met Alannah's.

"Let me guess," she said in a miserable tone, "you're halfway pro already."

"Hah!" Alannah gasped. She wiped her hands again, if only to steady them. No one else was wearing a gi. Was she supposed to wear a gi too? "This is my first lesson. I'm Alannah, by the way."

"Jules," the blonde said breathlessly. She finally stopped bouncing and settled beside Alannah. They both placed their hands on their hips and stared across the gym to where two men were clenched in a hold, down on the mat. One, blond hair buzzed down to his scalp, explained something to five young guys who stood at the edge of the mat. The other strained to escape, but the speaker seemed to hold him with no effort.

Was that her blond motorcycle rider? His face was away from her. She couldn't put a face to her mystery man.

"Damn," Jules said, "I could get used to having them around."

"Tell me we won't be doing that." Alannah sighed as a couple of teenage boys sauntered to stand nearby.

"No, that we won't," Lewis's cheerful voice said beside them. All female heads turned as their compact, muscular, young instructor walked up. He swept his bright gaze over all of them. "I'm Lewis." He planted himself in front of all of them, hands on hips, and grinned. "I'm a black belt in Brazilian Jiu Jitsu. I'll be your instructor. Welcome to your first lesson in martial arts."

"Yay," Jules said sarcastically.

"What?" Lewis turned and smirked at her. "Enthusiastic, are we? Well, step up. You'll be my first victim."

"Ooh, I'm so scared." Jules swaggered forward and held up both fists in a fighter stance.

"No, no punching." Lewis pushed her hands down. "We're going to warm up, that's all. Let's bow in."

No one moved.

Lewis waved them toward the mat. "Stand in a circle—" They arranged themselves into a lopsided ellipse, "—feet together, and bow."

Beside her, Jules dropped into a low, courtly bow. One of the teenage boys snickered.

"A small bow will do," Lewis drawled, "I'm not the queen."

"Really?" Jules said, straightening her gi. "But you smell like an old lady."

Muffled giggles came from behind Alannah. Alannah squeezed her lips shut to keep from laughing. Lewis stared at Jules incredulously, and shook his head.

Forty-five minutes later, Alannah was stuck on the mat with Jules' wiry legs wrapped around her. She dropped back. "Okay, okay already. I give up."

"Tap," Jules grunted.

"No, I'm not..." Alannah strained at Jules' body. "I'm not tapping. You're not... you're not Bruce Lee."

"Okay, let her up, Jules." Lewis helped Alannah to her feet and smiled into her eyes, "You're doing fine," he said in a low voice.

"I wish I had her energy." Alannah rubbed the back of her head and took her place on the edge of the mat as Lewis began to demonstrate with another student. She almost felt all her years, just now. She'd certainly feel this tomorrow.

"I'm too old for this," she muttered to the girl beside her.

"I know, right?" The slim blonde, who could have been Jules's sister, kept her eyes on Lewis and the young guy he was teaching.

Alannah wiped the sweat off her brow.

An hour later, Alannah sat on her bed with a blanket wrapped around her, drinking a glass of water. She pushed herself up to her knees and peered at the door of the Academy. The black motorcycle still stood outside, just below her window, illuminated by the streetlight. Alannah took a sip of water and tilted her head to the side. She was just about to turn around when the door of the school opened, and a dark figure emerged. He paused, as if locking the door behind him, before sauntering across the street to his bike. His face, wreathed in shadows, was hidden to her. In a moment, the bike revved, and he roared away.

Alannah picked up her phone and texted Jack, *Survived my first Jiu Jitsu class.* A little smile played on her lips.

You're a badass, he texted back about a minute later, *soon you'll be kicking butt.*

I'm no expert, but I haven't seen any kicking yet, she returned.

He didn't reply. She wondered what he was doing, far away. "Badass," she muttered to herself. "Yeah right." She hadn't travelled half a block from the flat in the last week. Maybe once she could manage that she'd be able to work her way up to Dresden. She could start working on it tomorrow.

∞

Alannah knelt on the bed and stared down at the door of the John Lin Academy. The motorcycle wasn't there. Alannah padded across the flat to the front window and watched the commuters in light coats or sweaters, carrying paper cups of coffee out of the cafe across the busy street.

"I'm not drinking another cup of that stupid tea," she said. Alannah walked back into the bedroom and rifled through the dresser for proper clothes. She knotted a wine-colored pashmina scarf around her neck and slung on her coat. The instant her boots hit the sidewalk, the butterflies were shocked awake in her stomach.

Alannah set her jaw. A black taxi cab sped past, and she scurried across the street and through the door into the back of the line. The aroma of espresso, the hiss of steam into hot milk, and the chatter of the morning crowd washed over her. Alannah sighed and tipped her head back.

She found a tiny corner table to set down her crescent roll, yogurt parfait, and macchiato. She leaned her head against the window and let the sun warm her face. As the foam from her macchiato tickled her top lip, her phone beeped.

Is now a good time to call? Idina.

Yes, now is fine. Alannah crammed a quick bite of the roll into her mouth to appease her grumbling stomach. She swallowed as the phone began to ring.

"Hey, Alannah," Idina's voice was brusque, hurried. "Whatcha doing?"

"Having coffee across the street at that cafe."

"Oh yeah?" Idina said. "I have an idea for you."

"Okay." Alannah stared at her coffee. Her stomach contracted gently.

"Would you be interested in a job?"

"What?" Alannah squeaked.

"Um, yeah. I have a contact who is looking for an immortal to fill a position if she can. Would you stoop to being a librarian?"

A choked laugh escaped from Alannah's mouth. She swallowed hard.

"Her name is Louisa," Idina said quietly, "she's very sweet, and I can vouch for her. She is a good friend."

The fact was that she needed an income. It wouldn't be right to live off Alexander's dole forever. "Where is it?" she asked in as even of a tone as she could muster.

"At the Central Library of Imperial College. It's in South Kensington."

Alannah licked her lips, trying to mentally work out how far away that was. Far enough. "Alright, what do I have to do?"

"I'll email you the details, and you can contact Louisa. It sounds like you could start right away."

Right away? Alannah sighed. "Okay, send them to me and I'll... I'll see what I can do. Hey, uh..."

"Yeah?"

She could hear Idina shuffling papers on the other end of the line. Alannah could imagine Idina's office in Schwalenburg, with a big, oak desk that had belonged to Daniel once, and a claymore sword hanging on the back wall. Was it still like that?

"Uh, have you found out anything about this Alexei?" Alannah asked.

The phone line was conspicuously silent for a long beat. "Right now," Idina said softly, "we only have more questions. Cyrus wants to chase down Ardovinni."

"Oh." Alannah said. "Well, alright. Did you tell Alexander about it yet?"

"No! No." Idina laughed under her breath. "God, no."

"Good. Okay, well, you'll send me the job posting?"

"Already did," Idina said.

Alannah carried her coffee and breakfast back up into the apartment, and sat for about five minutes with her knees pulled to her chest in the center of the bed. "Do it," she said under her breath. "Do it, Alannah." She pulled her laptop off the nightstand and flipped it open. In a few minutes she had typed her name into an online application to the job—a formality, the email from Louisa said. There was a box that said 'when are you available to start?'

Alannah typed 'immediately', shut her eyes, and clicked send.

CHAPTER 11
London, 1921

"Mr. Ardovinni is in the library, Sir," the butler said as he took Alexander's dripping umbrella and overcoat and eyed Daniel, who was stomping off his muddy boots by the door.

"Thank you," Alexander said, still somewhat breathless from the howling wind and driving rain. "Good heavens," he muttered to Daniel as they walked across the wide, bare floor where they'd danced the night before. "However much you've had to drink the night before, and however clear your head is now, next time we will still take a cab." Daniel's boots were still leaving damp prints on the wood.

"Quiet," Daniel muttered. "A walk didn't help worth shite." As the butler opened the library door, Daniel added, "Zoran better not chirp too loudly."

"Sir Alexander." Ardovinni stood from one of the wingback chairs. "Mr. Gunther."

Zoran rose out of the other with a little smirk on his face.

"Can I offer you coffee?" Ardovinni asked.

The Italian had dark smudges under his eyes, but he was immaculate in morning dress. Zoran had already sat down. He was without a jacket, and his collar hung open exposing his collarbone.

"Coffee would be excellent," Alexander replied.

"Stevens?" Ardovinni looked past him, at the butler.

The butler slipped out.

Ardovinni swept his gaze around the room and sighed almost inaudibly. "Is this room suitable to your purpose or would you prefer my study?"

"How discreet is your staff?" Alexander asked.

"How nosy, he means," Daniel muttered.

"Very nosy," Zoran said lazily. He propped his feet up on the little coffee table between the chairs. "I think there is very little of master Ardovinni's business that Mr. Burke hasn't... inserted himself into."

Ardovinni flinched, then rolled his eyes. "Mr. Kosar has his nose out of joint because I had Burke monitoring him yesterday evening. Use my study, then. I assure you no one will be listening at keyholes."

Stevens brought coffee. Alexander and Daniel ushered Zoran into Ardovinni's study and sat him down by the desk. Alexander took what was likely Ardovinni's chair. Daniel leaned against the wall behind him and took a slurp from his coffee.

Zoran laced his fingers together on top of the desk, and eyed them both. "So," he said, "I understand we have lost one of our own."

"Joseph Oswald," Alexander replied, "he was found drowned in his bathtub."

"Permanently drowned, Ardovinni tells me." Zoran licked his lips. His face lost his apathetic expression and his eyes took on a sharp glint. "How very fortunate for you that Signor Ardovinni has eyes in his head, or I would have come and went from London without anyone's notice."

"You did visit Oswald, then?" Alexander asked, "and didn't visit any other immortal for fear of Oswald's scheme being discovered?"

Zoran laughed. "I didn't visit any other immortal because I had no wish to. I was there at Oswald's request. He contacted me. They were his experiments and he conducted them, I presume, until the end."

Oswald's grey, distorted face returned to Alexander's memory. Under the desk, his fingers dug into his knees. The smell of coffee from the cup abandoned on the desktop wafted up to him. It turned his stomach. "What did Oswald want from you?"

Zoran opened his hands. "He knew I was interested in science, and despite my interest lying more in the area of heredity, I suppose he found in me a kindred spirit. He wanted help conducting experiments he couldn't conduct himself."

Daniel straightened from his position against the wall. "Such as cutting out his heart?"

"Indeed," Zoran said without emotion, "as well as drowning, as I'm sure you've already read in Joseph's journals."

"You're a sick man," Daniel growled.

Zoran laughed again. "You flatter me, Mr. Gunther. I never said I enjoyed cutting his heart out. Quite to the contrary, but Joseph was sedated every time. If a man wants to die, then what is sick about giving him his fondest wish?"

"You must have known it would fail!" Daniel slammed his empty coffee cup down. "We've had immortals drown. I was bayonetted through the heart not so long ago."

Zoran pressed his fingertips together. "Perhaps we did, but we were looking for patterns, for clues. We were conducting *science*."

"Given the patterns and clues you observed," Alexander asked slowly, "do you know what killed Oswald?"

"I wasn't there," Zoran shrugged. "How should I know that? Let me read his journals. Maybe Oswald himself can tell us."

"We read them," Daniel said.

"I would see them quite differently than you," Zoran said simply.

Alexander and Daniel glanced at each other.

"We'll consider it," Alexander said. "For the time being, Zoran, we must ask you to stay in London."

Zoran's face resumed its blasé expression. "I am quite content to extend my stay, but I don't suppose I could arrange to board elsewhere? Ardovinni's valet keeps watching me like I'm about to make off with the silver. Ardovinni has set a watchman, it seems."

Daniel chuckled under his breath.

Alexander surveyed Zoran. "If you give us your word that you will be at our disposal, you are welcome to put yourself up in a hotel."

"Good." Zoran pushed back his chair. "Let me know when I may read Oswald's journals."

Ardovinni was slumped in his chair in the library with a notebook open on his knees. The bleak morning light cast murky shadows across his face. He jumped up as they approached and clapped the book shut. His dark eyes fixed intently on Alexander's face. "Did you learn anything of use?"

"Only that we confirmed that Zoran was assisting Oswald," Alexander said. He pressed his fingers to his temple to fend off the dull beginnings of a headache.

Ardovinni's lips pulled tightly together for a moment. He tipped his head, began to speak but stopped himself. His hand lifted halfway into a gesture, then dropped to his side.

"What, Ardovinni?" Alexander asked.

"Did you ask Zoran about the vial he carries around his neck?" Ardovinni looked up at him.

Alexander stared at him. "A vial..." He recalled Zoran's open collar and disheveled person. "I saw no vial."

"Oh," Ardovinni looked down and nodded. "Oh, I see."

Alexander's brows knit together. "Was it a glass vial, something of a petal shape on a silver chain?"

Ardovinni inclined his head. "Indeed."

"Then I know the one you speak of," Alexander said. "He's had it for a very long time. I'm not surprised he didn't want to give it up."

"Ah," Ardovinni nodded. He didn't meet Alexander's eyes.

"Zoran will be taking himself off your hands soon," Alexander said, "he said he intended to take a hotel."

Ardovinni smiled for the first time that morning. "Well, that is most welcome news." He turned toward the interior of the library and dug one hand into his hair. "Though admittedly the more he spends on lodging, the less he will repay to me. I suppose that is a small price to pay for being able to walk around my own home and not be treated like something of a jailer combined with an insect."

"He owes you money?" Daniel snorted. "For what?"

"A—" Ardovinni turned to face them, and once again cut himself off, "Scientific research, I believe. He has a lab set up for himself in France, about which I asked very few questions."

Alexander nodded. "I see. Well, I appreciate this, Ardovinni. I truly do. I am sorry you've had to endure Zoran."

Ardovinni nodded.

"Is..." Alexander licked his dry lips. "Is Miss di Gaspare at home?"

Ardovinni smiled wearily. "She intended to sleep late. She supervised the cleaning up last night and sent me to bed."

"Oh, oh, of course," Alexander said. "Excuse us, Mr. Ardovinni."

"Glad to be of some help. I will call for a cab."

∞

"I understand you will be departing?" Giovanni eyed the suitcase through Zoran's open bedroom door. Shirts were scattered all over the bed.

"Yes," Zoran said and turned from the bookcase with a thick volume in his hands, "I think we would both like a little distance." He smiled, for once not at all mocking in his expression. Genuinely happy, it seemed. "Seneca? Cicero? Do you actually read these, Ardovinni?"

"Is it so difficult to believe?" Giovanni squinted at him. Zoran had tidied his appearance, now decent, if not quite faultlessly dressed. A silver chain gleamed against the burgundy of his necktie. The vial. It was stuffed into the top of his waistcoat.

Zoran fingered the spine of the book. "What proud history cannot be found in our own society, this we must find elsewhere."

"Roman history is my history," Giovanni said, "distant though it may be. But I am not ashamed of my immortal history."

"I am," Zoran said, gazing keenly at him, "perhaps I have done what I can to change things according to my principles, but they have not gone as I wished. We are a fragmented and backward society, Ardovinni."

This analysis took Giovanni aback. He had approached Zoran's room steeling himself to confront him about the mysterious vial, the identity and purpose of which continued to gnaw at him. Instead, he was receiving immortal quasi-political commentary.

"We shun science that might unlock the mysteries of our immortal condition," Zoran continued, his voice rising. "Instead the so-called Lords we have instated prefer fatalism." He fixed Ardovinni with his stare. "You aren't religious, Ardovinni, are you?"

Giovanni didn't answer. He didn't really expect Zoran wanted one. He was as religious as he was able to be. He attended mass, though not confession. Not ever.

"These close-minded men think science and religion are opposed, and perhaps religion as they know it is opposed to men who seek to unlock the secrets of immortal life and death by experimenting on their own persons."

So they had come around to it. "You know how he killed himself don't you, Mr. Kosar?"

A little smile formed on Zoran's lips. He shrugged. "I wasn't there."

Annoyance burned in the back of Giovanni's throat. "Yes, I am sure that is what you said to Sir Alexander, but I know codswallop when I hear it."

"I wasn't." Zoran spread his hands. "Alexander and Gunther need to pin Oswald's death on someone and it is a convenient figure you've brought them, Ardovinni. Mark my words, if they know the truth they'll do no good with it."

"And you will." Let the son of a bitch keep talking, and Zoran would give him information enough to use. Giovanni was sure of it.

Light kindled in Zoran's eyes. "It's perfection, Ardovinni. Immortal life as long as we wish, and death on our own terms. Simplicity, and right under our noses all this time."

"Ah." Giovanni smiled to himself. "All this time. So you do know how Oswald died."

Zoran's face froze, a word half-formed.

"You're wearing the vial again, I see." Giovanni pointed to the silver top of the vial, dislodged from Zoran's waistcoat by his gestures. "I wonder why you were so concerned that Alexander not notice it. Ah—"

Zoran had opened his mouth to speak again.

"—he didn't see it," Giovanni said, "I asked."

Zoran's face became rigid. His clear eyes had become hard, flat black. "What do you want from me now?"

Giovanni took a step closer and picked up the chain between two fingers. The vial slid out from under Zoran's waistcoat. Giovanni examined it, as Burke had, with the chain pulling Zoran's head forward. Zoran pulled back and the chain yanked tight between them. The same, transparent liquid sloshed inside the vial.

"Careful, " Zoran muttered, "you'll make your valet jealous."

Giovanni ignored him. "Is this water?"

Zoran was silent.

Giovanni released the vial and let it drop against Zoran's chest. The liquid slapped against the vial. "Water. Curious. Oswald drowned, no?"

"Ahh," Zoran growled, "you have it *all* figured out. I'll ask you again, Ardovinni, what do you want? This is a god-awfully strange way of making me pay back money."

Giovanni laughed. "Zoran, as I see it there are two things you want to protect right now. You want to keep that vial, and you want to keep your pregnant lover a secret. As I see it, if you will confess your role in Oswald's death to Sir Alexander in a thorough manner, I'll draw no attention to your forthcoming child."

Zoran eyed him. "I suppose the converse shall be that if I do not, you shall draw attention to the aforementioned child."

"Yes." Giovanni said.

Zoran sighed. "And the water?"

Giovanni shrugged.

They fell silent. Somewhere within the house a clock began to chime. Sharp footfalls approached. Giovanni glanced out the door and saw Burke coming down the hall, carrying a stack of shirts. He raised a brow but stared straight ahead as he passed by the door.

Giovanni turned back. Zoran's smoldering gaze was fastened on him. Zoran reached into his waistcoat and withdrew the vial again. "You know what this is?"

Giovanni nodded.

"No," Zoran shook his head. "You know it's water, and from the fountain, but do you know what this is? It is immortality for whoever you wish."

A sensation, like icy water, dashed over Giovanni's shoulders. "That is illegal."

Zoran shrugged. "Maybe, but we are immortal. What is a fine, or a jail sentence? It is but a slap on the hand if it meant keeping the one you loved forever." He shook the vial. "I will give you half of the contents to do with whatever you wish. In return, you will keep your silence."

Giovanni's heart began to pound painfully inside his chest. Zoran folded his arms across his chest, and the vial rested on his forearm.

He could take the water. Why not? He could keep it, and not use it.

Giovanni lifted his eyes and met Zoran's inky gaze. "Alright. But give it to me now. I'll not have you swap it for plain water."

Zoran nodded. "Then I will tell Alexander how I think Oswald died."

"What will you say about the fountain water?"

Zoran crossed the room to his suitcase and withdrew two brown, glass bottles of perhaps two ounces each. He took the chain from around his neck and began working the tiny stopper free. As Giovanni watched, he divided the water equally between them. He handed one bottle to Giovanni and pushed the other deep into the clothing in the suitcase. He hung the vial back around his neck.

"There," he said. "The vial is empty. If asked, the water is gone. I gave it all to Oswald."

Giovanni stared at the brown glass bottle, already warm from his palm. He closed his fingers around it and held out his other hand to Zoran. "Very well. It is a deal."

Zoran shook his hand. His fingers were icy.

CHAPTER 12

London, Present Day

"Alannah?"

Alannah, who'd been pressing her fingernails into her palms and craning her neck to look up the spiraling floors of the library, dropped her gaze and swung around. Her breath stuck in her throat.

"So pleased to see you." A woman with wispy blonde hair and a sweet smile stood behind her, holding out a plump, white hand. "I am Louisa. We spoke on the telephone."

"Pleased to meet you." Alannah grasped Louisa's hand and felt the tension that had balled up in her chest dissipate.

"Welcome to the Central Library," Louisa said as she released Alannah's hand. She flung one arm wide. "It isn't beautiful, but I daresay it is one of the finest libraries in London." With her other hand she fingered the cameo broach at the collar of her filmy blouse. She eyed the glass railing and functional metal trim and smiled ruefully. "Allow me to show you to your office, and then perhaps we shall take a grand tour."

Alannah smiled to herself as Louisa led her across the circular atrium, toward the offices at the rear of the library. Idina had said that Louisa was of the Victorian era. Though she wore slim black pants, her high-collared blouse and shawl-like, draping cardigan were reminiscent of another time. She'd safely managed to hang onto the past, it seemed.

Alannah glanced at her suit, the same slim-fitting suit she'd felt so self-conscious about wearing on the first day of classes in Winnipeg. She'd retained nothing of the wardrobe from her past life. She really had no desire to. But perhaps Louisa's parting with her past had been happier.

"This is Catharine," Louisa said as they approached the circulation desks. "Catharine, this is Alannah Krueger, our newest librarian for the social sciences."

"Oh!" Catharine stood behind her desk and held out a hand. Her luminous, dark eyes were huge in her thin face. Her navy cardigan draped loosely over her narrow shoulders. But as Alannah took her hand, she saw the spreading oak tattoo on her wrist.

"So pleased to meet you," Catharine said in a soft, French accent. "The three of us must have lunch together as soon as possible."

"Oh yes!" Louisa exclaimed.

A warm feeling suffused Alannah and her smiled widened. "Yes, we must."

"You are actually training to replace Catharine," Louisa said in an undertone as they passed the desks. She paused to open a door for Alannah. "She has lived here for nearly twenty years. She'll be moving on soon."

"Ahh," Alannah whispered.

Louisa licked her lips and glanced down, "You can imagine how relieved I was when Idina approached me with a qualified immortal for the job. I love my mortal coworkers, but you... you can't exactly let them deep into your heart, you know?"

"Yeah." Alannah sighed.

"But in any case, this is your office."

Alannah looked up and slid her gaze around the room, over the empty bookshelves, the bare walls that needed just a little bit of patching and paint, and the desk. A real wood desk, fortunately, and not that particleboard nightmare that she'd had in Winnipeg. And there was a window, bathing the whole room in bluish, spring light.

"This is nice," she said as she dropped her bag on the empty desk.

"You think so?" Louisa asked, twisting the edge of her sweater. "Well, good then. Oh..."

Catharine's light accent came from the other room. "Louisa?"

"One moment." Louisa slipped from the doorway.

Alannah sat down on the modern contraption of a chair and swung around. Her nerves returned, full force, to constrict her breathing and set her teeth chattering. She pulled out her phone, about to text Idina and ask her who Catharine was.

Why are you scared?

Idina didn't say there'd be a second immortal.

Did that matter? No, logically no, it was just that Alannah had mentally gone through the entire day, meeting Louisa, being friendly to another immortal woman that she'd never met, and now there were two, and what if they didn't like her?

I'm being ridiculous.

Alannah laughed under her breath. "You just think it's too good to be true," she said as she shoved her phone back in her bag, "you think it's impossible to actually belong here, don't you?"

She heard a soft throat clearing, and looked up into Louisa's blue eyes.

"I know how you feel," Louisa said gently, her eyes misting, "But don't worry. You're among friends now."

Alannah felt her throat seize and looked down, swallowing hard.

"In any case," Louisa said and cleared her throat once more, "here are your keys. The ones marked with the tape are for your office. The rest I will describe as we tour. I'll give you a few moments to settle in, alright?"

"Okay," Alannah said softly.

Louisa's face lit up. "Oh, and Cat reminded me that we're going out to dinner tonight after work. You should come—a lovely little bistro not far from here. Unless you have plans?"

"Plans?" Not hardly. She'd planned to curl up on the couch with one of Idina's novels, expecting to be too tired to do anything else. She was too tired to do anything else. She wanted to hide.

When's the last time you went out to dinner with a friend?

"No, I'd love to," she heard herself say.

"Great!" Louisa beamed brighter than the sun through the window. "I'll let Cat know. I'll see you in a few minutes."

Eight hours later, the sunny sky that had ushered Alannah into Imperial College was covered by low-flying, dirty-grey clouds. As Louisa, Cat, and Alannah piled into a little black taxi cab, the clouds opened up and poured down rain.

They ran, laughing, all with their heads stuck under Cat's umbrella, under the awning of the bistro.

"Patio seats, my ladies?" The host, a slim young man with bronze skin, grinned at them as Cat shook off the umbrella.

"The usual table," Louisa replied, and they sailed into the dining room behind him.

As they slid into the corner booth, Alannah's phone buzzed in her coat pocket. It was Jack, sending a picture of him, in gym shorts and a slim fitting t-shirt. He looked thinner—very thin—but he smiled. His forehead gleamed with sweat. Cyrus must have taken it. A second later, a text came: *Evening run with Cy.*

Looks nice. Better weather than here, she replied.

"Who're you texting?" Louisa slung her coat in the corner and slid in beside her. She grinned slyly and leaned in. She caught sight of the picture. "Oooh, the boyfriend is sending you sexy pictures?"

"What?" Cat half-laughed. She leaned in over the table, pushing her purse into the corner as she did.

"Oh, no." Alannah laughed. "That's Jack. He's not my boyfriend and that's just him being... stupid." She slid the phone back into her pocket before they got a good look at it, even if a man in sweaty gym clothes was hardly what she'd call a sexy picture.

"Cute," Louisa said.

"Young," Cat said, tilting her head as if still looking at the photo, "he still looks young. Once we get to a certain age, we don't look any age, really."

"He's fifty-two, I think." Alannah squinted at Cat's unlined face. No, Cat didn't look old, but really she didn't look young either. "About half my age."

"Half? Then you're practically a baby yourself." Cat laughed.

Alannah caught sight of a waiter approaching and lifted her chin in his direction.

"Wine?" Louisa asked Cat as the young waiter stopped beside them.

Cat nodded. "Hmm... a Riesling, I think." She glanced at Alannah with her limpid eyes. "Is that... alright?"

"Oh, yeah, yeah."

"What's the special today?" Louisa asked sweetly up at the waiter.

"Pan seared chicken with Jamaican Curry."

"Oooh, that's a bit too spicy for me." Louisa picked up the menu again.

"I'll have it," Cat said. A little smile played around her lips. After Louisa and Alannah ordered and the waiter retreated, she grinned devilishly. "Cowards."

"Oooh, I resent that!" Louisa said. She leaned toward Alannah and tapped her fingers on Alannah's arm. "So, Jack is not your boyfriend. Are you single?"

"Quite," Alannah said with a rueful smile. "Chronically, I'd say." It came with the territory, being a hermit from immortal society and all. The last man to even hint at a date was a young, lonely history professor, Miles Corder in Winnipeg. Poor Miles.

"Oh, me too." Cat sighed. "It isn't as if the dating scene is booming in our society, but England is the very worst place to be right now, I'm afraid."

"Very true," Lousia said. "We have exactly two immortal men in England right now, and both are married."

"Three," Cat said, "If you count Giovanni Ardovinni."

"Oh!" Alannah's heartrate began to accelerate. "He lives here?" Idina had never said that. Why hadn't Idina said that?

"Oh, only part time I think." Louisa waved her hand, completely unaware of Alannah's diminishing composure. "I haven't seen him in months." She leaned in, "We all think he has a boyfriend here."

"Oh goodness," Alannah muttered. "He isn't around now, then."

Louisa shook her head.

Cat eyed her for a moment. "Louisa has had some excitement recently, in that regard—men and boyfriends, I mean."

Alannah, still vaguely unsettled, turned to the blond woman beside her. "Really?" she asked in as light and interested of a tone as she could manage.

"Yes and no." Louisa wiggled a little in her seat. "Well, yes," she said as the waiter placed wine glasses in front of them with one hand, and the bottle with the other. He wrapped a white cloth around the neck of the bottle and poured for all of them. When he had gone, she continued. "I met someone when I was in Dresden, two weekends ago. Just a... handsome, blond, charming man."

Alannah tilted her head. "Daniel?"

"The lawkeeper? No, his name is Kristiaan. He's a doctor."

"Oh, I don't know him. I know of him, but I've never met him." Alannah smiled wryly. "I could have recommended Daniel to you—rather strongly. I dated him, many years ago. He's a good man. And," she added, "charming, blond and handsome."

"Yes, but taken," Louisa said, wiggling in her seat again. "Anastasie has laid claim to him."

Cat sipped her wine and raised an eyebrow. "He ought to be taken. He's more than four-hundred years old, and Anastasie is about his age. I'm sorry, Alannah, but he should have married her long ago instead of fooling around here and there with women a quarter his age."

Louisa laughed nervously.

"Immortal men are afraid of commitment," Cat continued, "They think they have to get it exactly right before they can settle down for eternity with a woman. It's nonsense. They would have been perfectly happy together two hundred years ago. Or," she added with a nod toward Alannah, "with you, I'm sure."

Alannah blinked. "I broke it off with him," she said softly, "though I'm sure we would have been happy if things had continued as... as planned."

Cat stopped, wine halfway to her lips. Her dark eyes fixed intently on Alannah's face. "Zoran's daughter, that's right."

Alannah flinched. And here was why it had been easier to stay in Winnipeg.

Cat set the wine down and touched Alannah's hand. "I'm very sorry. I've picked the wrong time and subject for ranting." She turned to Louisa. "Tell us about your handsome blond man, and I'll be quiet."

Louisa cleared her throat. Her cheeks turned pink. "Doctor den Hollander and I met at Schwalenburg when I went in. He is the doctor in residence there, but he also has a practice in Dresden..."

The tension began to ebb out of Alannah's shoulders. Perhaps it was the wine. She was exhausted, no longer happy to be with friends. She wanted to go back to the flat and go to bed. Except it was very likely she'd begin thinking about Daniel, and what could have been, and all the dreams that had died. This was what she had now, and it was the best new start she could hope for. She had to let the past go and stop wishing.

Halfway through their dinner, Louisa finally asked the question Alannah had been expecting. "What brought you to London?"

Cat, swirling her last bite of chicken through the curry sauce, looked up. Her gaze fixed intently on Alannah.

"Well," Alannah began, "I suppose it was time to move on. Alexander has been hounding me for ages, and then I had a bit of a close call..."

"Ahh." Louisa nodded, swirling the last of the Reisling under her nose. Her cheeks had a slight pink flush. "We've all had those."

"It's unfortunate." Alannah sighed. "I liked it there. I... well, there wasn't much society there."

Cat's doe eyes held hers and her head bobbed in an almost imperceptible nod.

"You, Louisa?" Alannah asked softly.

"I grew up here. My mother was Lady of the Bedchamber for Queen Victoria." Louisa set down the wine glass. "Of course, I've spent much time away. I lived in France, Germany, even Los Angeles for a time. I returned here a few years ago to live here for the fourth time." She sighed and her eyes misted. "It is the only place that truly feels like home."

Cat rolled her eyes. "You've had too much wine, Louisa."

Louisa clapped her hands to her flushed cheeks and laughed.

Alannah laughed too.

CHAPTER 13

Dresden, Present Day

"Idina? Sweetheart?" Cyrus called into the dark house.

Jack shuffled past him and set his bag down in the living room. The house was quiet.

"She said she was going to be here." Cyrus sighed. "Something must have called her away." He leaned against the doorway into the kitchen and pulled his phone from his pocket. "Want to get something to eat or should we take our chances and go up to Schwalenburg?"

"Last time you took me out to eat I met a psychopath," Jack muttered.

Cyrus's phone dinged. "Yes, Idina's at the castle," he said. "She says Zoran has posted to his blog again."

"I guess we'll go, then?" Jack kicked his duffle bag and turned around. "Not on the motorcycles, please. Last time I did that your wife tried to kill me."

Cyrus looked up from his text and raised one eyebrow. "Did she? I'm not surprised." He stuffed his phone into his pocket and flicked a set of keys off the key rack beside the door and caught them midair. "Idina took my car. We'll take Alexander's."

Jack nodded off before Alexander's BMW had left the city limits. Cyrus cuffed his shoulder to wake him in Schwalenburg's courtyard.

Slightly bleary-eyed and groggy, Jack stumbled after Cyrus through the big oaken doors. Anastasie, for once, didn't greet them.

"Up here." Cyrus led him up a staircase in the opposite direction of Alexander's office and the library, into a narrow hall, around a corner and through a half-open door.

Daniel glanced up from behind two large computer monitors, pausing mid-word. He tapped lightly on a silver earpiece and held up five fingers. Anastasie lounged in an armchair to the right of the desk with a book in her hands.

"Hello, Cy. Jack." She smiled and straightened.

Daniel continued a conversation in what Jack soon realized was French. His fingers flew over a wireless keyboard as he talked.

"Can I get you coffee?" Anastasie stood. "Daniel is on the phone with Martin Bertholette in London. He traced the IP address to a cafe about a block from his house."

"Bertholette?" Cyrus's eyes widened. "Bertholette? He's never corresponded with Zoran, not in the least. Although..."

"He was a known associate of Zoran back in the day," Idina's strident voice came from the door behind them.

Jack turned as she sidled in. He caught a whiff of tea. Idina handed a steaming mug to Cyrus and kissed him gently. She touched Cyrus's face and leaned against him.

"Was this for you?" Cyrus said in Idina's ear. He took a sip of the mug and settled her against his side.

"I'm sure you can make it up to me later," she muttered as she slid her arm around his waist and tipped the mug to take a sip. "As I said, Bertholette was a known associate of Zoran. We don't know how he could have received the materials, but we certainly know why he would post them."

"We're absolutely sure that Zoran wrote the article?" Cyrus asked. "What's it about? I should read it before we continue much farther."

"It's in support of Lia's death experiments, and denouncing the Lords for squashing inquiries over the deaths of Joseph Nils Oswald and Jurgen Zeigler." Daniel jerked his chair around and pointed at Jack. "Are we going to talk about this in front of him?"

Cyrus shifted Idina and glanced at Jack. "I guess so."

"Alright." Daniel nodded. He gazed at the screen for a moment. "I'm just bringing the article up."

"So, Zoran has somehow heard a great deal about what happened to Jack?" Cyrus asked.

"Well," Daniel said and squinted at the computer, "I would say so. Some of these appear to be direct references to different experiments. I'm not sure though."

"Let me see." Jack shoved past Cyrus and Idina and leaned over Daniel to see the screen. Daniel moved his chair so Jack could get in closer. "It's in German."

"This is a translation." Daniel flicked the mouse, bringing up a new page, this time in English.

...we should not be surprised that death experiments are undertaken again. Where there is a desire to die, or a desire to kill, some will be desperate enough to take great risks. These risks would be wholly unnecessary; however, if the history of the immortals had not been kept from them. They do not know that an immortal may not be killed by any poison, nor by electrocution, not even if all the blood shall be drained from his body shall his heart stop beating for all eternity.

A chill skittered down Jack's spine.

History is a commodity immortals possess in great abundance, yet these so-called Lords have censored it for their purposes. Do they know how Oswald and Zeigler died? Absolutely.

Jack swallowed hard.

"What do you think, Jack?" Daniel asked quietly.

"Uh, he..." Jack could feel sweat beading up on his temples, "he mentions draining blood. They didn't do that to me. They did that to Koenig." The image flashed in front of his eyes: Marcus's waxy skin and blood running through a silicone tube into a bucket. His stomach twisted.

"Right," Daniel said under his breath. He scrolled down, scanning Zoran's words before adding, "And they also tried electrocution, as I recall. He also makes mention of cutting your heart out."

"Sick bastard," Idina muttered under her breath. "He's done that one before."

Jack turned to look at her. "So this *has* happened before?"

"Oh definitely." Idina glanced back at Cyrus. "Just before we were married. Joseph Nils Oswald. He experimented on himself, though, which you have to admit is at least more ethical even if it is no less sick."

"And he actually died?" Jack said slowly.

"Yes." Idina nodded, eyes distant. "He is dead and buried in South Kensington."

The question was on the tip of his tongue: how? But the words would not come out.

The room was silent. Daniel's forehead was tightly furrowed. Zoran's words reflected in his eyes.

"What did Bertholette say?" Cyrus asked, in the quiet.

"He said he didn't know." Daniel turned his chair and squinted at Cyrus. "Granted, I don't know why he would post something from a cafe when he has his own computer at home. He's a known supporter of Zoran. He was under surveillance for years. Why would he post something like this? It doesn't make sense."

"But," Cyrus said, "would he aid Lia? Would loyalty to Zoran transfer over to loyalty to Lia?"

"She is Zoran's niece," Anastasie spoke up for the first time.

"She is?" Jack interjected.

They ignored him. "She's never made contact with Zoran," Cyrus continued, "Not while he was in prison. We'll have to go back into the records and see what we can dredge up. Maybe there is a connection between Lia and Martin, or with his wife. Maybe Camille and Lia knew each other at some point? I don't recall them living in the same community. Idina?"

Idina shook her head. "No, never."

Her eyes flickered. She leaned her head against Cyrus's shoulder. "They do have something in common, though. It needn't be a coincidence." A deep sigh came from between her lips before she continued, "They've both lost children. We took them away."

Her words thudded into Jack's chest like a physical blow, not enough to stagger him but enough for him to feel sharp pain. "Because it was illegal?"

Idina nodded. The tip of her tongue traced her top lip. Her eyes focused on the floor. In an uncharacteristically small voice she said, "It is the very worst thing about this profession, Jack."

Jack's breathing came shallowly as a memory came sharp and hot into his mind.

"You would appreciate this if you were even a hundred years older." Lia, *her dark eyes spitting fire and the scalpel pressed against his skin biting like an adder, "Not having to live while the world dies around you. You'd don't know what it's like to watch your child die!"*

He swallowed hard. "Did the child die?"

Idina blinked. "I don't know. She would be..." her eyes flickered rapidly as she made her mental calculation, "Eighty-two. She could have passed away. We haven't had her under surveillance for about fifty years, since we'd realized she was most certainly mortal." She took a deep breath through her nose. "Why do you ask?"

"Because Lia... I remember her saying something." Jack shook his head and rubbed his eyes. "I'm too tired for this."

"It *has* been a very long day," Cyrus said apologetically. "Daniel, where are you going with this next?"

Daniel reached over and took Anastasie's hand and laced his fingers through hers. "I'm going archive diving," he said, "if you will keep me supplied with coffee, Mon Coeur?" He smiled up into Anastasie's face.

"Always," she touched his cheek with her free hand.

Jack flinched. He was surrounded by happy couples. What did that make him? A fifth wheel? And what was more, he had nothing to contribute to this conversation. His tired mind was bogging itself down in thoughts of Clarissa, and Lia's mysterious, dead child, and death experiments. The old urge for a stiff drink and an hour or two of oblivion on the business end of a gun was creeping back like a persistent sickness.

"Jack," Cyrus said, "do you want to curl up in a corner for a bit while I brief my wife on all that transpired in Italy?"

Jack raised his head wearily, "Yeah, yeah I suppose."

"We have two cars here," Idina said. She twisted out of Cyrus's arms and straightened her shirt. "Which did you take, Cy? Alexander's?"

"Yes."

"Well, then give Jack the keys and send him home. He can go to bed."

In the time since they'd arrived at Castle Schwalenburg it felt like the temperature had dropped ten, maybe fifteen degrees. His hands shook on the steering wheel, his heart beat erratically.

He was shivering violently when he got to Alexander's house. He shut the door behind him hard, and didn't even bother to turn on the light. He plunged into the kitchen and yanked open the fridge. He scanned the contents, then left it open. By the bluish light he began opening the cupboards, rifling through them, until finally his hands closed around a thick glass bottle. He pulled it out and opened the cap. He took a deep whiff, and his eyes watered with the fumes mingled with the sweet aroma of peaches.

Jack swiped the first cup he found, a china teacup, and poured it full. He held the first sip, sweet and burning, in his mouth then gulped the whole cup down. His stomach was empty. His head swirled just a moment, then clarity returned. The Schnapps thawed the ice in his belly.

He slumped against the counter and poured another teacup full. He drank half in two gulps, then stood with his fingers wrapped around it like it was actual hot tea he was holding. His eyes fell on the twelve ebony handles of the kitchen knives.

If I died, I'd see Mary Rose. No more fifth wheel.

"Don't you dare." He sniffled and wiped his nose. He took another sip. "What the hell is wrong with you?" He tipped back the cup and let the Schnapps pour down his throat. His hand trembled around the cup.

He grabbed the bottle, but it was empty.

Jack sank down in one of the kitchen chairs and put his head in his hands. His mind swam, but he wasn't confident it was the alcohol.

"You don't know what it's like to watch your child die!" Lia's screech echoed in his head.

"Well, I will," he groaned. Jack pressed his palms to his face.

A clunk nearby brought his head up. It was followed by a rattle of a key in the door and then the gentle creak of the hinges. The light flicked on, and Alexander's blond head came around the corner. "Hello, Jack." His eyes were bright, though underlined by dark smudges, "Are you home alone?" He eyed the empty bottle of Schnapps.

"Yeah," Jack said in a low voice. He pushed the bottle away and stood up.

He could feel Alexander's gaze on him, "Jack," he said quietly, "if you need someone to talk to, I have ears to hear."

"I have nothing to say." Jack ran his hands through his hair and looked up. Alexander had taken a few more steps into the room.

He smiled wearily at Jack. "Fair enough. Are you hungry? When did you get in from Italy?"

Jack froze. "I, uh..."

"Adolf said you'd asked for permission to go into Ardovinni's house." Alexander crossed to the fridge and gave Jack a little grin over his shoulder as he opened the door a little wider. "My lawkeepers, always so clever. Did Cyrus find what he was looking for?" Alexander set a butter dish and a block of cheese on the counter and shut the fridge door. He opened the breadbox.

"Not really," Jack said hoarsely, scrambling for what he'd say if Alexander continued this line of questioning.

Alexander pulled a frying pan out of a drawer and set it on the element. For a few minutes he asked no more questions, and set to work putting together plain cheese sandwiches and setting them into the heating pan. The aroma of melting butter filled the small kitchen.

Alexander turned and leaned against the counter. "I've already mentally composed an apology to Ardovinni. Perhaps it was alright in the legal sense, but that man is fastidiously private and I can only imagine his reaction when he finds out."

"He isn't answering any of his calls," Jack protested. "He can't just show up in Winnipeg, scare the shit out of Alannah, and leave!"

"Well, to be fair—" Alexander turned abruptly and flipped all of his grilled cheese sandwiches. The pan sizzled. "Scaring her wasn't his intention. He was trying to delicately introduce me to this mysterious young man..." Alexander trailed off and dropped his gaze to the stove in front of him. "Once again, Mr. Ardovinni knowing things I do not know and unwilling to relinquish his knowledge easily."

"I bet," Jack said.

"But his secrecy makes sense. The young man's parents will face the council, though." He sighed and said to the frying pan, "I would never want to be in their place."

The silence in the kitchen was loud amidst the faint sizzle of the frying pan and the kitchen clock ticking.

"Am I crazy to be jealous of... them?" Jack said slowly.

Alexander shook his head and flicked off the element. He turned around, holding the frying pan, and fished a plate out of the cupboard. He slid the plate of sandwiches on the table in front of Jack and sat down opposite him. Alexander pulled a napkin from the holder beside the window and fished a stub of a pencil from somewhere.

He began drawing, sketching out lines on the notepaper.

Confused, Jack picked up one of the oozing cheese sandwiches and began to eat, all the while watching.

Before three minutes had passed, Alexander lifted his hand so Jack could see the napkin clearly. It was faces, three miniature portraits not two inches tall each, but in remarkable detail. A young man with a shock of light hair and eyes that, even in pencil, sparkled. He had the same chiseled chin as Alexander. Two young women with braids coiled around their heads completed the collection, both with rosebud mouths and rapturously happy expressions.

"My children," Alexander said. He touched each penciled face in turn. "Augustus, my son and heir. Annette and Konstanze, my beautiful daughters. All of them gone more than six-hundred years, but I remember them." He rolled his pencil between his fingers and began to draw again, this time in slower, loving strokes. The soft, oval face of a woman appeared. Her eyes fastened on them with a tender expression. "My Idonia."

Jack pressed his lips together, against the sudden pain in his throat. The grilled cheese hung forgotten from his fingers.

"I wonder sometimes..." Alexander rubbed his chin and gazed at the paper with soft eyes, "I wonder if that is actually what they looked like, or if it is only as I remember them. But... so it goes." He sighed, folded the napkin and put it in his pocket. "There have been moments when I've imagined that they were here with me. Now there is another immortal child among us, of course. Of course it has crossed my mind. What if it were my August?"

Jack felt sick. He could imagine exploding joy if Clarissa was proved to be immortal, and yet crushing guilt in having passed that burden on to her.

Alexander grimaced. "But, given that our one example of an immortal child coming from immortal parents is due to... shall we say, tampering on their part, it is no stretch to think that somewhere along the way these parents also deliberately immortalized this child. That itself will be a great investigation. Once again, Ardovinni's secrecy makes sense."

Jack blew his breath out slowly.

"I don't suppose you are going to tell me what you found about him?" Alexander asked wryly, "since Cyrus went to such trouble to be secretive, until Adolf spoiled it for him."

"No, I better not," Jack mumbled. He stared at his half-eaten sandwich.

Alexander picked up a sandwich. "I'm an old man," he said. "I can wait a little longer."

∞

In the morning Jack stumbled down the stairs late. Cyrus, Idina, and Alexander were already at the kitchen table with coffee cups in their hands. Idina had her feet up on Cyrus's knee, her loose red hair the brightest thing in the room. Rain spattered against the window behind them, punctuating Alexander's rapid-fire German.

"Bitte," Cyrus held up his hand and inclined his head toward the door where Jack stood.

"Hey." Jack wiped his hand across his eyes as he padded into the kitchen. The smell of toast lingered in the air, along with the telltale bagel crumbs on the tabletop. "What did you guys find? Are we taking a plane somewhere else?"

"Maybe," Idina said over her shoulder. "There's bagels on the counter. Fresh this morning. I picked them up on my run."

Jack eyed the rain streaming down the window. "You did?" He picked up the plastic bag and fished out a fragrant, cinnamon-spiced bagel, studded with raisins.

She shrugged. "It only started raining a few minutes ago. I was lucky. As we were saying..."

Alexander raised his head from his coffee cup. "Daniel has sent Lia's and Peter's pictures to Benjamin Turner in London. He is going to the cafe where the blog post was allegedly posted and he'll ask the staff there if they've seen them."

"Peter?" Jack didn't remember them talking much about Lia's burly blond side-kick, never mind identifying him and having a picture.

"Bouwmeester. Peter Bouwmeester," Alexander said, "Marcus Koenig was able to identify him yesterday. He was a known associate of Zoran's before Zoran was incarcerated. A bit of a goon."

"Yeah, I'd say," Jack muttered. He leaned against the counter and took a bite out of the bagel. "What about the American? He identify him?"

"Nope," Idina said.

"We actually have no idea who he might be," Cyrus said sheepishly, "there is no American immortal named Jordan that we know of. There isn't even any American immortal that matches his description, or non-American, for that matter. We showed Koenig pictures of a few people we thought *might* be your American, but he didn't recognize any of them."

A gust of wind rattled the window.

"Daniel said Benjamin was *very* suspicious of the Bertholettes," Cyrus said. "He said he'd gone to the Bertholette home to pick up a book, and Camille had seemed very reluctant to let him into the house."

"We'll see what Benjamin turns up." Alexander nodded slowly. "Cyrus, I would prepare to go to England. You too, Idina."

"Yes!" Idina pumped her fist. "We never get to travel together."

"Do I get to go too?" Jack drawled.

"No." Idina leveled a dark stare at him. "You already got to go to Italy with my husband."

Jack held up his hands. "You sent me."

"Alexander can babysit," she said.

Alexander laughed. "I am a terrible babysitter, I do assure you."

"You can't be any worse than I am," Cyrus said wryly.

"That's not much of a standard," Jack said. "All he has to do is keep me from falling into the hands of a psychopath intent on cutting my heart out."

"What could possibly go wrong?" Alexander held out his hand. "Pass me a bagel, Jack."

Two hours later, Cyrus got a call from Daniel. A barista in the cafe had recognized Lia.

CHAPTER 14

"About Zoran's blog post," Jack said. It was mid-morning. He and Alexander were in the car on the way up to Schwalenburg after dropping Idina and Cyrus off at the airport. "Is it true what he said about you withholding the death method?"

Alexander's hands tapped on the steering wheel. "Yes, it's true. In a way."

Jack licked his lips nervously. "What do you mean?"

"We withheld the death method, as per the wishes of the community." Alexander continued to drum on the stitched leather of the steering wheel. "Just over fifty years later we revisited the decision and upheld it, and within a year from now we will revisit it again."

"Oh."

"Zoran is aware of this, and no doubt wishes to influence it. Lia, I cannot say. I wonder as to her mental health. Idina mentioned to me that her child died recently." Alexander frowned and glanced at Jack. "I reminded Idina that Lia spent time in Harwin Nervenheilanstalt after her child was taken away."

A lead-like weight settled in Jack's stomach and the faintest, creeping desire for drink and oblivion. "It doesn't seem right," he said roughly.

"No." Alexander shook his head. "But in the greater scale of things, neither does spreading immortality to further generations. It seems better to us to penalize ourselves than to curse our children." He slowed the car and turned off the paved highway, onto the smaller road leading up to Schwalenburg.

"What if you're the dad?"

The words were out of Jack's mouth before he'd thought about it.

Alexander turned his head and looked at Jack. "I've thought of it," he said. "I thought of it the moment I looked into the eyes of that unidentified young man. Cosima's eyes."

Jack sat silent, staring at the dashboard, hands on his knees.

"It brings all the pieces together." Alexander shook his head slightly. "It does so rather poetically, even." The car bumped across the bridge. Schwalenburg loomed on the crag above them. Alexander shifted down as the car rounded a tight corner and began ascending the narrow drive up to the castle.

The BMW rolled into the courtyard and into a parking spot between a silver SUV and a slick black motorcycle—Daniel's. Alexander switched the car off and tilted his head back against the seat. He sighed heavily.

Alexander's face, so young in appearance despite his years, twisted in a myriad of emotions. His blue eyes were ancient, haunted. He pressed his lips together, as if holding back a tide.

"If he is my child," he said hoarsely, after a moment had passed, "I will pay the price for myself, and for Cosima if I may. It's my fault. God help me, I will pay."

Jack walked into Schwalenburg in Alexander's wake.

"Hello Alexander!" Anastasie's voice floated cheerfully down from the head of the staircase.

119

"Hello," Alexander's reply was almost inaudible. He stopped, nearly causing Jack to slam into him, squared his shoulders and turned to look up the stairs. "Hello, Ana," he said clearly, "is Daniel in his office?"

Anastasie's feet appeared on the first stair, and then the rest of her came into view. "Hello Jack. Yes, Alexander, Daniel is in his office. He was on the phone when I left him, which was only a moment ago. Would you like any coffee sent up to your office?" Anastasie paused in front of Alexander and peered into his face. "Is everything alright? You look pale."

"Yes," Alexander said softly, "everything is alright, for the present."

Anastasie leaned in and kissed his cheek. "Text me if you need anything sent up."

Alexander seemed to regain his composure completely as he led Jack up the stairs toward his offices. His face was completely placid when he glanced back at Jack. "Will you be going exploring?"

Jack shrugged. "Yeah, I'll poke around."

"You can take the car if you want." Alexander put one hand on knob of the office door and fished in his pocket with the other.

"Yeah, I..." Jack grimaced. Considering what had transpired last time he'd explored on his own, he wasn't ready to go exploring *that* far and wide. "I'll stay close for now."

Alexander shrugged. "Suit yourself."

Jack hadn't wandered very fall before he found the doors to the Library. He poked his head inside. Light shone, pale and lethargic through the library windows, which were supplemented by wrought-iron chandeliers between the beams of the room. Jack glanced around and saw no one, but his ears caught the sound of someone singing. The words were French, sung in a high, bird-like voice.

Jack smiled and slipped inside. Anastasie perched on a high stepladder in front of the family tree, leaning toward it with a fountain pen in her fingers.

"Hello again, Jack," she called down.

"Hello." Jack craned his neck up toward her and caught a glimpse of his own name, Jakob Gerhardt Krause, dangling from a spindly line below 'Gerhardt Krause, Mortal.'

"I'm on the map," he said.

"Yes Sir!" Anastasie turned again to her work, squinting at the parchment with a critical eye.

"What are you doing?" Jack asked.

"Restoring a few faded sections." She applied the fountain pen, turning a light line to a hard black one.

"Can I look once you're done?"

"Certainly." Anastasie immediately put her pen back into a little bag and began to descend. Jack reached to steady the ladder, but she jumped the last two steps to the floor.

"Have a look." She motioned for him to go up.

Jack clambered up and perched on the third-last rung. He glanced at his name and then looked straight to the top where Alexander's name was. He followed the branches of the tree only a few generations down and found Zoran's name. Two generations down, he found 'Lia Brenner."

Jack turned around on the ladder, "Anastasie, did you know Lia?"

Anastasie's blond head peeked around the corner, gazing flower-like up at him. For a bare moment Jack knew exactly why Daniel had fallen for her.

Anastasie twisted the end of her braid. "Well, I saw her around, but no—not really."

"Zoran is her great-uncle, looks like."

"We just say uncle," Anastasie explained, stepping nearer, "because we have so few kin, why should we add extra words? But yes, her great-uncle."

"Did he raise her?"

"Raise her? No, not hardly. I doubt they knew each other for the first twenty-five or thirty years of her life. But I am no expert."

Her face became a thoughtful pout, her chin in one hand. "You may be able to find that in the digital archives. You can access it here in the Library. You need a password, but I can let you in."

That sounded interesting. Jack sprang down the ladder and followed her to a computer kiosk, hidden in the corner. Anastasie sat down, and opened a window on the computer. "They are publicly accessible, but some of it is password protected so only lawmen can access it—confidential things, you understand."

"Could you write all that stuff down?" Jack asked.

"Alright," Anastasie said, tapping a couple keys, "there you are." She straightened. "Do you need a tutorial, or will you figure it out?"

Jack peered at the search box on the screen, allowing him to search by name, clan, key word, date range, or city. "Seems intuitive."

"Alright then. Would you like coffee?" She took a few steps toward the door. "I was about to get some."

"Sure," Jack said absently as he sat down. As soon as she'd disappeared behind the stacks, he typed in 'Lia Brenner' and hit 'search'. A whole page of links showed up, with snatches of articles in them—all in German.

"Damn," Jack said.

He clicked on the link at the very top of the list. As the page loaded, a scanned paper image, a box appeared beside it with 'See translation?' in it, and several languages. Jack clicked on 'English' and another page opened.

Lord Alexander von Katlenburg welcomes Amalia Theresa Brenner, immortal, into his clan and the greater Society of Immortals...

Jack squinted at the dates. She was still quite young. Well, less than a century older than him, anyway. He scanned the rest of the file, and sure enough, Zoran Kosar had found and assimilated her. Jack clicked shut the window and picked another, further down the list. It was of little consequence—a mortal newspaper, mentioning her as a part of a committee or something.

"Jack?" Anastasie set a pottery mug of coffee in front of him.

"Huh?" Jack looked up.

Anastasie just waved toward the cup, and disappeared.

Jack clicked a link about ten down on the list and found his way into the translation. It was a birth record. Jack bit his lip and slipped one hand around the coffee cup. The ceramic nearly burnt his hands. He let it go.

To Amalia Brenner and an unknown mortal father, a daughter. Born September 17, 1930.

The rest was blacked out. Jack clicked on it, and a box popped up, requesting a lawkeeper's password.

"Damn." He could make out one thing, though. Idina had signed it. Idina had taken away Lia's baby.

An unexpected surge of anger went through Jack, making his heart pound. He pushed back from the desk.

Why am I angry? What do I care about that psycho bitch?

He had this image in his head of Mary Rose, holding a tiny, red, wrinkly Clarissa in the delivery room. In the memory he leaned over beside them, staring in mingled terror and delight at Clarissa's ten tiny fingers.

Jack swallowed hard and sat forward again.

As the mouse hovered over the 'x' to close the window, Jack realized there was another tab titled 'photo archives'.

Jack raised an eyebrow, momentarily wondering if he'd be able to dredge up photos of Daniel and Cyrus in plaid Fortrel, or Idina with poufy eighties hair. After squinting at the screen for a moment, however, he typed 'Zoran Kosar' into the search box and hit enter. Three files popped up.

Jack clicked the first one on the list. It was a distant, black and white shot of three figures standing on a rocky plateau, looking out over snowy mountains. One man glanced back but all Jack could make out of his face were his obsidian eyes, glittering in the sunlight of that past, summer day.

A vague vision pinged off his memory, of dark eyes peering at him through a cell window.

Jack clicked the next photo.

A man lounged languidly on a bed, his head tipped back against a whitewashed stone wall. His dark hair curled over the collar of his standard grey shirt. His face was relaxed but his eyes fixed intently on the camera. Black eyes. Jack flinched as he looked into them and looked away. He didn't know why.

"Zoran," he whispered. "So that's you, you bastard."

He'd seen Alannah in his glimpse of the delicate mouth, the high cheekbones, even the vaguely amused expression.

Why did he feel a cold lump deep in his belly? Jack spun away from the computer toward shadowy, silent stacks of book.

An icy chill went down his back, like Zoran was still watching him.

Jack reached back and grabbed for the warm coffee cup without looking, his hand scrabbling across the desk. Jack turned. His fingers encountered the hot porcelain for a moment, then the cup toppled. It crashed to the floor and shattered. Coffee splattered on Jack's ankles.

"Jack?" Anastasie's voice floated over the bookshelves.

Jack looked up and met Zoran's fixed black gaze. He jerked toward the computer to close the window. The wheels on the chair skidded and slid out from under Jack as Anastasie came around the corner. Jack fell forward. His head bounced off the desk as something bit into his palm. He landed on his hands and knees.

"Oh goodness!" Anastasie stood over him. "Are you alright?"

"Ahh, I'm okay. I'm okay." Jack reached out for the top of the desk. Blood smeared as he lifted himself to his knees. He held up his hand and a rivulet of blood ran down his wrist, from a deep slash in his palm. "I'm just bleeding on your library."

"Stitches," Anastasie said, "you'll want stitches for that."

"Oh goody," Jack groaned, "I suppose that can be done in house?" He pressed his unhurt hand to the cut as he staggered to his feet.

A smile was threatening to form on Anastasie's mouth. "Dr. Kris isn't in today."

"Well damn." Jack grimaced. He was pretty sure a goose egg was forming on his temple.

Anastasie giggled. "I'll let Alexander know, and I'll take you for stitches."

A few moments later Jack was sitting on the circulation desk with his hand wrapped in a paper towel when Alexander poked his head into the library. "I've failed as a babysitter already," he said. "I'll take him."

They ended up at a hospital on the outskirts of Dresden. Alexander explained the situation to the triage nurse and they found seats in the crowded waiting room. "This could take a while," he said, "would you like a coffee?"

"Coffee," Jack said with a laugh, "yeah sure. I dumped mine on the floor."

"I'll be back." Alexander stood up. "I think there's a place down the street."

Jack tipped his head back against the wall and shut his eyes. His mind wandered, first to Zoran's glinting, dark eyes, then to Lia's baby, now gone.

"Jakob Krause?"

Jack lifted his head. "What?"

A plump, blond nurse smiled at him. "Jakob Krause?"

Jack staggered to his feet. "Uh yeah, that's me."

She said in heavily accented English, "You may come in."

Jack glanced around for Alexander. Had he dozed off? How long had it been? He was led down a hall among curtained off cubicles. His phone buzzed and with one eye on the nurse he pulled it out and read it.

Alexander: "*Sorry. Bumped into someone and got to talking. Be there soon.*"

"*Going in now*," he tapped out, just as he was seated on a gurney thing in a curtained off cubicle. The nurse left him, and Jack pulled out his phone again.

"Wie geht es dir, herr—" a voice said at the door.

"I don't speak German," Jack said as he checked his texts.

"Pardon me. I speak English." The doctor's English was nearly unaccented. It was, in fact, American, sending warning signals off in Jack's consciousness.

Jack lifted his head, and the doctor met his eyes. Dark, beady eyes, fat face, wire-rimmed glasses. The American. He was just missing the bloody lab coat.

"You!" Jack leapt off the gurney.

The American peddled backward, spun around and clawed his way out of the door.

Jack caught the door with his injured hand and shoved his way after him. "Come back, you son of a bitch!"

The American skidded around a corner in the hall, Jack on his heels, past two full cloth bins of laundry. He shoved them as he passed, and one began to lumber across Jack's path.

Jack grabbed it and hurdled over, past two startled orderlies. The American was nearly in reach. He glanced back, wild-eyed and shoved through a door. Jack reached for it as it slammed shut. All his momentum flung him forward. His palms slapped the glass and smeared blood, but Jack wrenched it back open and pelted out into the cool air. He could see the American, unveering, running heavily across the parking lot.

He's going for his car.

Jack put every bit of energy into his long legs, pumping his arms. The heavy American, laboring, stumbled. Jack pounced, and they both rolled on the asphalt, behind a parked Mercedes.

"Help!" the American struggled against Jack's body weight.

"Shut up, Jordan." Jack slapped a hand over his mouth, pinning him with both arms and legs. "I'm going to wring your neck, and then once you rebound, I'm going to wring it again just for fun."

"No!" the American gasped through Jack's fingers, smearing blood as he wiggled.

"Don't worry. It won't hurt," Jack grunted as the American heaved against his arms. "Shut up!"

"No!" he wheezed, "don't kill me. I'm... not... immortal."

Jack paused.

"Well damn," he said. "Then you better cooperate."

He heard heavy footfalls pounding toward them and someone calling "Jordan? Jordan?"

Jack clamped his hand tighter, and for good measure, grabbed the American's throat. "You keep quiet." He pressed them both against the wheel of the car. He could feel Jordan's pulse pound beneath his thumb.

The footfalls passed and paused nearby. Jack heard faint tones, and suddenly the American's phone began to vibrate between them. Jack tightened his grip, both on mouth and throat.

Jordan whimpered. The phone went quiet, and the footfalls receded in the way they had come.

"I'm going to reach for my phone. If you squeak, I'll hurt you. I swear." Jack released the American's throat. Under his bloody palm, the man gasped for air.

Alexander picked up on the second ring. "I'm coming. Are you seeing the doctor?"

"Uh," Jack whispered, "I found the American, Alexander."

"What?" Alexander's voice dropped automatically into a whisper. "Where are you?"

"In the parking lot, behind the hospital! Between some cars! Come and get us!"

"Are you sure?"

Jack glanced wildly at the American, then out into the parking lot. "Yes!"

"Alright, I'm coming."

What they'd do when Alexander came, Jack had no idea. Jordan jerked in his arms as soon as he hung up. Jack redoubled his grasp on Jordan's throat. The man wheezed, but lay still.

Alexander managed to find them quickly, despite Jack's whispered, vague directions. Jack heard the whirr of his silver BMW and lifted his head cautiously above the hood of the Mercedes as Alexander drove past. Alexander glanced over and saw them, looped around and came back.

Alexander got out. Jack saw a flash of metal in his hand. He jumped between the cars and knelt down beside them. "You can let go of him," Alexander said in a low voice. He pressed the snub-nose of a pistol into Jordan's fleshy jaw.

Both Jack and Jordan recoiled. There was a glint in Alexander's eye that Jack had never seen before.

"Holy shit," Jack breathed.

"I'm not... immortal," the American squeaked through Jack's hand.

Alexander's face went white. "Then you better cooperate, sir."

"That's what I said," Jack grunted.

"You can let go," Alexander said again.

Jack eased his grip and rolled back into a squat, against the car behind him.

"We need to get him into my car," Alexander said softly. "Is anyone around?"

Jack shuffled to the end of the vehicle and looked around. The parking lot was deserted, except for an older couple walking slowly up toward the entrance of the hospital. "We're good."

Alexander shifted the pistol into Jordan's gut. "Stand up slowly."

A minute later the BMW peeled from the parking lot onto the busy street, sloshing two cups of coffee in the cup holders up front. Jack sat in the back seat with the pistol in his lap, aimed at Jordan beside him. Alexander drove with a grim expression on his face.

"I hope you're very sure about this, Jack," he said.

"Yeah," Jack said, brandishing the pistol at Jordan, "I'm pretty sure this jackass's face is burned into my brain. He kinda gave himself away by running."

"They're looking for me," Jordan said, "the hospital."

"Shut up!" Jack jabbed the pistol toward him.

"We'll take care of it," Alexander said without looking back. "Relax, Jack. This is the American? The doctor?"

"Yes!"

"Where are you taking me?" Jordan's voice rose in pitch.

"I haven't decided yet." Alexander's fingers tapped on the steering wheel. He glanced in the rear-view mirror at them.

"They'll look for me." Jordan's voice took on a hint of determination. "You can't just chase me from the hospital and expect them to—"

"Jack, get his wallet," Alexander cut the man off. "Find his identification."

"He's sitting on it," Jack said.

Alexander eyed him in the mirror. "I'm sure you can persuade him."

Jack eyed the gun in his lap. Instead he opted to heave the American face first against the window and dig his wallet from the back pocket of his khakis. Jack flipped it open and hunted for something that looked like ID.

He squinted at a driver's license. "Jordan Booth, thirty-seven. One hundred seventy-two centimeters, one hundred thirteen kilograms—" he eyed his captive, "seems a little optimistic don't you think?"

"Address?" Alexander asked sharply.

"Uh... 624 Muhlenstrasse, Dresden."

Alexander tapped the navigation screen in the center console of the car. "Look through his wallet carefully. Is there any signs of a wife, children? Jordan, answer me truthfully. Do you have a wife and children to be... extremely alarmed if we take you to your house and, shall we say, interview you?"

The American's breath shuddered out. "No."

"Do you have a roommate?"

Jordan paused.

"Jordan," Alexander said, "do you have a roommate that might get hurt if he walks in on us?"

"No," Jordan whispered.

"Jack?" Alexander asked over his shoulder.

"Yeah, I've got nothing." Jack stuffed cards and receipts back into the billfold.

Alexander nodded and faced forward. He tapped the screen again and in a moment Daniel's voice came over the speakers in the car.

"Hello?"

"Hello Daniel, it's Alexander. We have an unexpected opportunity."

"Oh?" Daniel sounded slightly out of breath, like he'd run to the phone.

"Jack found his American doctor."

"Where are you?" Daniel said fiercely.

"Can you meet us at 624 Muhlenstrasse?" Alexander made a right turn onto a wide thoroughfare. "It's a private home."

"Got it."

"Bring your computer. And Daniel?" Alexander's voice became much more stern, ominous, "He isn't one of us."

Daniel's voice took on a much more solemn tone. "Got it. I'll be there in twenty five minutes."

"Isn't this illegal?" Jack asked quietly.

"Absolutely," Alexander said, still facing forward. "But Dr. Booth isn't one of us. We can't process him by our laws. We have to get as much information as we can, while we can."

"You're going to ransack my house?" Jordan's voice came out small and distant.

"Yup," Jack said, popping the 'p'.

"But you can't press charges against me?"

"Not by our laws," Alexander said coldly, "but believe me. We'll think of something."

Jordan pressed his lips together and hunched his shoulders.

"He doesn't have to talk," Alexander said as he took an exit. "In my experience, Daniel can extract a lot of information from his personal computer, and for that matter, find plenty of material to make sure this good doctor doesn't bother us anymore."

Jordan's eyes bulged, but he kept his mouth shut.

In about five minutes they pulled up in front of a brick faced, two-story house. Jack squinted at it, trying to visualize the night he met Lia—trying to visualize more than a drunken haze and her hands tangled in his shirt. The house felt familiar.

"Stay here with our dear little friend." Alexander opened the glove box and pulled out a short knife in a leather scabbard. He tucked it under his arm as he got out of the car. "I will check the house."

Well, I'll be damned. Jack watched Alexander disappear alongside the house. *The old guy is a lot more badass than I thought.* He could feel Jordan vibrate beside him. The American's eyes were round, slightly glassy in the greyish light. He twitched.

"Don't move." Jack brushed the gun along Jordan's side. "I've always been a bit trigger happy."

It took Alexander five minutes to slip back into the car. "The house is empty. We'll drive around to the back lane where we can bring him in quietly."

Alexander crawled the car down the empty street, into a nearly invisible driveway that led to an alley. Jack could hear him counting houses under his breath. When he'd counted to eleven, Alexander wedged the BMW onto a little asphalt pad behind the brick house.

"Hold still," Alexander said. He got out and opened Jordan's door. Jack saw the wink of a blade as Alexander snugged the knife up against Jordan's ribs. "Get up nice and slow." Alexander caught

Jack's eye over the American's head. "The kitchen door is unlocked. Go and open it for me."

Jack bounded across the eight square feet of lawn and yanked open the kitchen door. It was a little loose on its hinges, and creaked in a loud complaint. As he turned back, he heard Jordan yelp.

"Don't think it," Alexander said calmly. He shoved Jordan past Jack into the kitchen and plopped him onto a wooden chair. "Give me the gun, Jack."

Jack handed it over. "Since when do you carry a gun?" he asked.

Alexander gave him a tight little smile. "I've always carried it." He gestured to Jordan with the pistol. "See if you can find me a towel."

"Clean or dirty?" Jack eyed the overflowing sink and the crusty dishes piled all over the small counter. He picked out the corner of a coffee-stained towel and tugged it from the wreckage.

"I don't care. " Alexander held out his hand for the towel. He forced Jordan's jaws open and tied the towel through his teeth and around his head. Jordan coughed behind the gag and groaned.

"Oh, this is nothing," Alexander muttered, "I haven't brought out a buzz saw or anything."

Jack laughed. "Damned if you don't have a mean streak, Alexander."

Alexander grimaced and shook his head. "Only as needed. Check the door. I hear footsteps."

Jack pressed himself along the door and peered out the narrow window beside it. "Daniel," he said. Daniel, clad in black leather and carrying his motorcycle helmet, had his eyes intent on the door. In a moment he rapped softly.

Jack opened the door.

"Just me," Daniel said softly as he pushed his way in and closed the door behind him. He deadbolted it shut. "Who do we have here?"

"Doctor Jordan Booth," Jack said. "He's the guy Lia had chopping me up."

Alexander picked up a grimy plate from the kitchen table and brushed crumbs onto the littered floor. "Jack identified him as one of Lia's associates. Mr. Booth has neither confirmed nor denied this."

"Naturally," Daniel said.

"Not immortal," Jack added.

Daniel flexed his fingers. "Will you be conducting the interview, Sir?" he said to Alexander.

Alexander unbuttoned his jacket and hung it on the back of one of the kitchen chairs. "I'll see what I can glean from him. In the meantime, Jack, do you have his phone?"

Jack pulled the smartphone from his coat pocket. It was smeared with blood from his cut hand.

Daniel gave him a questioning glance and held out his hand.

"One moment, Daniel." Alexander intercepted the device. "Doctor Booth needs to excuse himself from work. Give me five minutes."

"Very well. Let's find his computer." Daniel turned and marched into the interior of the house. "Come Jack," he called over his shoulder.

"Daniel," Jack said slowly, "I think this is where Lia brought me. Does that make any sense?"

"Well, you said Lia took you to a house but Lia lived in an apartment." They paused in a den area with a ripped faux leather couch, books and papers on every surface, and a sixty-inch plasma TV hanging over it all. Daniel glanced at the front entrance. The bare spot in front of the door was perhaps the cleanest part of the house. Daniel sucked in a deep breath through his nose and curled his lip.

"If this is the place, no wonder Lia kept you well occupied. No woman ever stayed two hours here." He fixed Jack with his grey eyes. "*Is* this the place?"

Jack licked his teeth. "I don't know."

"Take your time." Daniel turned, swung his head right and left until he caught sight of the stairs leading to the second floor. "I'll try there. You take a look through those—" he shoved his finger at the papers and books on the American's coffee table. "Walk around a bit. See if anything seems familiar.

"Okay." Jack faced the front door again and tried to conjure that night. He touched the door with one finger—as if that could give him some sort of flashback, which it didn't—then turned and pressed his back to it as if Lia were there, legs wrapped around him, mouth wrestling with his.

Idiot.

Mary Rose, I'm so sorry.

Tell me you didn't have your eyes shut the whole time.

No, he hadn't. When they'd stumbled, laughing, through the front door, Lia hadn't even switched the light on. She'd slammed the door and shoved him against it. Over her shoulder he'd seen a flash, a reflection of orange streetlight. Jack looked up, across the room, and there hung three framed diplomas hung opposite him, beside a closet.

That was something, Jack guessed.

They'd made out for a few minutes after that.

Jack squeezed his eyes shut and tried to picture it, and to push past the onslaught of physical stimuli. What had he seen, heard, felt?

She'd reached for something with her right hand, then she'd stuck him with the needle. No way she'd kept a syringe in that little spangled dress she'd had on. So where did she reach to?

There was a bookshelf beside the door. But no one ever left a syringe of some sedative lying on a bookshelf, right? Did Jordan prep it? Probably.

"Where would I keep my sedatives?" Jack slid down to a crouch against the door, suddenly weary and feeling in need of a shower.

Shower.

Bathroom.

Jack staggered to his feet. He found the bathroom on the second door he tried. It held one of those bathtubs with the clawed feet, a cracked, beige porcelain toilet, and a pedestal sink with a mirrored-front medicine cabinet, speckled with water stains. Jack swung the door open and scanned past the toothbrush and paste, the three bottles of pills, and saw a small zippered bag. He dumped its contents into the sink—four brand new syringes, two vials labeled Midazolam.

"Bingo," Jack breathed. "Daniel!" he spun around, jamming his hip against the sink.

"Yeah, I got it." Jack heard the thump of Daniel's feet overhead, pounding down the stairs. "I got the computer."

"I got something else." Jack poked his head around the corner and dangled the bag as Daniel reached the bottom of the stairs.

"What's this?" Daniel tucked the shiny black laptop and the spaghetti of cords under his arm and reached out to grab the bag with two fingers.

"Syringes, and Midazolam."

"What's Midazolam?" Daniel shook the bag gently.

"I don't know. Look it up. But she stuck me with something and it knocked me out. I'm guessing this is it."

"Alright." Daniel handed it back. "We'll take it with us. Let's see what we can do on this thing." Daniel led him into the kitchen.

Alexander sat on a wooden chair, facing Jordan, legs crossed, and drinking the cold coffee he'd bought an hour earlier. Jordan's gag lay on the empty table, but his lips were tight pressed together. "The doctor is a silent fellow," Alexander said, lifting the cup to his lips.

"We'll see." Daniel brushed a few crumbs from the kitchen table and laid the laptop down and opened it and tapped his finger on the mouse pad until the screen lit up. "Pass me my bag."

Alexander reached behind his chair and slung a backpack, which had gone unnoticed to Jack, over toward Daniel. Daniel pulled out a silver laptop and opened it beside Jordan's computer.

"Ten minutes," he said.

"There's still another cold cup of coffee," Alexander said with a wry smile.

"I'm fine." Jack turned the bag over, and the medicines and syringes clattered onto the tabletop. He picked up a vial between his thumb and forefinger, "So, Jordan, what happens when you inject someone with Midazolam?"

"It is a sedative," Jordan said, deadpan.

"Why do you have a sedative?"

Jordan looked away.

Jack leaned over him and brandished the vial in his face. "Did Lia call you that night? Did she tell you she was bringing you a lamb to slaughter, and you should get a needle ready? How'd you meet her anyway?"

Jordan pointedly moved his eyes.

Jack grabbed his face and forced his eyes up. "Look me in the eye, fuckface. How did you meet her?"

"Lia works at a bar. How do you think?"

Jack glanced back at Alexander. He nodded. Carry on.

"Did she take you home too?"

"No," there was a hint of a growl to Jordan's voice. He twisted his face from Jack's grip and his lip curled. "Idiot."

Jack's palm cracked across his cheek.

"Jack." Alexander half rose from his chair.

Jack leaned in, and despite the contempt in Jordan's face, the American flinched. "Then what made you believe her when she said she was immortal?"

"And I'm in," Daniel said softly from behind his two screens. "Let's see what Mr. Booth has been up to."

Jordan swallowed hard and pressed his lips together again. Jack leaned back and crossed his arms. "Yes, Daniel, do tell."

Daniel ignored him, leaning over the keyboard, clicking furiously.

"You have a lot of pornography, Mr. Booth," he said after a few minutes had passed.

Alexander looked up slowly and took a deliberate sip from his coffee.

"That's not a crime," Jordan said in a low voice.

"No." Daniel grimaced. "But it is if it is child pornography, you sick bastard."

Alexander, Jack and Jordan all froze.

"I think I can figure out which is your boss's email." Daniel watched Jordan's face over the screen of the laptop.

"Don't," Jordan said softly.

"Where is Lia?" Daniel asked.

"I don't know."

Daniel typed away at the laptop and flicked at the mouse pad. "I have an email with your kiddie porn in it, ready to send to about five different email addresses, all of them work addresses."

"I don't know!"

Daniel's finger hovered, as if over the send button.

"I don't!" Jordan wrenched against the zip ties that held him. His voice was laced with panic. "She said she didn't need me where she was going, and she'd get in touch when she did, but I think she went to England."

"Did she mention a specific place? A specific person?"

Jordan's eyes rolled from side to side. Jack could hear his quick, gasping breaths. "I don't know!"

"Do you know where Peter Bouwmeester is?" Alexander asked.

"He's probably wherever she is, lying low. I don't know!" Jordan looked like he was going to pass out. His flabby face was beaded with sweat.

Daniel narrowed his eyes. His fingers twitched over the keyboard. Finally, he tapped a few times on the mouse pad. "Alright. You're safe for now."

Alexander slid his chair a little closer to Jordan and looked up into Jordan's face. Jordan flicked his eyes away.

"Look at me," Alexander said in a low but firm voice.

Jordan looked up, bleary eyed.

"Who asked you to be involved in this?"

Jordan hesitated, then said, "Lia."

"And you met her at the bar where she worked," Alexander said.

"Yes."

Alexander's eyes narrowed. "She disclosed that she was immortal?"

"Yes," Jordan squeaked.

"And you believed her?"

"She uh..." Jordan licked his lips, "she shot herself in front of me."

Jack snorted. "Figures."

Alexander straightened and regarded Jordan for a moment. "Sir, as a doctor, you had no qualms about harming innocent immortals?"

"I-I..." Jordan stammered and glanced at the snub-nosed pistol, now resting in Alexander's lap, "I mean, whatever you guys have, wouldn't it save people's lives? It would be irresponsible to—"

"You don't know what you're talking about." Alexander jaw hardened. "You cut my friend's chest open, froze him, and bled Markus Koenig to death among other things. You weren't trying to save lives. You were torturing innocent men."

Despite Jordan's soft, quivering jaw, his voice managed to gain strength, "Markus's body had the ability to regenerate its own blood. In the case of a blood shortage that could save a life. Or if he can grow a new heart or kidney, then someone who needed one to save their life—"

"So you could make a nice little immortal organ farm, is that right, you sicko?" Jack growled.

"Daniel," Alexander said softly, "are you looking for his research files?"

"No, don't take them!" Jordan cried.

"I'm looking," Daniel said.

"Jack," Alexander's voice was quiet, even, "go look around the house for any other electronic devices. I mean hard drives, cameras, memory sticks. See if he has any notebooks or written records of his experiments. We are going to comb through this house."

He leveled his gaze on Jordan. "Perhaps your motives are pure, sir, and you think that it is right to forgo the wellbeing of the few in favor of the masses. Tell me then, should we forgo your wellbeing for the sake of our masses?"

Sweat dripped onto Jordan's upper lip. "Don't kill me," he squeaked, "I'll tell you where it all is."

A flicker of a smile crossed Alexander's face.

Between Jordan's direction and Jack's searching, they unearthed an external hard drive filled with notes, pictures and videos of Lia's experiments as well as several notebooks.

Jack stood, wiping his watering eyes in the kitchen. His nose ran from the clouds of dust and mold he'd disturbed when he'd rummaged under Jordan's bed. Daniel plugged the hard drive into his laptop. A window opened on the screen. After a few clicks, Daniel opened the first file. A video popped up. The little wheel spun as the computer lagged, then through the tinny laptop speakers came the shrill wine of the circular saw.

Jack gasped.

Daniel slapped at the keypad and the noise stopped, but a cold sweat had already sprung up on Jack's brow. He began to pant, and squeezed his eyes shut, shaking his head, trying to rid himself of that sound.

"Shit," Daniel muttered under his breath. He looked up at Jordan, who slumped in the chair with his head down. "Care to watch this?"

"No," Jordan said.

"Here is the plan," Alexander said as he laid both his hands on the grimy Formica tabletop and leaned forward to look into Jordan's eyes. "We cannot press criminal charges, because we don't exist. We cannot send you to jail for your crimes, and I object to killing you outright. What we *are* going to do is make sure you are prosecuted for crimes of the mortal sort. For instance, that child pornography you seem to own so much of. I believe Mr. Gunther has already sent out a few emails to that end."

Jordan made a little choking noise.

"I believe," Alexander drawled, "that it would be to our advantage that you lose whatever credibility you may retain. To that effect, I believe we'll treat you to a sampling of hallucinogenic drugs and ensure you are found in said condition."

Jordan jerked forward, but Alexander calmly pointed the pistol at him.

"Are you satisfied, Daniel?" he asked.

"I found his banking information," Daniel said. "I may alter this information. Actually, Mr. Booth, you might find a great deal of your history isn't what you remember it to be. But what can we say? You're an addict."

"Don't do this," Jordan whimpered. "Please. I'm sorry! I'm sorry Jack. I'm sorry she did that to you."

"Shut up!" Jack spun around, still vibrating; the sound of the buzz saw still reverberating in his ears. "Shut the fuck up! I have to live with this too. You're getting off easy!"

Alexander held up his hand. "Jordan, I have one more question for you, and if you give me a satisfactory answer we'll at the very least leave your money alone. Did Lia say why she was doing this?"

Jordan swallowed hard and bobbed his head. "She said she needed to know how to kill immortals f-for revenge."

Alexander let out a long slow sigh. "I see." He nodded. "Very good. Let's clean up our mess."

They left Jordan slumped on the floor in front of his chair, in the grips of an injected drug that Jack had no desire to identify. There had been a bottle of wine in the fridge, half-empty and covered with plastic wrap. Alexander dumped most of it on the kitchen floor, in a puddle around Jordan.

When they were a few blocks from the house, Alexander placed a call to the police and sent them to Jordan's house, feigning the need for a wellness check.

Jack realized, when they were almost home, that his hand had never been stitched and his jeans were streaked with his own blood.

At Alexander's place, Jack slumped at the kitchen table. Alexander paced in the living room on the phone with someone up at Schwalenburg. Jack poked at the cut on his hand. It had stopped bleeding anyway. He should wrap it up.

Alexander ended his phone call a few minutes later and came into the kitchen, still in his coat. He shrugged it off and tossed it over a chair. "Good heavens," he said, "Daniel has his hands full tonight."

"With Jordan's stuff?" Jack looked up wearily.

"He'll set up surveillance on Jordan, credit cards, passport and the like—"

"How?" Jack said sharply.

Alexander grinned sheepishly. "Daniel has his fingers in many wells of information. Where we cannot insert a person, Daniel can find the back door."

Daniel's a hacker. Geez.

"Clever," Jack said wryly.

"A matter of necessity," Alexander said quietly, as if he regretted it. "Men like Jordan are exactly why we keep our secrecy. Men like him, and those who actually have the power to work out their ideas." He sat down opposite Jack. "You did well, Jack. It was providential, lucky perhaps one might say. Nevertheless, your quick thinking paid off. We'll hope for a less risky scenario next time."

"Next time." Jack laughed under his breath. He clenched and unclenched the cut hand.

"Ah yes,"—Alexander sighed—"you never got it stitched."

"It's fine. It stopped bleeding," Jack said.

"I'll find some gauze." Alexander got up and began rummaging through drawers. As he approached, holding out a first aid tin, his phone began to jingle in his pocket. He set the tin on the table in front of Jack.

"Guten abend." Alexander turned away from Jack. "Ja." A long pause. A deep line appeared between Alexander's eyes as he listened.

When he hung up, he sat down opposite Jack. "Two things: First, Cyrus and Idina found no traces of Lia or Peter, except to confirm that Lia had been at the cafe with a blond man. They haven't determined who that was yet."

"Okay."

"And second, Giovanni Ardovinni has arrived in Dresden. He will come and talk to me tonight."

Alexander's ageless face looked old then, old and tired...and scared, Jack thought. Jack didn't blame him.

CHAPTER 15
London, 1921

Zoran left Giovanni's house just after noon. Burke carried out his luggage with a face so impassive that only Giovanni could detect the mutinous glint in his eye. A hired car sat out in the bright sunlight.

"I'll stay at the Kenrick Hotel." Zoran paused by the open door and looked back at Giovanni.

"When will you speak to Sir Alexander?" Giovanni asked.

Zoran glanced back, his eyes fastened on something just over Giovanni's head. "I'll send him a message when I arrive."

"I will know if you haven't done it," Giovanni said. "Mark my words."

Zoran laughed under his breath. "You enjoy having me by the tail, don't you? Well you mark *my* words: the turn of the wheel shall bring me back up to the top, and you down below. I'll relish it when it does."

Giovanni kept a stoic face. Burke, just passing back into the house, curled his fist at his side. The valet's eyes met his.

Keep walking, Giovanni thought, *keep walking, John*. Burke only made a slight inclination of his head, and disappeared into the house.

"Send word to your mistress," Giovanni said in a low voice. "She will not see you for some time, I'll warrant."

Zoran shrugged and took a step toward the door. "I told her not to expect me until late summer."

"When is the child to be born?"

"That," Zoran spat, "is none of your concern." He strode through the door and into the waiting cab.

Giovanni let out his breath. He would send the mistress a letter, lest she not be cared for when the child came. At very least she would know where Zoran had gone and what was keeping him.

"He's grown more insufferable since last I saw him." Cosima's low voice came from behind him.

Giovanni turned. She stood, watching him with a little smile on her lips. She had a thin, filmy sweater wrapped around her pale blue gown. She blinked at the sunlight as Giovanni shut the door.

"Did you sleep well?" he asked.

"Quite."

"Sir Alexander was here."

"Oh," her face fell, "I would have gotten up."

"He was here to see Zoran." Giovanni took her elbow and guided her back into the house, "In regards to the matter with Mr. Oswald."

"Ahh," she breathed, "then his mind will be very full," she said tenderly, "and I have no pretense to see him."

"You'll see him soon enough," Giovanni said firmly.

Cosima looked searchingly into his face. "Don't be angry with my weakness, Giovanni," she said with a sigh. "You know I've never stopped loving him."

He knew. "I am not worried about love," he said, "but commitment."

It was commitment that was on his mind, not just that Alexander would finally promise himself to Cosima, but also the commitment of immortality, and if he should ask it of John Burke.

Late that afternoon, he returned to his library and found Burke there, standing by one of the bookshelves with a volume open. Whatever Burke's errand had been, it was now forgotten. Giovanni stood by the door, aware that Burke had not yet seen him.

The golden sunlight shone across Burke's face, burnishing his dark brows and mahogany hair and lighting a mark upon his cheek, the scar left by a bullet that had winged him in the Great War. Burke was thirty-five now, old enough to have a few threads of silver at his temples.

Giovanni had always found him handsome. For that very reason, when Burke came in response to his advertisement, Giovanni had almost passed him over. But something about his erect, military bearing and closed, clipped way of speaking during the interview had convinced Giovanni that there was no danger of him getting too close.

How remarkably wrong he'd been.

How had Burke known his master's isolation? At first, Giovanni had rebuffed his overtures of friendship, his attempts to engage Giovanni in the books he'd left lying in his rooms. Finally Giovanni had the courage to answer with more than two or three words and found he could talk to Burke as if they were old friends. He was well read and well travelled. The only thing he'd remained tight-lipped about was his past. He'd never married. Burke said he didn't care to.

Could Burke hear his heart pounding when, purely by way of his duties, the valet would lean near to adjust his neckerchief, or brush lint off his coat? Could Burke read the lust, mingled with despair, in his eyes? How had Burke known, without Giovanni telling him, what he was?

For it was Burke who had seduced him.

Burke looked up from his book, finally, and met Giovanni's eyes. Giovanni straightened from his position against the doorframe and shook himself out of his reverie.

Burke smiled, but his eyes glanced past Giovanni. "Is everything alright, Sir?"

Giovanni detected footfalls in the hall behind him. "Our houseguest has departed."

"I'll notify Stevens," Burke said. He sighed almost imperceptibly and slid the book back onto the shelf.

"What were you reading just now?" Giovanni asked.

"Keats," Burke said softly. "'Thou wast not born for death, immortal bird. No hungry generations tread thee down.'"

Giovanni flinched. The footsteps came nearer. He glanced back and saw Cosima. "I need to talk to you," he said to Burke. "Come tonight."

Burke's smile was tinged with melancholy. "I will."

∞

They sat, side by side, against the headboard. The room was almost pitch dark, the candles long since burnt out. Downstairs, the grandfather clock had just finished chiming three. Giovanni could no longer see Burke's face, but he could hear his quick breathing.

Suddenly a sharp laugh burst from Burke's side of the bed. "This is all a joke on you, Giovanni. He's leading you on, giving you plain water."

"I don't think so," Giovanni said in a small voice. "I have a good inkling of when Zoran is lying, John."

"I cannot," Burke said. "I cannot drink it. My god! When I think of my days stretching on forever and ever? I fear it more than death! I am a soldier, Giovanni! Do you think I fear death?"

Giovanni sat silent, sick to his stomach. He felt as if Burke, though solid and full of life beside him, were already slipping from his grasp by the pull of the hungry years. Bitterness stung at the back of his throat.

What had Cosima said, only yesterday? She'd told him Burke's coming was providential.

"Not providence," Giovanni had said. "Providence would do no such thing. Likely it is a devil's snare that will choke me in the end."

And Cosima had laughed because she'd thought he was joking.

"Forgive me," he said to Burke. "Forgive me, I didn't mean—"

Suddenly Burke seized his hand and pressed it to his lips. "No, no, forgive me. Oh Giovanni, I did not think of you, I..."

"No, I should never have asked such a thing of you," Giovanni cried. "I know the burden of the years!"

Burke folded Giovanni's hand up inside his much larger one and clutched it under his chin, rocking back and forth. His breath came fast. "I have to admit, I would gain some satisfaction from finally seeing the inner workings of your society, finally speaking openly with your so-called great men."

Giovanni choked a laugh.

"But to live forever..." Burke sighed. He fell quiet.

"Don't do this for me," Giovanni said finally. "Don't you dare, or in fifty or a hundred years you will curse my name. Think about it, perhaps, but choose to do it or not to do it for your own reasons."

Burke nodded, his chin rasping against their hands. "I'll... I'll think about it." He slumped down and leaned his head against Giovanni's shoulder. Giovanni could almost hear the thoughts running through his mind.

Please say yes, Giovanni thought, but guilt gnawed at his belly.

∞

That morning, Alexander was compelled to take his Bible to the table with his tea. What had once been a habit as engrained as breakfast had now become a rarity, but a strange sense of desperation had overtaken him. He felt as if he, like King Saul, would consult a medium if it could make Joseph Oswald's spirit rise out of the ground and tell him how he had died.

He'd just opened the Bible and raised his tea to his lips when Daniel came in carrying a message from Zoran.

Come to see me at the Kenrick Hotel. I need to speak to you.

Daniel eyed him.

"Zoran wishes to speak to me," Alexander said. He tossed the paper aside and it fell to the floor.

"And?" Daniel said. He dropped into the chair opposite Alexander and pulled the day's newspaper from under Alexander's Bible.

"I suppose I'll go," Alexander said with a sigh. "There must be half a chance he has something of use to tell me." He fingered the pages of the Bible and shut it again. He got up, tea forgotten.

"Now?" Daniel looked up.

Alexander shrugged. "Best to get it over with."

It had been two centuries at least since Alexander and Zoran had lodged in the same house, but in that time Zoran's habits had not changed. His hotel room was already littered with papers and open books. Zoran received Alexander civilly, this time neatly dressed and solemn-faced.

"What can I do for you, Zoran?" Alexander asked quietly, when he was seated in Zoran's tiny hotel sitting room.

Zoran sat down opposite him and clapped both hands on his knees. His obsidian eyes fixed intently on Alexander's. "I know how Oswald died," he said.

Alexander's breath froze in his lungs for a second. "How?" he said, when he was able.

"I gave him water from the Immortal Fountain," Zoran said. "I told him to put it in the water and drown himself with it. Clearly he succeeded."

Alexander stared at him. His mind spun in circles—water? How had Zoran come by it? Could this be true? Zoran had not been with Oswald? How could it be proven? They could not try it again.

"How can you be certain?" Alexander said sharply.

Zoran spread his hands. "Truly, I cannot be at this time. But you have the water at your disposal, and there is more than one immortal who would welcome death."

"You know I wouldn't—"

"Yes, yes," Zoran said impatiently, "but water is what I gave Oswald, fountain water, and there is little doubt in my mind that this is what happened. You were in his apartment. Did you find any vials of water? Small, brown bottles?"

Alexander strained to visualize the contents of the apartment. They'd cleaned many jars, dishes and bottles. Small bottles of water? "I don't believe so."

"Well, then we shall likely find ourselves at an impasse. I have no more water, and I did not kill him." Zoran sat back. "But that is what I told him to do, and he is dead."

Alexander let out his breath in a shaky stream. *Dear God! Dear God, what do I do?* He pointed one, trembling finger at Zoran. "Where did you get that water? The fountain is sealed in its cave."

Zoran smiled, "Indeed, but you took me there once, remember? That was many, many years ago but I have kept it ever since."

Alexander sat immobilized on the edge of his chair. "I—" He had nothing to say. What could he say? Finally he said, weakly, "Surely there is another way we could confirm...?"

"Let me read Oswald's notebooks," Zoran said eagerly. "But truly, there are immortals who would jump at the chance to—"

"No!" Alexander half rose from his seat. "I need to think. Have the journals if you wish, but we shall not begin drowning immortals!"

Zoran laughed. "See, this is exactly why I didn't tell you in the first place. I would not have told you, if Ardovinni didn't have his foot on my throat—"

"Ardovinni?"

"—I knew that you'd do no good with this revelation." Zoran's eyes snapped at him, "Perhaps we can live immortal, and then die

149

when we are tired of this life? Is that not perfection? Tell me, Alexander. I know you have some moral argument against this."

"Be quiet," Alexander cried, "I need to think about this. Stay here, Zoran. Do not leave or we shall hunt you down like dogs."

Zoran laughed again and slouched in his chair. "Very well. Send me the notebooks. I am entirely at your leisure."

Alexander bolted from the hotel room but stopped in the hall, suddenly ashamed of himself. Zoran was playing him like a stringed instrument, whether what he said was true or not. There had to be at least some way to make more certain whether fountain water had been the death of Oswald. The notebooks, as Zoran said, would surely hold some clues. They would sift again through the detritus of Oswald's little apartment.

And he needed to talk to Ardovinni. What did Zoran mean, that Ardovinni had forced him to tell this?

Alexander almost turned back to say to Zoran that by no means would he receive Oswald's notes, but he thought the better of it. He needed a calmer, more rational mind to help him work this through. He was yet too emotional.

No, he was terrified. As he emerged onto the street and the warm, late spring air, his heart was still hammering. There was a picture in his mind of plunging his head and shoulders into the icy fountain, which flowed underground at Schwalenburg, and finally sleeping that never-ending sleep. It shot him through with apprehension, like it were an actual appointment he was dreading.

He was torn for a moment between returning home to speak to Daniel or going immediately to Ardovinni. He recalled that Daniel had meant to go out on other business that morning, so he hailed a cab and made for Ardovinni's house.

Instead of Ardovinni, it was Cosima who received him in the sun-filled library. She rose out of one of the chairs to greet him, her coffee-colored curls burnished by the light behind her.

Alexander was momentarily taken aback by her appearance. In the confusion of the morning, he'd forgotten she was in the city. "C-cosima," he stuttered, "I came to see Ardovinni."

"Giovanni has departed on business." Her smile faltered as she surveyed his face. "Alexander, what's wrong?"

"I-I…" Alexander slumped against the doorframe and pressed his palm to his eyes. When he took his hand away, Cosima stood right in front of him.

"You're pale," she said.

"Zoran told me how Oswald died." In that one, positive statement, Alexander suddenly realized Zoran had convinced him. Oswald had drowned, in water from the Immortal Fountain.

Cosima's eyes narrowed. "He's certain? You're certain?"

"Yes… maybe… I don't know." Alexander rubbed his jaw.

Cosima frowned deeply for a moment, then turned away abruptly to pull a little cord beside the door. A moment later, Stevens appeared. "Stevens," she said sternly, "bring brandy for Mr. von Katlenburg."

A few moments later he was seated, sipping the searing liquor. Cosima sat down opposite him, surveying him gravely.

"Better?" she said gently, when he'd finished the glass.

Alexander nodded and laughed hoarsely. "I'm embarrassed at my lack of composure, truly I am. I…" The words began to flood from him, "Since the events in Verdun, and since Camille's child was taken, Zoran has never missed an opportunity to prod and poke at me with his needles and barbs. I should be inured to it by now. How can I possibly trust that he tells the truth? He says he wasn't in London when Oswald died."

"But he knew?" Cosima's dark eyes contained skepticism, mingled with trepidation.

"He says…" *Should he tell her?* "He says he told Oswald what to do. A theory, I guess, and now Oswald has confirmed it."

"Ah." She nodded. "It is but a theory. Still, Oswald is dead."

"We can hardly test his theory. We cannot kill one of us to confirm a theory of Zoran's."

"Someone would be willing to do it," Cosima said quietly. "I know you don't like to think it, dear Alexander, but it is true."

"I... I cannot." Alexander *did* know it was true, but that didn't mean it was right.

"No." Cosima looked down at the Persian rug below their feet. "No, perhaps not. There must be another way." She breathed a laugh. "Immortal animals perhaps."

"There has to be another way." Alexander swallowed hard. "I don't understand how Ardovinni got all of this out of Zoran. He said Ardovinni forced him to tell me this."

Cosima gazed at him, forehead scrunched, for a moment. Suddenly she nodded. "Money. Zoran borrowed money from Giovanni, and a lot of it. I told Giovanni he'd never get it back, but it seems to have provided Giovanni with leverage over him. Well, that is good." She shook her head. "Giovanni hasn't discussed this with me, Alexander. He's only told me why he brought Zoran in the barest of terms, but it seems his intuition told him Zoran was involved in Oswald's death."

"And he was right." Alexander tipped his head back toward the ceiling. "Ah, dear God, if he's telling the truth. If this secret has been here the whole time, if..."

Cosima's hand came down on his and gripped it firmly. "Then I would begin to fear for your life, dear Alexander."

He turned and stared at her blankly. "No, no, I..."

"Never mind your convictions." Her ebony eyes were stormy. "For if things are as they were last time we were together, then they sit on a cracked foundation. Next time your black clouds roll in, perhaps they would capsize you and send you to the abyss!"

Her words stung him. He pulled away his hand, but she caught it back and kissed his fingers. "Alexander," she said earnestly, "don't pretend you don't know how I care for you."

Pretend? He knew he didn't deserve her love, and he'd convinced himself not to expect it of her. "But after Lisbon..."

Lisbon. Ardovinni's house in the quiet suburb had become his refuge after he was wounded in the Boer war. He had no place to go to convalesce, no one to take care of him. Ardovinni had agreet to put him up in his house in that city with some servants and Cosima to look after him.

As swift as she was to begin putting his ruined health to rights, she was equally swift to see the bitterness that had taken root in his heart: anger for his lot in life that had burned down to embers and continued to eat away at his spirit.

∞   ∞   ∞

"Is it unjust that we live this life?" She stamped her foot, her dark eyes sparking with fire. "Are we too good for our fate? Can we not be happy with what we have?"

"Are you happy?" he cried, "are you?"

"I am loved by good people," she shot back. "I am a free woman, treated with respect and well cared for all my days by a good man."

He hated that she meant Ardovinni, and not him. He said so.

"Whose choice was that?" she snapped.

His. It was his, because he'd been unwilling to take her as his wife and risk conceiving a child together. There could be no platonic friendship between them. In the week she'd been with him, despite having been apart for nearly a decade, his desire for her had flared into a blaze.

Alexander was half asleep on one of the settees in the dark library, a book shut on his chest, the candle burnt down beside him. Cosima sat down beside him. Before he could think it through he reached for her and pulled her down on top of him. She returned his fervent kisses with equal passion, and her hands were as free as his, but she at least had the sense to disentangle herself and pull away.

"We used to be good for each other," she breathed.

The next day Cosima left Lisbon, and he did not stay much longer, fearing Ardovinni's return.

∞ ∞ ∞

So perhaps Alexander was justified in thinking she'd tired of him. But in the way she was looking at him, there could be no mistake that Cosima still cared.

Cosima scooted her chair closer to him and leaned toward him. She cupped his chin with one gentle hand, and traced the outline of one of his eyes with her fingertips. "Sometimes I've imagined lines here," she said as the pads of her fingers slid along the outer edge of his eyes, "and here," she traced his mouth. "I've pictured you old and grey as you will never be and wished it for you." Her ebony eyes held his. "I thought perhaps you would be happier then, Alexander, but I don't think that anymore." She laid her palm flat over his throbbing heart. "Your happiness must come from a peaceful heart. That is what I long to see in you."

Alexander's shoulder's sagged. "How can I be peaceful now?"

To his surprise an impish smile crossed Cosima's mouth. "What did Giovanni read to me this morning? 'I have somewhat against thee, because thou hast left thy first love. Remember therefore from whence thou are fallen, and repent, and do the first works.'"

Alexander smiled despite the rebuke hidden in her quote. "Ardovinni reads to you from the Scriptures?"

"This may surprise you," Cosima said archly, "but Giovanni goes to Mass every week, and he knows that I also have faith in my own way."

To this Alexander could not find a satisfactory reply and looked down at his hands.

Cosima touched his face again and stood up. He stood also.

"What are you going to do now?" she asked softly.

"I need to return to Mr. Gunther and discuss this with him," Alexander said. "I hope that Oswald may have left us some clue among his things about how he died."

"Shall I send Giovanni to you when he returns?" she tilted her head.

Alexander nodded. "I would be grateful."

"Then I will do that."

Alexander found himself on the street; his heart was warm, as if Cosima's hand still lay over it, yet his mind was as heavy as ever.

CHAPTER 16
London, Present Day

Finally Alannah wasn't the one on the bottom. Jules, flat on the mat, pinned under her legs, abandoned all technique and swung her fist at Alannah's stomach.

"No, no, no!" Lewis shouted from the side of the mat. "Trap and roll, Jules. Trap and roll."

Now I've got you. Alannah pressed her lips together, suppressing a smile. Jules, in her panic, had forgotten to tuck her elbows and now she was in no position to trap her foot. Jules struggled again, baring her teeth. Finally, she went limp and started giggling.

"Okay, get up." Lewis rubbed his hands over his short hair and smiled blearily. His voice had the slightly muffled quality caused by a stuffed nose. "Jules, you panicked!" He said as Alannah and Jules dusted themselves off.

"Well, Alannah usually doesn't get me," Jules grumbled. Her green eyes glinted with fun.

"Yeah, yeah, you're always the one on top. Good job, Alannah. Your form was excellent." He clapped his hands. "Leslie, step up. Alannah, you'll go again. I'd demonstrate with you, but I'm afraid I'll drip snot all over you." He pulled up the front of his shirt, exposing toned abs, to wipe his nose.

Alannah turned aside. She collected the tail of her loose, black t-shirt and tucked it into the waistband of her gi pants. She wiped the sweat off her forehead. "Alright. I'm ready."

Half an hour later, she carried her gym bag out into the golden evening sunshine and checked her phone. There was a text from Jack.

Idina and Cy are coming to England. It's about Lia.

Alannah paused on the sidewalk to shoulder her bag and felt tightness creep into her chest that wasn't from a vigorous roll in the dojo.

This doesn't concern me, she thought resolutely. *It's a massive city, and Lia doesn't know me.* She texted him back: *Did they say if they planned to stay here?*

No, he returned a couple moments later, *how was Jiu Jitsu?*

Good, she returned. If Cy and Idina hadn't texted her then they probably didn't intend to stay in their flat. They were probably on the far side of the city somewhere. She sighed and unlocked the building door.

As she dried her hair, post-shower, her phone dinged on the vanity counter. She wiped the condensation off the screen with one hand and slung the towel into the bathtub. It was Louisa, returning an earlier text asking about her evening plans.

Kris said he would call, Louisa wrote.

Alannah grinned wearily and carried the phone to the bedroom. Oh Louisa. How many word-for-word accounts of Louisa's phone calls had she and Cat had to endure? Louisa had fallen hard for the good doctor. Alannah could only hope Doctor Kris reciprocated at least half of her friend's enthusiastic feelings.

She sat cross-legged on the bed and gazed down at the John Lin Academy, lit by pale grey streetlights. The motorcycle wasn't there, and hadn't been at any point that she'd been home. It was stupid to think longingly of the anonymous rider—she'd yet to identify him at John Lin; it seemed her class and his hours did not coincide. He was, undoubtedly, not single, and not interested, and above all, not immortal.

Alannah drew her knees to her chest and wrapped her arms around them. Well, she'd left Winnipeg, gotten a job, and started taking Jiu Jitsu lessons. Maybe she'd soon work herself up to a boyfriend.

Jack?

Alannah giggled. She could maybe, *maybe* picture that. Objectively, he was a nice looking guy in a scruffy *Canadian* sort of way, though he made Daniel the huntsman and soldier look positively refined. They got along really well. He made her laugh, and she felt safe with him.

It was a little hard to picture kissing him, though. It made her shudder a little, then laugh.

"Well, who knows what a couple of decades could do, right?" She sighed and stood up to boil the kettle.

It had taken her a little time to fall for Daniel too. Of course, that had a great deal more to do with him being about four hundred years her senior.

∞   ∞   ∞

Alannah and Daniel arrived in Dresden on the same train. It was the early seventies, and she had just finished the school year at Humbolt University in Berlin. He'd been in Berlin on a lawkeeping mission. Alexander must have told him that she was on her way to Dresden, because he didn't looked at all surprised when he spotted her in the train station. He smiled wryly at her and sat down on the bench beside her.

"Miss Krueger," he said.

"H-hi." She shut her book quickly and smiled.

He held out his hand.

"You have all your fingers!" she blurted before she could compose something proper to say.

His blue eyes gleamed. He leaned in and said confidentially, "A little accident put them to rights." He flexed the restored digits.

"Alexander missed you," he said as he straightened. "It will be good to have you in Dresden."

∞ ∞ ∞

She missed Alexander now. She missed Dresden.

Two days later, when Alannah arrived home from work, she realized the black motorcycle was still in its parking spot. Half an hour later, when she emerged from the building again with her gym bag over her shoulder, it was still there.

She walked into the Academy, glancing around the entire way to the locker room, hoping to spot the rider. No dice. There were a couple of teenage guys at the far side of the room practicing on the heavy bags, and the usual girl was at the front. The rest of the occupants were her classmates.

A few minutes later Alannah had her palms flat on the floor, bum up, pain rocketing through her tight hamstrings. She heard Jules bounce up to the mat.

"Aggh…" She straightened and pressed her palms to her lower back.

"Hello, 'Lannah," Jules chirped.

"Hey," Alannah grunted as she pressed her palms flat to the ground again.

"Good evening," a deep voice said, somewhere in the region beyond her backside, "Lewis is ill and spreading mucous and plague, so we have sent him home. Unfortunately, that leaves you with me."

The voice had an odd accent to it. The blood rushed out of Alannah's head as she straightened; for a moment she was blind and dazed.

"I will be instructing you until he is fully functional."

Alannah's eyes cleared, and there, wearing blue 'gi' pants and a snug black t-shirt, stood the blond man from her doorstep. His ebony eyes met hers, the same eyes that had arrested her on her doorstep in Winnipeg.

Alexei.

CHAPTER 17
London, Present Day

Alannah sucked in a breath, nearly choking. Alexei's face mirrored her shock for a bare instant before the dark line of his brows tightened and erased every sign of recognition. He turned away and began the lesson. Alannah felt sick. Momentarily she considered rushing into the locker room and locking herself in a bathroom stall, but Jules had caught her eye and was mouthing 'What?' at her.

"Nothing," Alannah muttered. There were lots of people here. She'd be fine. She'd gut it out and figure out what to do afterward.

For the next hour, Alexei's eyes passed over her every time she was in his line of sight and Alannah tried to look at him as little as possible. It was hard not to, because she realized as she lay pinned under Jules, completely helpless, that with his short blond hair and broad shoulders, he was probably her motorcyclist.

As soon as he dismissed them, Alexei turned and presented them with the rock-hard line of his shoulders. He stalked away without looking back at her.

Alannah staggered on trembling legs back into the locker room. She could feel tears welling up in her eyes.

She yanked off her t-shirt and whipped the clean tunic and leggings from her locker.

Where am I going to go now?

I just got a job. I just got friends.

"Alannah!" Jules bounded into the room. "Is he your ex?"

In spite of herself, Alannah burst out laughing and the tears rolled out of her eyes. "No, he's not my ex."

Jules' eyes grew rounder. "Your ex's best friend? Did you—"

"Whatever you're going to say—no." Alannah held up her hands, searching for an explanation Jules might accept, "I'm sorry. I don't know what's wrong with me, I—" She swiped at her streaming eyes.

"But the way you glared at each other!"

"We had a run in," Alannah said desperately as she pulled her tunic over her head. "Just once. I'm sure he's a nice guy, and we were just having bad days." She shimmied into her leggings. She was getting out of here, no matter what stupid questions Jules threw her way.

"Aw…" Jules pulled her fluorescent orange backpack from her locker. "I was hoping for a juicy story and I sense you're not going to explain this 'run in' at all."

"No, no I'm not." Alannah closed her locker with forced gentleness. "See you next week."

Despite her calm explanation, fear prickled down her spine as she stepped out of the locker room and surveyed the dojo. Alexei's blond head was nowhere to be seen among the sparring young men and women.

Alannah shouldered her gym back and skirted around the open room toward the door. The brisk breeze chilled her sweaty skin as she swung around to push the door shut. As she straightened and fixed her eyes on the door of her apartment building, her eyes found the black motorcycle, the beacon of adventure in her life. There, in a gunfighter stance behind it, stood Alexei di Gaspare. He gripped his helmet in one hand.

Alannah almost did an about face back into the school. She'd rather brave Jules's prying. She'd rather…

"What the hell are you doing here?" His harsh voice carried across the street. "Why are you following me?"

Anger ignited in her belly, and with it came fresh tears. Alannah hitched up the gym bag that threatened to slide off her slumped shoulders and felt her face burn. "I'm not following you. What are you doing here?"

"I work here!" he said. His face, which had been hid partially by shadows, became clear as he took a step toward her. He was pale, every line of his face tight. "I thought that was evident. How did you find me?"

"I didn't!" Tears continued to stream. Now she was angry and embarrassed. "I left Winnipeg and picked the one neighborhood in this whole damn city that you happened to be in! What do you want?"

Even across the street, she could see the hard glare of panic in Alexei's eyes, the battle of fight or flight in the lines of his body. A modicum of calm, even control ebbed into her limbs. "I swear, I didn't know you were here," she called. "I promise."

There was a long pause.

Alexei glanced up and down the street, set down his helmet, and stalked across the narrow no man's land between them. His ebony gaze searched hers as he approached. He stopped quite close to her, and said softly, without his eyes leaving hers, "You're serious. You didn't know I was here?"

"If I had, I wouldn't have come," Alannah said with a helpless, breathless laugh. He was too close. She shivered with cold and nerves and edged away. "I just live here."

The door swung open behind them and both of them jumped.

Jules barreled out, saw them, and skidded to a halt. "Oh shit!" she said.

Alexei glared at her.

"Okay, okay!" She held up her hands and backed away. "I'm going!" Then she said under her breath, "Wanker."

For a moment Alannah wanted to cry out, "No, stay!" But Jules kept walking, leaving her alone with Alexei.

"Alright. You live here. I live here. Great." Alexei said in a low voice as soon as Jules was out of earshot, "And now I suppose I can expect the law keepers to come calling."

"Well, yes, I suppose you can." Alannah lifted her chin with much more bravado than she really felt. "They've been looking for you, you know, ever since you tried to push your way into my house in Winnipeg."

His jaw tightened. Fear, yes that was genuine fear in his eyes, but Alannah wasn't ready to feel sympathy yet.

"I guess..." Alexei looked down at his boots and raked his hands through his hair, "I guess it doesn't make a difference anyway."

Alannah stared at him.

He looked up. "Giovanni landed in Germany this afternoon. He'll see Alex... He'll talk to your people tonight. So..." he shrugged and let out a long breath. "So whatever. Call them."

Alexei turned around and began to cross the street toward his motorcycle.

"No wait!" Alannah cried. She clapped her hand to her mouth, appalled by her bravery.

Alexei turned back, glanced down the street, and crossed to the other side as a car rolled past. "What?" he called.

She could feel her hands shaking uncontrollably. "Alexander is my friend. What did you want from him?"

His face twisted. "Oh, now you want to know? Well, I'm not talking about that here."

She was committed now, Alannah realized. She was talking to him. She scooted across the street and stood a safe distance from him, within bolting distance of her building's door. "Can we talk somewhere else, then?" she asked.

Alexei's mouth opened a little.

"Please?" she asked, "I won't call anyone yet. I promise."

She saw his Adam's apple bob as he swallowed. "There's the coffee shop over there." Alexei pointed to the corner of the building hiding the familiar cafe.

"Give me fifteen minutes?" Alannah asked. "Just to ditch my stuff?"

Alexei glanced at his motorcycle. "Yeah. Okay."

For the course of the next fifteen minutes, Alannah talked herself into texting Idina despite her promise, then cried as she put on clean clothes, then talked herself out of texting Idina, then washed her face to hide the evidence of tears. She wrapped her wine-colored scarf around her neck, jammed her feet into her boots, and clambered down the stairs out the door.

Alexei stood in the falling shadows, beneath the awning of the cafe. His scuffed leather jacket was zipped right up to his chin, one hand thrust into his pocket, one holding his motorcycle helmet.

"It got colder in fifteen minutes," Alannah said. Her bottom lip quivered uncontrollably, though not from cold.

Alexei peeled himself away from the wall and held the door open for her. "It's hardly Winnipeg," he said, much more mildly than before.

"True."

"I don't plan to return there, if I can help it." Alexei glanced back and forth around the full coffee shop. His hands clenched at his sides.

"It isn't so bad when it isn't winter."

Alexei glanced back at her, taking her in with a serious look. "Then why are you here?"

"Because you and Ardovinni scared me away." Instantly, Alannah was sorry she said it. It was laughable, really, that two men showing up at her doorstep would chase her from a city, a country for that matter.

Alexei just stared at her, but to her surprise Alannah could see understanding in his eyes. "I'm sorry," he said, so soft she could hardly hear it over the coffee shop noises. His shoulders dropped as he turned toward the empty queue. "What can I get you?"

"I'll get my own coffee."

Alexei's eyes glimmered under his lashes. "I always pay for the lady, no matter what she feels about me. My mother drilled me mercilessly."

Alannah gave him a weak half-smile. "Medium roast, then, with room for cream. And thank you."

"There's an open spot over there." Alexei lifted his chin toward two faux leather chairs under a lamp in the corner. "Can I give you this?" he held out his helmet to her.

Alannah took the helmet from him and wound through the tables to the corner where she plopped down in the chair facing the window, and set the helmet down on the little table beside her. She sat, perched on the edge of her seat, and let out a shuddering breath. She stayed like that, with her foot bobbing in midair until Alexei set down a steaming porcelain mug beside her, another for himself, and a paper bag.

"One moment," he said. He slipped across the restaurant and brought back the cream pitcher and packets of sugar.

"One sugar," Alannah said.

He dangled the cream pitcher over her cup. "Tell me when."

Once he'd given himself a solid shot of cream as well, he carried them back, and sat down opposite her. One foot bounced incessantly, though his upper body remained still. He slid his hand into the paper bag and pulled out a very grainy looking muffin.

"Excuse me. I haven't eaten much today," he said, "I have another, if you'd...?"

Alannah waved it away. Her stomach was firmly knotted anyway.

Alexei took a bite of his muffin and sat chewing, not meeting her eyes. Alannah was silent, trying to assemble a complete question to ask him.

"I..." she began, "I wanted to ask you... what did you come to Winnipeg to see Alexander about?"

He looked up and squinted at her. "It's complicated."

Alannah paused and took a sip of her coffee, but her eyes never left his face. "Well, I gathered that," she said quietly, "but I'm a close friend of Alexander's. Alexei, I promise you that I'll treat it as delicately as I can."

He nodded. "As I said, it makes no difference. Giovanni is in Dresden right now." He sighed and pressed his hands to his knees. "Cosima di Gaspare is my mother. I am her immortal son."

Alannah let out a breath she didn't know she was holding. She felt pressure mounting in her chest. If Alexei was Alexander's child, he would be distraught. If Alexei was Cosima's child by another man, Alexander would also be devastated.

"Alexei," she asked softly, "is Alexander your father?"

He nodded again.

"Oh," she whispered. She felt a tangible stab of pain. This would hurt Alexander so badly.

Alexei picked up his coffee and eyed her over the rim as she reflected. "What will your close friend think about that?" His voice ground with bitterness.

Alannah swallowed hard. "I think," she said in a small voice, "I know, rather, that Alexander is a kind and good-hearted man." Her voice gained strength, "Given that he took care of me, the immortal child of his enemy, with all the love and self-sacrifice one might expect of a close family member, I would expect very much that he would do the same for you."

Alexei blinked away and stared into his coffee cup. The coffee shop noises filtered in to Alannah's consciousness, the bell over the door tinkled, the espresso machine hissed.

Alannah wondered, then, for how many decades this question had haunted Alexei. She'd been lucky, in a way. She'd been raised since she was a baby by her loving Mama and Papa Krueger, and until her adult years she'd never had an inkling that she didn't belong.

"I mean it," she said belatedly.

"I see you mean it." He raised his head, his mouth twisted wryly. "But as my mother has said, *Sir* Alexander did not want children and that is why he didn't marry her."

"I'd like to think it was more complicated than that," Alannah said.

"That's how I heard it." Alexei ripped a piece off his muffin and popped it in his mouth.

Alannah pressed one hand to her mouth and wrapped her other hand tightly around her warm coffee mug. Compassion suffused her and silenced her for another long moment.

Up close he didn't resemble Alexander so closely. Certainly, he was taller and more muscled. He was, Alannah thought, very handsome. His face didn't have the same refined bone structure of Alexander. His jaw was a little more square, his brows a little heavier. The total effect, combined with large, ebony eyes was a palpable sense of intensity. He couldn't hide his tension, it radiated from him in an aura. He drew her eyes to him. It was very difficult for Alannah to stop looking at him.

"What does Mr. Ardovinni plan to tell Alexander?" Alannah asked finally.

"That I exist," Alexei said, "and that I want to become assimilated into the society."

"You do?" she said, surprised.

He nodded but did not elaborate.

"Will you go see him?"

Alexei shook his head. "Not now. Giovanni and I have been travelling for a long time and I need to return to my career here. I can't disrupt it right now or I might not have anything to come back to." He paused, "I just... I just don't want to look over my shoulder anymore, or for my mother to for that matter. I'm not a criminal. It isn't my fault that Alexander couldn't keep it in his pants."

Alannah flinched.

His eyes gentled. He fiddled with the snaps on the cuffs of his jacket. "I don't want to cause him trouble, I really don't. That's why we came to Winnipeg. I'm sorry we scared you."

Alannah sighed heavily and said, "I thought you were there about something else. I don't know how much you know about immortal history..."

"Not much."

She shrugged. "I have my own baggage, is what I'm saying."

"We can be civil, then?" he asked tersely. "I will be at John Lin for your next class."

"Of course!"

"Are you going to call your law keeper friends immediately after you leave?"

Alannah opened her mouth and shut it again. If Giovanni Ardovinni was that very moment telling everything to Alexander, then it wouldn't be long before the law keepers knew everything. "No, I guess not."

She wanted to say, "Let's be friends, then," but she couldn't get the words out when she looked into his tightly drawn face. Why, she couldn't pinpoint.

They parted ways with very few more words, both very subdued.

Upstairs in the flat, Alannah went immediately to the window and watched Alexei mount his motorcycle and drive away down the dark street. She clenched her hands tightly together. It felt incredibly peculiar to think that her motorcycle rider fantasy was Alexander's son. No matter what she told herself about it being an innocent fancy, she couldn't shake off the unease. She felt like some sort of pervert.

The thought reminded her that Mr. Ardovinni was probably, right then, telling Alexander that he had a son in Alexei. She texted

Alexander, *Hey, I heard that Ardovinni was at your house. Is everything okay?*

She didn't really expect him to text back. He didn't. And she couldn't stop thinking about Alexei, or get his dark eyes out of her head.

CHAPTER 18

Dresden, Present Day

After Alexander told Jack about Ardovinni's imminent arrival, he disappeared into his room without elaborating further. Jack had observed the other man's hands trembling, despite being clenched tightly against his sides. He didn't envy the old guy at all.

Jack glanced at his still unbound hand and grimaced. He'd have to fend for himself then.

He managed to unwrap an antiseptic pad and swab away the crusted blood from the wound, blinking against the sting. The gauze was a little tougher to affix, but he managed a fairly knobby, bungled looking bandage. After that, he started digging in the fridge for food that didn't need cooking.

Alexander came out of his bedroom half an hour later. He'd changed his clothes, now in dark jeans and a grey, long-sleeved shirt. His face was placid, even serene.

"Did you find something to eat?" he asked calmly.

"Yeah," Jack said, looking up from his phone. He was scrubbing at it with an antiseptic swab, attempting to remove what was fortunately his own blood from the cracks.

"Mr. Ardovinni will be here soon," he said. He crossed the kitchen and picked up the kettle. Behind Jack, water rushed out of the faucet. A moment later the kettle clanked onto the element. "When he arrives, Jack..."

Jack set down the phone and turned to give Alexander his full attention.

Alexander turned on the flame under the kettle and leaned against the counter. "I've given some consideration to how our interview should proceed. *You* were actually there with Cyrus in Italy, and probably know more about the official case than I do."

"Well not that much," Jack said. "Cy was basically babysitting me."

Alexander nodded. "I don't think it would be wise for you to sit in on my conversation with Ardovinni," he said. "Our good will toward each other is somewhat tenuous. I don't want to betray his trust by bringing in someone he may perceive as an outsider."

"Yeah." Jack frowned. "Yeah, that makes sense. I guess I can make myself scarce." It did make sense, even if he really wanted to hear what Ardovinni would say.

Alexander smiled tightly. "I would appreciate it."

Jack took the phone and slowly climbed the stairs to his bedroom. He laid down on the bed and shut his eyes. It was too bad he'd finished the peach Schnapps. He wanted a drink something fierce, something to numb him before the day's events swirled back in. It was a little too much to process right that instant.

He thought he heard the door open, and Alexander speak. Ardovinni must have arrived. Jack was tempted to put his ears to the door, or the air vent on the floor, but before he could pursue that any further his phone began to ring.

Jack sat up and clapped the phone to his ear. "Hello?"

"Hello," Cyrus said tersely, "Jack, I've been trying to call Alexander. Do you know why he isn't answering his phone?"

"Uh," Jack said, "probably because he's talking to Ardovinni right this instant."

Cyrus was quiet so long that Jack thought the line had gone dead.

"Hello?" Jack held the phone away from his ear, but the call was still live.

"Yes, I'm still here," Cyrus said in a subdued voice. "So, I suppose our schemes will all be undone?"

"They already were," Jack said. "Alexander was born at night, but it wasn't last night."

"Hmm."

"What'd you call about?" Jack asked as he settled more comfortably against the wall.

He heard Cyrus sigh softly. "Because the Bertholettes aren't home. They seem to have departed and no one knows where they've gone."

"Shit," Jack said, "they run off with Lia and Peter?"

"We don't know, but the timing is suspect."

"What are you going to do?"

"Well, we were going to get Alexander's recommendation, but we're trying to see if Daniel can get any sort of information about them," Cyrus said. "Alexander will see my call, but we'll continue without him. He may have a lot on his mind."

Indeed.

Cyrus hung up, and Jack was alone again in the room. He laid back down and shut his eyes. If he fell asleep, he wouldn't have to think about any of this: not Lia's child, whom she never got to raise, nor Zoran's sphinxlike gaze, nor Jordan's fat, terrified face as Alexander stood over him, nor the very likelihood of Alexander having just gained himself a son.

His mind swirled, and the days' events blended together as he approached sleep. Suddenly he felt a sharp prick in his neck. He was sliding down the door in Jordan's house again, but this time instead of just passing out, he was paralyzed. The ghostly image of Lia appeared, dragging another woman. She looked up: blond curls, peaches-and-cream skin, delicate face. Mary Rose? No, Clarissa. The buzz saw whined...

"No!" Jack sat up in bed, drenched with sweat.

Below, he heard Alexander's voice—loud but unintelligible. Jack pressed his hand to his pounding heart—the new heart.

His fists clenched at his sides as if he could fight the confusion, the disturbance within him. He wanted death for a few hours of silence in his head.

Jack jerked upright and swung his legs off the bed. He couldn't take this train of thought. He needed relief. He needed—

Unthinkingly he swung the bedroom door and plunged down the stairs. He arrived at the bottom and nearly collided with a slight, dark-haired man in a suit. Jack's eyes met the stranger's startled, black gaze, and then looked up into Alexander's bloodshot gaze and pale face.

"Jack," Alexander said hoarsely, "this is Giovanni Ardovinni."

Ardovinni nodded gravely. "Mr. Krause. Welcome to our society."

"I-uh—" Jack's heart was still racing, his breath still quickened, "thanks?"

"Mr. Ardovinni was just leaving," Alexander said.

Ardovinni bowed his head, a slight gesture of acknowledgement. He departed without another word.

Alexander sighed and leaned heavily against the wall. "Jack," he said in a hollow voice, "congratulate me. I am a father."

Jack swallowed and said nothing.

"Oh God," Alexander whispered as he turned and banged both fists against the wall. "Oh God! What have I done?"

Jack turned away awkwardly. He glanced back.

Alexander was still slumped against the wall. His back heaved with sobs.

Jack sighed and rubbed his eyes. He slunk into the kitchen and put the water on to boil. He wasn't going to be able to go to bed any time soon. He sat there, drinking bitter cups of black coffee, listening to Alexander pace around the living room. Every now and again an animal moan came from beyond the kitchen door.

"Shit," Jack muttered. Was he supposed to do anything? If it were him in there, blood would be running already.

He was about to get up and check on Alexander when a phone rang. It wasn't his. His was upstairs on the bed. Jack stumbled to his feet and spotted the lit phone screen on the counter, halfway stuffed under the breadbox. It was an incoming call from Idina.

"Idina!" Jack hissed into the phone.

"Jack?" Idina's voice was momentarily confused. "Jack? Is Ardovinni still there?"

"No, he's gone," Jack said softly. He took a few steps toward the kitchen door and peeked out. Alexander was crouched in the center of the living room, his face in his knees. He rocked slowly back and forth.

"And?" Idina said, her voice distant.

"Yeah, it was exactly what we thought," Jack said. "Alexander is falling apart." He paused. "Should I be doing anything?"

"I..." Idina sighed and continued, "Alexander isn't in the habit of hurting himself. Just don't let him leave the house."

Once Idina hung up, Jack crept past the living room to the front door and slid down against it with his cup of coffee. Coffee or not, he was tired. His head drooped against his chest and after a while he dozed off.

∞

A tremendous thump on the door woke Jack up. A moment later, the door smashed into his back.

"Holy shit!" Jack jumped up and out of the way. Coffee sloshed all over the floor.

"Jack?" Daniel boomed. The door thunked against the wall. Daniel's broad shoulders almost filled the doorframe. He stood, motorcycle helmet still in hand, phone in the other. "Jack," he said tersely, "where is Alexander? He's not answering his phone."

"I don't know," Jack said hoarsely. "He would've had to climb over me to leave."

"Well, he does have a back door. What is going on?"

"Shit," Jack said under his breath. "Daniel, that Ardovinni guy was here yesterday. You don't think Alexander would do something stupid, do you?"

Daniel's eyes narrowed. "So it was what we thought?"

Jack nodded.

Daniel's gaze dropped. His eyes flicked back and forth in thought. "I don't think he'd hurt himself," he said after a moment. "With any luck he is still in bed, asleep."

"Somehow I kind of doubt it," Jack said.

He and Daniel ascended the stairs. Daniel poked his head into Alexander's bedroom and quickly withdrew his head. "He's in there. Asleep."

"Not dead?" Jack asked.

Daniel turned. "If he is, it is only temporary. I'll go down and make some coffee. I'll wait for him to wake up."

Jack took this opportunity to go back into his bedroom, find clean clothes and some mouthwash for his sandpaper mouth. When he got downstairs, Daniel was sitting at the kitchen table, tapping one hand on the tabletop, scrolling on his phone screen with the other. "I take it you both had a rough night."

"I guess." Jack pulled out a carton of eggs.

"So, I don't know how Alexander will balance this with last night's revelation," Daniel said, "but someone posted to Zoran's blog last night, and it wasn't Zoran." He pulled out his phone. "It's all in German, but I can give you the gist."

"Okay." Jack leaned against the stove.

Daniel's expression wavered between amusement and anger. "It says, 'abandon the cowards to their fate and take back the secrets to immortal life. Take back Schwalenburg from the Lords and their henchmen, take back the fountain. With the fountain, we would never have to suffer the loss of our children. I will never forgive them for taking my baby. I will never rest until I have vengeance. I will kill the immortal lords."

"Oh shit!" Jack stood up straighter. "Lia wrote that, I bet."

"She goes on, but it's all about the same." Daniel rubbed his forehead and squinted at the screen. "She's kind of raving. I know this isn't Zoran, because Zoran's posts are of a completely different style. His grammar, his use of the language, they are all different. With the line about taking the baby, it could be Lia." He scrolled down the screen. "What concerns me is that she alludes to an event that she's planning; 'All will take notice on that day, and the revolution will begin again.'"

Jack snorted. He turned and pulled out a frying pan with his cut hand. It stung, and he shook the offending hand.

"Don't laugh yet," Daniel said wearily. "You should do your research. Zoran had an entire little society. Alannah was part of it. Zoran would hold lectures about immortalizing our kids and forming an immortal race, out in the open. He'd go to the council sessions of the Lords and rant for an hour. That all ground to a halt when he killed Jurgen Zeigler, but his mystique hasn't quite evaporated yet." He paused. "Transcripts of the lectures are in the digital database. You could read them. They're a little sick, some of them."

Jack cracked an egg into the pan. "Yeah, maybe some other time."

"I think if he hadn't gone to jail he would have told everyone how he killed Jurgen, but doing it from prison wouldn't be the same, or something." Daniel opened his hands. "I don't know. He's out in about twenty-five years. Before that we'll have revisited our decision to withhold the death method. If the society wants to know, we'll tell them."

"You'd let them kill themselves if they want to?" Jack asked quietly with his back to Daniel, focusing on the frying eggs.

Daniel sighed. "I don't know."

"If we could make our children immortal—"

Daniel held up his hand and said impatiently, "I don't have children. How should I know? Whatever you think, it has already been thought. Lia can say what she likes, but after Joseph Oswald died the immortals voted three to one to keep the alleged death method secret and to continue to disallow immortalizing children."

Jack bit his lip hard. "Okay fine. So, what are you going to do? Do you know where she posted from?"

"It was uploaded from an English mobile phone, registered to a Greta Morgan." Daniel drummed his fingers on the table. "There is no such person, as far as my research can turn up."

"Smart," Jack muttered. He scraped at the eggs, scrambling them into a white and yellow mess.

"I don't have any way of tracking the phone, unfortunately." Daniel's fingers continued to tap unrelentingly on the table. "'All will take notice on that day, and the revolution will begin again.'" He swore in German and jerked the chair back. "Coffee, Jack?"

"Yeah, sure. Black."

By the time Daniel had poured two mugs, Jack had his eggs on a plate and sat down opposite the lawkeeper at the table.

Daniel set the coffee in front of Jack, and sat down. He didn't drink his own coffee. He just sat again, staring out the window, his fingers drumming on his knees this time.

"What would she do?" Jack said around a mouthful of eggs. "How would she get everyone's attention?"

There was a soft clunk behind them.

"Was that the door?" Daniel said. He peered out the window. "Hmm," he laughed softly, "Alexander got past our defenses. He's gone for a run, looks like."

"Uh..." Jack half rose from his seat.

"Let him go," Daniel said, "he doesn't want to talk to us. He'll feel better when he comes back." He leaned back and crossed his arms behind his head. "What would Lia do? Who knows? If she was up to death experiments she could be up to anything."

"Well, can't she fly a plane?" Jack muttered, slumping in his seat, "because she could always drop a bomb on Schwalenburg. That would get our attention. Ours and everyone else's."

"Don't talk about that lightly," Daniel growled. "Maybe you don't know history very well, but Dresden has a history of being bombed."

"Geez. I'm sorry." Jack shoved the last of the scrambled eggs in his mouth.

"She wants to kill the Lords," Daniel said thoughtfully. "Given her penchant for kidnapping, she might nab one of them."

"Mhmm," Jack swallowed his eggs.

"Von Schwalenburg is in Rio." Daniel steepled his fingers over his coffee cup, which he still hadn't touched. "That leaves Adolf Hardwin and Alexander."

"Shit, we just let the geezer out the door." Jack slapped the table. Daniel's coffee sloshed onto the table top.

Daniel grabbed for napkins from the little holder by the window. "Well, we will just have to take our chances for now. I don't know what Lia would do to him."

"Besides hurt him."

"Besides hurt him." Daniel pressed his lips tightly together. "That would be her style."

"Oh yeah." Jack got up and poured more coffee. His head was starting to ache from a short night and far too much caffeine. "So what, we lock up Hardwin and Alexander?"

"I don't have the authority to do that, and Alexander would never go for it." Daniel held out his cup for more coffee. "I'll think of something."

Alexander came back about an hour later. His blond hair, pulled back in a messy knot, was plastered to his head with sweat. His face was red and shiny, but calm, and he had a little light back in his eyes. "Daniel," he said as he pulled his phone out of the pocket of his shorts, "forgive me for avoiding you. I am composed now."

"Good run?" Daniel said gruffly.

"Eight miles." Alexander crossed briskly to the coffee carafe, but found it empty. "What brings you here?"

Daniel paused, frowning deeply at Alexander's back. "Someone posted to Zoran's blog. It wasn't Zoran."

Alexander turned, holding a coffee cup, his face guarded. "Go on."

"Based on the wording, it may be Lia. She calls for vengeance on the Lords and promises an event that will make all take notice, and start the revolution again."

"Zoran's revolution," Alexander said. "It is the only revolution we have, thus she must refer to it. I fear no vengeance, but an event that makes all take notice? What does this mean, Daniel?" Alexander started another pot of coffee, and sat at the table.

"There's no chance she has water..." Daniel began.

"Her actions toward Jack suggested she did not," Alexander said, glancing at Jack. "However, there is always the possibility that Zoran has water stashed somewhere. "Since..." his breathing staggered, "since it seems I have an immortal son."

Daniel looked down and said quietly, "Yes, him. Somehow Cosima must have gotten water. From Zoran?"

"Not from me!" Alexander cried. "Where else could she get it?"

Jack and Daniel shifted uncomfortably.

"We will talk to Zoran," Alexander said. He leapt up out of the chair. It teetered on two legs and clattered to the floor. "We will pay my old enemy a visit."

"Alexander," Daniel said as he leaned forward, "Lia may attempt to kidnap you! We need to watch you."

"No, No. I am not tying up more lawkeepers." Alexander turned slowly. He pressed his palms to his eyes. "Daniel, do you still have those tracking chips?"

"That sounds nefarious," Jack muttered.

"We considered planting them into each immortal to make watching over them easier." Daniel rolled his eyes. "Someone," he said while jerking his chin toward Alexander, "shot that down."

"Wonder why?" Jack's lip curled.

"Give me one," Alexander said. "Give me one and give Adolf one. If Lia takes either of us, you'll find her."

"She'll hurt you," Daniel said.

Alexander looked up. His face might have been composed, but his eyes were bloodshot. "I don't care."

Daniel raised an eyebrow. He got up stiffly from his chair. "Alright, the chips are at my house. I'll go get them. Call Hardwin. Please."

"I will," Alexander said tersely, "after I take a shower."

Jack was left alone in the kitchen again. "Well," he muttered, "if anyone needs me, I'll be sleeping." Actually, with all the caffeine he'd ingested, he'd probably just lie there vibrating. Jack sighed.

CHAPTER 19
London, 1921

A month had passed since Zoran's quasi confession to Alexander, and the case remained at a stalemate. There was nothing in Oswald's files to suggest he'd been given water from the fountain. There was no correspondence with Zoran that spoke of it. If the container that had held the fatal liquid had been present in the apartment, it was not so now.

"Simply, we cannot know," Alexander said. He, Daniel, Cyrus, and Idina sat around the dinner table in Alexander's little house. "But we cannot hide the fact that Oswald is dead any longer. It is dishonest."

Idina opened her mouth, but Cyrus spoke first. "What explanation do you mean to give?" he asked calmly.

Here was the question that had kept Alexander awake at night, even more than his thoughts of Cosima. "I suppose we could say that we have a theory, but are unable to test it out for obvious reasons. We then could open the floor to discussion."

"Discussion?" Daniel said wryly. "Open to volunteers, perhaps you mean."

"No! Certainly not," Alexander cried, "unless, perhaps, Zoran would like to make himself our laboratory rat. It seems only fair."

"I asked him that," Idina said archly. "He warmly declined. So at the very least, he is convinced of his own theory."

"So am I," Alexander said quietly, "but that isn't good enough." He got up and began to pace beside the table. His footfalls made the tea cups tinkle lightly against their saucers on the table. "Perhaps Ardovinni would allow us to assemble in his house."

"And perhaps he would send away his servants," Daniel said.

"Mmm, true."

"We would fit here," Idina assured him, "and Daniel makes really quite tolerable tea."

"Alexander made this…" Daniel pointed to his cup.

"Very well," Alexander said, "I will call for a meeting."

The immortals assembled in Alexander's crowded room two days later. To his great relief, Cosima and Ardovinni were the first to arrive.

Cosima clasped his hands and drew him aside. "Of course, I already know that Oswald is dead," she said softly, "but I suppose you are preparing for quite a reaction?"

"I fear so." He pressed her fingers to his lips, then leaned his cheek against their folded hands.

"What will you tell us?" she asked, gripping his hand earnestly. "I know that Giovanni has a theory, but he keeps it to himself. It isn't his to tell, is what he said."

"We will say that we have a theory," Alexander said, lifting his head and glancing toward the door where Louisa Spencer had just made her entrance and was greeting Idina cheerfully. "From there on we have to submit that we don't know the best way to proceed, and that we'll have to convene a council to discuss it further."

"Good heavens," Cosima breathed. She disentangled her fingers from his and stepped back. "I hope you have said your prayers this morning, my love."

Alexander said nothing.

The little circle of nine immortals were forced to sit knee-to-knee in Alexander's little sitting room. Zoran was not among them.

He had not been invited, and he apparently hadn't managed to catch wind of the meeting either.

They drank tea that Cosima had belatedly prepared after tasting Daniel's apparently 'passable' tea and declaring it unfit for consumption. Alexander sat at the head of the room, bracing himself for what he had to say, and sending belated prayers ceilingward for the right words, and for calmness among the immortals.

"Friends," he said hesitantly. No one heard him.

"Friends!" he said, louder. Louisa Spencer lifted her head and signaled to the Turners that they should all pay him attention.

"I..." Alexander felt a lump come into his throat, "I have truly unfortunate news for you, news that I hope you will take with a spirit of great constancy."

Every eye was on him now, and every teacup forgotten.

"A few of you have inquired with me about Mr. Joseph Oswald and his whereabouts," Alexander continued, "and about him I must deliver this unfortunate announcement. Mr. Oswald... is dead."

Louisa gasped. There was a moment of utter silence, and then every voice broke loose.

"Dead? You can't be serious!"

"Under what circumstances?"

"You're sure?"

"Where is the body?"

Alexander held up his hands. "Friends," he said, "we have known of his death now for a while. He is, in fact, dead. We kept watch over his body for a long, long time."

"How long?" Benjamin Turner broke in.

"Long enough for putrefaction to set in," Daniel said grimly from behind Alexander, where he leaned against the wall.

Once again, the assembled were quiet.

"Mr. Oswald was a troubled man." Alexander sighed and braced both hands against his knees. "He was experimenting and attempting to find a way to die. We found him drowned in his own bathtub."

"But—" Louisa's voice trembled. Tears had welled up in her eyes. She was fanning herself furiously. "You can't... we can't..."

"Sir Alexander!" Benjamin Turner exclaimed. "Many of us have drowned and recovered! He cannot have drowned."

"No," Alexander said gently, "we cannot drown. Many of us know this. We—"

"He was no true immortal, then!" Turner continued. His searching eyes roved the other faces, as if looking for someone to second this motion.

"He was one hundred forty-three years old!" Daniel said. "Tell me he looked even fifty-three!"

"Well... no," said Turner.

"We do have a theory," Alexander said. "Mr. Zoran Kosar was in correspondence with Mr. Oswald and has supplied us with his theory. Unfortunately, we don't have proof that his suggestion was the actual method of death."

He let this sink in for a moment. He could see Turner's mind whirling. Miss Spencer's fan waved so fast as to be nearly invisible, still her teary face was flushed red.

"You can't test it," Sarah Turner said, her clear voice ringing out for the first time, "unless you think us in immediate danger."

A ripple of whispers went around the circle.

"We do not," Alexander said, "and you are very right, I do not believe we can test it in good conscience."

"You are absolutely certain we cannot stumble into this death?" Sarah said.

"Well," Alexander said defensively, "how can we know that for sure? How can we know anything for sure? An immortal has died. A perfect oxymoron!"

"You must do something!" Louisa bleated.

Sarah jerked her head toward Louisa and gave her a scornful look. "Surely you can perform more research. We cannot make a hasty decision, not for a discovery of such enormity!"

"What? How? By killing ourselves?" Louisa's tears streamed afresh.

Alexander caught Cosima's eye across the circle. Her face was one of the calmest, more composed than Ardovinni's stoic face and haunted eyes. Silently she got up, knelt before Louisa and took her hands. She began to speak in a low, soothing voice to her.

"Ardovinni," Alexander said, "what do you think?"

Ardovinni's head rose. He looked at Alexander in surprise. For a moment he didn't speak, then said, "I do not care to die myself, and certainly we cannot kill an immortal to test a theory. Nevertheless, we should expend all intellectual channels to unravel this mystery."

"Yes, yes indeed, Mr. Ardovinni," Sarah Turner said. Her husband glanced at her with a perturbed expression.

"I would assist," Ardovinni said softly, "if anything is needed. Mr. Kosar, I believe, does keep a laboratory."

"Yes, Zoran," Benjamin Turner said. "Where is he and what does he have to say for himself?"

"He is being investigated for conspiring with Mr. Oswald," Alexander said.

Turner rubbed his chin and sighed.

"I can already tell you what he'd say," Alexander said with a grain of annoyance, "that we should test on the first willing candidate. After all, to have the power to die at our fingertips couldn't be anything less than the pinnacle of perfection. Death on our own terms."

"Willing candidate?" Louisa said over Cosima's head.

Alexander ignored her. "The moral implications of this are far reaching indeed. We will have to consider what cost might come with playing God."

"I think," Ardovinni said quietly, "that Zoran would say that we are immortals, and standard conventions of morality do not apply."

Every eye was upon him, then, even Cosima's.

"That is blasphemy, Sir," Benjamin Turner said in a low, menacing voice.

"I did not say they displayed my sentiments." Ardovinni's face was tight, stoic. "But if we are to truly study all angles and debate morality, then perhaps we must also discuss if our unnatural state calls for new rules."

Alexander flinched and turned his head away, wondering at Ardovinni's words. The immortals around him also fell into contemplation. Truly, Ardovinni had captured a thought he himself had not been able to utter. Alexander had, for most of his long life, suspended judgment on the fact that the Scriptures he professed belief in seemed to make no allowances for immortality. He and Zoran had debated it once, and Alexander had demonstrated multiple "general principles" that applied to immortality.

Oddly, he could not remember them now.

But belief, or at least intellectual consent to an idea, and practice are two very different things. Faithful practice had grown incrementally harder as time wore on.

When the immortals dispersed they had only made one decision: that they could make no decision now. Not without the input of the entire society of immortals.

∞

Giovanni and Cosima were greeted at the door of their house by an alarmed looking Stevens.

"Sir," he said, his hands straining slightly from their tight clasp behind his back. "Sir, there is a woman here to see you. I do apologize. She said she was looking for a Mr. Zoran Kosar. I cannot imagine what—" He pressed his lips together for a moment. "Sir, I couldn't turn her out into the night in her condition. She speaks no English."

Alarmed, Giovanni glanced at Cosima. She gazed back, equally at a loss.

"Zoran's mistress?" Giovanni said quietly, half to himself. "Thank you, Stevens. Cosima, if you will come with me?"

He and Cosima followed the butler into the library. The instant Giovanni showed his face in the door, a woman rose out of a chair. She had bedraggled coffee-colored curls, and her ample curves were overshadowed by the burgeoning swell of her belly. She swayed slightly and almost fell back into the chair.

Giovanni sprang forward. "Miss," he faltered, he did not know her surname, "Miss Marie, please sit," he said in French. He turned. "Stevens, tea if you will." Marie sat and stared down at her hands.

The butler nodded and backed out of the room. Quickly Giovanni sat down in the chair beside her. Impulsively he took her hand and pressed it with his own. "Miss Marie, what can I do for you? You cannot have just come from France!"

She nodded miserably and lifted her pale face. "Mr. Ardovinni, where is my Zoran? Why does he not return, or even write me when his child comes at any moment?"

Giovanni heard Cosima's soft intake of breath. He leaned forward to look into her eyes. "Miss Marie, Mr. Kosar has been detained because of some of his experiments. There is an investigation."

"Why?" Her brown eyes grew round.

"One of the immortals has died."

"What do you mean?" She said in a small voice.

As Giovanni looked at her blank face, a sinking feeling came over him. He'd made a mistake. He'd assumed her immortal also, but what if she were not? "Miss Marie, are you aware of the society that Mr. Kosar belongs to?"

She nodded and sank down in the seat. Her eyes welled up with tears. "I know of it, Sir. I've never met any of them."

"Ahh..." Giovanni sighed. He glanced at Cosima. She shook her head. He should not question, nor enlighten her further.

The young woman covered her face and began to cry in earnest.

"My dear lady," Giovanni said, "you are unwell. You are very tired. I cannot take you to Mr. Kosar this evening. It is very late. Allow me to have a room made up for you."

Marie looked up with relief on her tear-washed face.

"Come," Giovanni said, "my sister will make sure you are taken care of."

"Certainly!" Cosima said, though he could feel her gaze on him, burning for an explanation.

"Giovanni!" she hissed to him as he slipped out to give the orders to Stevens.

"Later," he whispered. "She needs rest, in her condition."

An hour later, when Cosima had seen that Marie was safely ensconced in bed, she returned to Giovanni in the library and grabbed his arm in a tight grasp. "Explain this!" she said.

Giovanni pointed to the chair beside him. She sat.

"She is Zoran's mistress," he said quietly, "as I am sure you'd deduced."

"Indeed," she muttered, "there can be no doubting it."

"I knew of her, but Zoran asked me not to say anything because of the child," Giovanni said. "When I realized how long Zoran was detained, I wrote her a letter to reassure her and to offer her assistance if she had need of it."

"And apparently she does!" Cosima threw up one hand. "You can't keep Zoran's secret any longer. Not when she is asleep in your own house, liable to burst out the child at any moment. Travelling in that condition!"

"I gave him my word that I would not," Giovanni said in a low voice.

"But I did not!"

He inclined his head. "Indeed."

"Then I will inform Alexander," Cosima said. "I must send him a note immediately."

"Not now!" Giovanni said. "It is nearly midnight."

"First thing tomorrow, then."

"But Cosima," Giovanni leaned toward her and said softly, in case of listening ears, "I don't think she is immortal."

"Right," she said as if she had not thought of this. "No, who is to say she is. Ah, damn!"

"I need to sleep on this." Giovanni rubbed at his temples. "Good lord..."

"Giovanni," she said a little softer, "she is exhausted and unwell. What if she gives birth here? Good lord, she will give birth in England! What then?"

"If Zoran will not perform his duty by caring for her," Giovanni said as he ran his hand through his hair, "then I will."

Cosima snatched up his hand and pressed her lips to it. "You are a good man, Giovanni."

In the morning when Burke was helping him dress, he informed Giovanni that Miss Marie had caused a ruckus during the night by crying and running into the hall.

"What?" Giovanni turned to Burke as the valet held up his coat. "Who..."

"Miss di Gaspare attended to her," Burke said, then quieter, "I believe it is her time."

"Damn!" Giovanni pressed both hands to his cheeks. "Ah God, already?"

"The exertion of the trip must have caused this," Burke said. "A woman in her condition, I cannot imagine—"

"Has a doctor been sent for?" Giovanni demanded.

"Of course. As soon as it was light, Miss di Gaspare sent someone to fetch him. He should arrive at any moment." Burke took a deep breath and smiled slightly. "She says you are to do nothing. This is not your realm of expertise."

Giovanni's eyebrows rose, despite the heavy pit in his stomach. "Expertise? Miss di Gaspare has no children."

Burke leaned and said in his ear, "Do you have children, Mr. Ardovinni?"

Giovanni laughed and clasped the back of Burke's head for a moment. "Heavens no."

"Then it isn't your realm of expertise. Let the women attend to her." Burke kissed Giovanni firmly on the cheek and then began to brush the lint off his jacket.

A few minutes later Giovanni traipsed cautiously into the hallway, listening for agonizing cries of childbirth. He heard nothing.

Cosima sat calmly at the breakfast table, drinking tea and reading the morning paper.

"Good morning," Giovanni said as he plopped down beside her and Stevens poured coffee. "Burke informs me that we can expect a small guest."

"Indeed," Cosima said. She folded the paper and regarded him. "I've sent for the doctor, and sent a letter to Sir Alexander already informing him that Zoran's mistress is here."

"Good lord," Giovanni muttered, "exactly how did you explain that?"

"I sense you shall be the one explaining," she said mildly, "and I shall be the one repairing the damages to your spirits."

"They're suffering already," Giovanni said. He tasted his coffee. "Exactly when do I enlighten Zoran about the arrival of his mistress and his child? Is she agitated? Is she asking for him?"

"Oddly no." Cosima cocked her head.

"Then perhaps we can put off the matter. I'd do well to consult Sir Alexander on the matter." The plot would thicken a great deal if he did, but now that Marie was here and her child about to come forth in his own household, Giovanni didn't want Zoran to be able to slink away with his child and lover before his deeds could come to light.

Whatever, exactly, were his deeds?

The doctor arrived only a few minutes later, and was shown up to Marie's bedroom by one of the servants. Giovanni had just relaxed enough to peek at the newspaper when a muffled cry came from upstairs. He started, and glanced at Cosima.

"Good heavens," she said under her breath. "I'm so glad that isn't me up there."

"I think..." Giovanni bit his lip, "perhaps I should intercept Sir Alexander and meet him at his house?"

"That might be wise," Cosima said without looking up from her teacup.

Giovanni promptly got up and called to Stevens to send for a cab.

He found Sir Alexander about to depart from his house.

"Ardovinni!" Alexander said in confusion, "I received Cos... Miss di Gaspare's note. I was about to come to you."

"Well, uh," Giovanni said, "our guest's time has come. The child shall arrive today."

"Oh!" Alexander's blond eyebrows rose. "Oh. Oh, I see. Well. Come in, then. Can I give you tea?" He laid aside his hat and umbrella and led Giovanni into the house.

Giovanni observed that Alexander had dark smudges under his eyes, like bruises. His face was pale and strained. His shoulders drooped.

"About the woman..." Giovanni leaned against the door of the small kitchen as Alexander put the kettle on and stoked the stove.

Alexander raised his head, the poker poised at the door of the stove.

"I knew that she existed," Giovanni said, "but Zoran begged me to say nothing about her, or the child."

"Ardovinni, you know very well it is illegal for us to reproduce," Alexander said sharply.

Giovanni nodded. "I was more concerned with the matter of Oswald's death. I decided to let it pass." This, of course, wasn't the most accurate version of the story, but he felt he deserved a modicum of privacy yet.

Alexander's eyes narrowed, but he said, "There is some sense to that I suppose." He hung the poker in its place and led Giovanni into the dining room to sit. "Forgive me, this must seem like very poor accommodations to you," he said with a note of embarrassment.

Giovanni knew very well that Alexander could afford better. He inclined his head and said nothing to this. "There is another thing," he continued quietly, "I am concerned... that is, I don't know for sure, but the woman may not be immortal and thus I wasn't sure what to say to her about Zoran's detainment, or about-about anything."

"Ahh," groaned Alexander, "good God, Zoran, what are you on about this time?"

Giovanni watched him, unsure if he was expected to reply. "And," he said finally, "what are we to do with the woman? I'll not send her on her merry mortal way with a child in tow."

"No! No, certainly not," Alexander said into his hands. In the other room the kettle began to sputter but Alexander did not seem to hear. "There are homes that take unmarried mothers," he said softly, "and I would certainly pay any fees incurred."

"As would I," Giovanni said.

Suddenly Alexander jerked upright and stood up from his chair. He rushed into the kitchen and returned a few minutes later with a steeping teakettle and two cups hooked over his thumb. "A thought has occured to me," he said as he set them down. "This is a bona fide criminal offense. There is no question, by our laws."

"Yes." Giovanni shifted in his chair.

"Thus, we now have grounds to detain Zoran against his will."

"We do."

Alexander rubbed his chin, then seemed to recover himself. "Tea, Mr. Ardovini?"

"Please."

Alexander poured the tea for both of them and wrapped his slender fingers around his cup. He rocked back and forth slowly, deeply in thought. "Granted, we still cannot punish him for conspiring with Oswald. It isn't an offense to consult in experiments, and we cannot prove that he killed the poor man. But, it buys us time in which we can keep track of Zoran while we decide on what to do."

"If the woman is immortal, though," Giovanni said, "you shall take the child, as you did with Camille Bertholette's."

Alexander fixed him with a weary, blue-eyed gaze. "I take no pleasure in it, but yes."

Giovanni gazed down into his tea. Should he say anything? When Camille's child was taken, he'd said very little. He'd thought it none of his business at the time, and second-guessed it ever since. Now with the mother in his house, the thought of her child being taken away made his stomach sick and the earthy aroma of the tea turn sour. "I hope, then, for her sake that she is mortal then."

"As do I," Alexander said.

"How shall we enlighten Zoran of her arrival?" Giovanni asked, swirling the tea in the cup.

Alexander hesitated and surveyed Giovanni keenly. "Leave it to me," he said, "for I have many questions for that man."

Giovanni sipped his tea so as to not have to say anything since he had nothing further to say on the matter.

Alexander sat slumped in silent contemplation. After three or four minutes had passed, he raised his head and said, "Ardovinni, if you will forgive me for changing the subject..."

Giovanni inclined his head. "Go on."

"Cosima recently mentioned you being interested in religion. I had always thought that to... not be the case." Alexander smiled sheepishly. "Not that we've discussed it in one or two centuries."

Giovanni laughed under his breath. Had they ever discussed it? He couldn't remember. "I am interested," he said, toying with the handle of the teacup. "I have been for some time. It seems to me that immortal creatures can only find comfort in the care of other immortal creatures. But," he grimaced, "it is difficult to resolve to run the race when one feels they are hamstrung from the gate."

Alexander glanced away. Giovanni pressed his lips together. Another thing they had not discussed for a century or two, perhaps never, was the fact that he was, always had been, what Alexander would call a homosexual. He knew that by not speaking of it, Alexander was attempting to avoid disagreement and maintain a peaceful relationship with him. But silence was tiresome. Giovanni's life was full of silence.

"Ordinary people cannot understand how fortunate they are," Giovanni said. "They take it for granted completely."

Alexander sighed. His shoulders remained taut.

He left that thought to simmer. Giovanni turned the teacup in a slow circle as he continued, "The mortals can never know such complete loneliness as we do."

Alexander nodded, his eyes tired and dark.

"And there is no need for you, Sir, to know such complete loneliness as I do." Giovanni leaned forward. "There is a good, immortal woman who would marry you in an instant. I am doomed to love transient mortals."

"I do mean to marry her," Alexander murmured.

"When?" Giovanni fixed him with a stare. He'd heard that before.

"I haven't asked her."

"When will you ask?" Giovanni said in more of a biting tone than he'd intended. Still, he didn't regret it.

"Good God, Ardovinni!" Alexander dug one hand into his hair. "Not right this instant, not with a dead immortal and Zoran's child about to be born in your house. I will have to haul him back to Dresden. It could detain me any number of months!"

"And she cannot go to Dresden with you?" Giovanni said in an undertone, "Don't you desire her at all, Sir? Doesn't she tempt you at all?"

"Good God, of course she does!" Alexander cried. "But you are talking about your sister, Ardovinni!"

"No, I am talking about your sanity," Giovanni said under his breath. "Forgive my coarseness," he said aloud. "Sir, do not delay any longer. Ask her tomorrow, once the child is safely born."

"I cannot promise that." Alexander's chin jutted.

Now the man was just digging in his heels.

Fine, Giovanni thought, but one way or another Alexander would repent—either when she gave up, if indeed Cosima had it in her, or when he took her into his bed for the first time.

He laughed silently. Cosima had been a bit more frank, perhaps, with him than most sisters were with brothers. After all, he knew Cosima when she was still a harlot.

"I do not understand your hesitation," Giovanni said finally. "Sir, if I had my way not only would I be dead long ago, but I should have also been married to a good wife and have several children to my heritage. And if marriage were now an option to me, I would do so." He swallowed. "But it is not. Now Sir, if you will excuse me I will take my leave."

"Yes, yes, thank you Ardovinni." Alexander looked him in the eye, but just barely.

Giovanni delayed returning home for another few hours by going to the building where Joseph Oswald had once lived, and informing the landlady that Oswald's apartments could be leased out again. He then went to the bank, before finally going home.

Cosima seized him the instant he showed his face.

"Giovanni! Where have you been?" She pulled him into the library. She looked up, ebony eyes round in her drawn face. "Giovanni, the woman is dead!"

Giovanni pressed his hand to his mouth.

"She hemorrhaged. There was too much blood lost, she..." Cosima leaned her head against him.

Woodenly, Giovanni lifted his arm and wrapped it around her shoulders. "The child?" he asked in a hoarse whisper.

"Alive, a girl," she said into his chest. "Oh Giovanni, what will we do?"

He rocked slowly, his movement carrying her with him. The house was silent, but as they stood Giovanni heard the weak cry of a newborn. Giovanni raised his head. "Who has the baby now?"

"She's with Bernadette," Cosima sniffled. "I've sent someone to look for a wet nurse until-until we decide what to do with her."

"I need to go back to Sir Alexander," Giovanni said weakly, "but if he's gone to Zoran already, then what?"

"Send someone with a note." Cosima looked up. "Send Burke."

Giovanni nodded slowly. In his mind the note was already forming.

Burke left within ten minutes. Giovanni climbed the stairs and stood outside the room where the dead woman lay. He discerned, again, the mewling cry of the newborn somewhere down the hall. He followed the sound, and found Cosima's maid, Bernadette, holding the infant.

"Sir," she said plaintively, "the baby needs a nurse. Is one coming?"

"I..." Giovanni pressed his lips together a moment before he said, "I hope so." He bent closer to look at the red-faced, wrinkled baby. She was no thing of beauty, her face all screwed up under a thatch of dark hair. At very least, she probably had Zoran's dark locks. Still, Giovanni had the overwhelming desire to hold her. He held out his arms. "May I, Bernadette?"

"I—yes, of course." Bernadette shook herself slightly and passed the tiny child over with a look of slight concern on her face.

Giovanni settled the warm bundle in the crook of his arm and cradled the baby's little head. All at once the baby seemed to tire of crying, and fell silent with one tiny squeak. Giovanni gazed down at the crescents of her closed eyes, as small as the curve of his fingernail but fringed with delicate, dark lashes.

"Ohhh"—he sighed—"you poor creature."

"Does her father yet live?" Bernadette asked tentatively.

"He does," Giovanni said, not lifting his eyes from the baby's face.

"Might he... take her?"

Oh dear God, Giovanni thought. *What does Zoran want of a child?*

∞

When Burke returned, saying he'd just caught Alexander at home, Giovanni and Cosima feared that Alexander and Zoran would come at any moment. But only the wet nurse arrived to care for the child. At about six in the evening, Cosima finally decided to see to the washing of Marie's body to prepare her for burial. She disappeared up the stairs with two of the maids, her face set in grim resolution.

About ten minutes later, Cosima rushed into the library where Giovanni sat looking at the same page of his book as he had been when she had departed.

"Giovanni," she leaned closer, "Giovanni, the woman is healing."

The book fell to the floor. "What?"

"She's healing. The tear in her—" Cosima grimaced. "It has closed. Even her stomach is beginning to look like there was never a baby."

"She *is* immortal," Giovanni breathed. He passed his hand over his mouth. "Good lord, Cosima, can you make an excuse to the maids and get them out of there?"

Cosima licked her lips. "I'll think of something."

Giovanni drummed his fingers on the arms of the chair he sat in. "Now I shall have to send another message to Alexander," he said.

CHAPTER 20

London, Present Day

When Alannah arrived at John Lin Academy early for her Tuesday evening lesson, Alexei's black motorcycle was parked across the street. She stood along the wall watching Alexei spar with a massive, muscled young man. She gasped as Alexei landed a knee to his antagonist's midsection. The other man reeled, but caught his balance in time to block the next attack. They broke away from each other. Alexei's face twitched with a slight smile. His wiry body poised, alive with energy, clad in a snug black t-shirt and tights.

He has a great butt.

Stop it!

Alannah bounced her gaze away, across the gym in time to see Jules stagger in under the weight of a car seat and diaper bag. For once, her face was flushed and screwed up into a frown. Alannah peeled herself off the wall and walked toward her.

"Jules, who's this?" She peeked into the baby-seat, at an apple-cheeked infant with streaming blue eyes.

"Um, this is Nan," Jules panted. "She's just..."

"What a darling!" Alannah straightened. "Is she yours?"

"Uh huh." Jules bit her lip. "Mum couldn't take her like usual and I couldn't get another sitter, and... I sure hope it's okay if she's here."

"I hope so too." Alannah stroked Nan's chubby cheek, brushing away a stray tear. "I'll try to help out as much as I can. I'm out of practice with babies." She followed Jules into the locker room and occupied Nan with a squishy toy mouse from Jules' bag while Jules climbed into her workout gear. Then, while Jules stretched and warmed up, she swung the car seat back and forth while Nan burbled.

"Aw, she's a doll," Alannah cooed.

"Out of practice, my ass," Jules grunted from her upside down, stretching position.

At that moment, Alexei stalked past, wiping his face on the pulled-up front of his t-shirt. His skin-tight pants left little to the imagination. Alannah saw Jules, her head still on level with her knees, jerk her eyes up, then down.

Alexei glanced over and raised a casual eyebrow. He stretched his arms over his head, exposing a four-inch strip of his toned stomach, and yawned.

Jules squeaked and nearly lost her balance.

A laugh burst from Alannah's mouth. Hands full with Nan's car seat, she pressed her mouth into her shoulder. Alexei caught her eye with a droll twinkle in his, and kept walking.

"Wanker," Jules said as she straightened. "What an asshole. Damn hot asshole, but asshole all the same. Is he still bothering you?"

"No, we talked and cleared the air. It's okay." Alannah felt a bit of heat in her cheeks.

Alexei swaggered back out of the men's locker room in gi pants and a dry t-shirt. Two of the young guys from the class followed.

"What's with the baby?" he asked sharply. "Is he yours, Alannah?"

"*She* is Jules' baby. Her name is Nan," Alannah said, shaking off her discomposure.

Alexei knelt and peered into the car seat. One of Nan's fat fists waved in the air near his nose. "Aww, dolcezza."

"I couldn't get someone to watch her," Jules stammered. "She's just been fed, and she'll sleep I think and..."

Alexei lifted his hand. "No, it's okay Jules. I understand. We can take turns watching her, I'm sure." He stroked Nan's cheek, and ran one finger down her button nose and then stood. He clapped his hands as he walked out on the mat. "Alright, then! Bow in."

"I take back what I said about him being an asshole," Jules hissed to Alannah as she sat down beside the car seat, and Alannah walked out onto the mat. "What did he call my Nan?"

"Dolcezza? It's Italian. I think it means, like, sweetie, or sweetheart."

"You speak Italian?" Jules asked as they faced Alexei.

Alexei must have heard, because he caught her eye.

Alannah shrugged. "Just a little." She'd been learning, just before she'd left Dresden in the seventies. She left Jules behind and faced Alexei with the rest of the class.

"Alright, Mama. Out!" Alexei said as they finished their first exercise. He padded off the mat and reached out a hand to hoist Jules to her feet. "I'll sit with bambina." He plunked down, cross-legged. "You can work with Alannah. Get to it." His eyes flicked away. "James, you're using your arms when you should be using your legs. Come on."

Jules glanced back as she took a ready stance in front of Alannah.

"She'll be okay," Alannah said under her breath.

About the time Jules got Alannah on the ground, the sound of a squeaky cry came from the side of the mat.

Jules faltered, and Alannah relaxed for a moment as she looked over.

"Can I pick her up?" Alexei called.

"Uh... yeah?" Jules' voice pitched upward.

"It's all good." Alexei waved her away as he began to unbuckle Nan from her car seat. "I won't break her."

A while later, Alannah, under Jules' side mount, saw Alexei's bare feet.

"What do you need to do to get into a half-guard?" he said.

"I don't... know..." Alannah grunted.

"Pause, Jules. Hold it."

After Alexei walked her through it, step by step, Alannah successfully maneuvered her way into a better spot.

"Good. Alright, hold up everyone," Alexei said. "Let's pull it in. Bow out without me. I have my arms full."

As Alannah stood up, she saw Alexei plant himself at the end of the mat and sit down, cross-legged. Everyone plunked down around him and began stretching or doing other cool-down exercises, and that was when Alannah realized that Nan was nestled in Alexei's arms. Her chubby cheek pillowed on his chest, and his hand cupping the back of her head. The baby was asleep.

"Aww, Jules, look!" Alannah poked Jules.

"Aww!" Jules crawled over to Alexei's side and peered at her child. "You got her to sleep. Marry me, Alexei."

Alexei laughed softly and peeked at Nan's face. "It just sort of happened, I can't take credit. But sorry, Jules. I'm already taken."

Alannah's heart skipped a beat. She swallowed. Well, there it was. He was taken. The last little bit of her motorcycle rider fantasy had evaporated.

"Too bad!" Jules stroked Nan's head. "I'm not taking her back just yet. She seems perfectly comfortable where she is. Do you have kids?"

"No." Alexei looked down. "My partner and I can't have kids, so I borrow them when I get the chance."

"Aww, that's too bad." Jules plunked down beside him. "I'm sorry."

"Yeah, I'm sorry too."

"Can I take a picture?" Jules fished out her phone.

"Go ahead."

"Aw, this is precious." Jules passed Alannah the phone, showing an image of Nan, thumb popped in her rosebud mouth, flushed chubby cheeks and Alexei's protective hand over her downy blond hair. Alexei's head had been tipped down toward the baby, and Jules' camera had caught just a glimpse of his ebony eyes. Instantly, Alannah longed to have the picture in her collection.

"Will you send it to me?" she asked.

"Sure!"

Ten minutes later, Jules was out the door with Nan. Alexei stood at the window, absently rubbing the spot where Nan's cheek had rested. Alannah came to stand beside him. "You like kids?" she asked as casually as she could manage.

"Yeah." He glanced over with a wry smile. "When I lived in LA I used to babysit the two neighbor girls. They were one and three years old. It still sort of surprises me that their mom let a couple of guys take care of her kids, but I guess she figured she could trust us."

"Us?" Alannah asked without thinking.

Alexei laughed once quietly, and for a moment his face was almost rueful. "Giovanni and I are together. You might as well know."

Alannah's mouth formed the word 'Oh' but no sound escaped.

She was wrong. There had been just a thread of her daydream holding on, and now it was snapped. A pit settled in her stomach.

Alexei glanced at her, then out the window. "By the things Giovanni's said, I thought you would have conjectured that already. I guess I was wrong."

"Yeah, well..." Alannah waved one hand helplessly and said, "I don't really know Mr. Ardovinni. I just know of him."

"Yeah," Alexei said. He turned away from the window. "If I give you my number would you send me the picture of sweet Nan? Giovanni would like it."

"Yeah, of course." She paused. "Listen, uh, how did Mr. Ardovinni's meeting go? I thought maybe I'd hear from Alexander, but..."

"He said it went well," Alexei said faintly. "I can go to Dresden whenever I'm ready, or he'll come to me. Whatever I like."

"Do you know when you'll go?"

He looked at her, his dark eyes inscrutable. "No." He let out a heavy sigh and said, "Anyway..." in a tone that suggested he wasn't going to let her pursue that topic. He gestured toward the locker room. "I'll grab my phone."

Alannah managed to stumble back home on her tired legs, and make it into her bathrobe before tears spilled out of her eyes. She plopped down on the edge of the bed and laughed softly as she wiped at her eyes. What was wrong with her? It had been a dumb fantasy. That was all. And she was attracted to him, like she hadn't been attracted to a man since Daniel. That was all. She was a grown up. She'd get past it in a day or two.

For goodness sake, he was Alexander's son. That would be weird, right?

Half an hour later, Alannah was curled up on the bed with a book and the last of her evening tea, when her phone dinged. Alexei.

Thanks for the pic. Giovanni says I am to invite you to dinner. He's back in London tomorrow. Are you free Friday evening?

Alannah laughed wryly and set her tea on the nightstand. This just took the cake. Dinner with Mr. Ardovinni and Alexei? Just what her jangled heartstrings needed.

And once she finally worked up to calling Alexander, things were going to be difficult to explain.

Nope. She had no good excuses, and she was done with being anxious, so she texted back: *Yes, I'm free, thanks. What did you have in mind?*

In fifteen minutes, she was engaged to go to Alexei and Ardovinni's condominium on Friday. Giovanni would cook, and Alexei assured her he was a good cook.

Alannah laughed and rubbed her eyes. This was absurd.

∞

"What would you think of a weekend trip to Dresden?" Louisa asked, across the table from Alannah in the lunchroom.

Alannah looked up from her phone and the salad and chicken she was picking at. "Huh?"

"Well, not *this* weekend," Louisa continued, twisting the end of her fishtail braid, "but I was thinking I could fly to Dresden to see Kris, maybe two weeks from now. I'll ask Cat too. We could make a weekend of it and do some shopping. It would be fun. "She gazed at Alannah with a puppy dog expression. "It *would* be fun, Alannah."

Alannah had explained her anxiety to Cat, but she'd never taken the time to tell Louisa exactly how big a deal things like weekend trips were to her. A far bigger deal than it should be. Alannah sat silently, motionless, considering this. If they'd fly to Dresden, she'd have to visit Alexander and *that* would be really nice. As much as she was settling in here in London, she did miss the guy. She'd also have to go to Schwalenburg, see Idina, Cyrus, Daniel... She'd be able to see Daniel without regret, she thought.

But this would bring her very, very close to Zoran again, and all the old haunts and memories. She wasn't sure she could do that.

"I don't know," she said finally, forcing lightness into her voice. "I'll have to think about it. It-it would be fun to go on a trip with you girls."

"Yeah," Louisa said brightly. "I'll mention it to Cat. She'll want to look at flights and stuff. Think about it, m'kay?"

"Alright."

"How about this weekend. Do you have plans?" Louisa delicately picked up the crumbs of her chocolate cake and licked them off her finger.

Alannah was about to say no, but instead she laughed and said, "Actually, I'm having dinner with Mr. Ardovinni and his partner this Friday."

Louisa paused mid-lick, her mouth open, and her eyes round. "Why?" she demanded.

Alannah blinked. "Well... why not? Is he unpleasant?"

Louisa blushed a little and put her hands back on the table. "Well, no. No, he's actually quite a sweet man when you talk to him. Last time I saw him he remembered to ask me how my trip to Fiji was. Did I tell you about that trip? That was last summer."

"No, I don't think so, but really Louisa, why not visit with Mr. Ardovinni?" Alannah put down her fork.

Louisa's delicate face screwed up. "No real reason. It was just a surprise. He's so... private. Have you met his boyfriend?"

"Yes," Alannah said reluctantly. "He seems nice."

"Oh." Louisa shrugged. "Well, alright." She lowered her voice and leaned toward Alannah. "I thought perhaps you were borrowing money from him."

"Ohhh." Alannah nodded slowly. "No, nothing like that. A friendly visit, really."

Louisa sat back, apparently satisfied. "Fiji was beautiful. We should go."

Alannah laughed silently, but she felt a little knot of anxiety in her stomach. It would be alright, right?

∞

Ardovinni had cut his hair since the last time Alannah had seen him. That it was now short, slightly longer on top to show off the natural curl, was the first thing she noticed, but she was far too shy to say anything about it. He greeted her at the door with a winsome smile and ushered her in. The savory aroma of bread and herbs washed over her.

"I'm glad to meet you again under—" Ardovinni's mouth twisted wryly "—friendlier circumstances."

"Yes," Alannah said sheepishly. "I assure you my gun stayed home."

"Oh good," Alexei said wryly as he emerged from the hallway.

Alannah couldn't help but look him over. He was dressed in dark jeans and a slim-cut, charcoal oxford shirt with the sleeves rolled up on his forearms. His damp hair looked like it had been combed, and then he'd raked one hand through it.

Despite all her attempts to derail her nerves, Alannah had gone through everything in her meager closet when she was getting dressed. At the last minute she'd settled on the black sheath dress and simple gold necklace. Now it seemed a bit much, even if Ardovinni was in dark pants and a crisp white shirt.

They stood awkwardly for a moment, and then Ardovinni held out his hand toward the set table. "The antipasti is ready, the entree not far behind. Please, let's be seated."

Alexei silently pulled out a chair for her. As Alannah sat, she took a quick glance around the apartment. The kitchen, from which Ardovinni was carrying a basket of bread and a covered tray, was small but well-appointed with stainless-steel appliances. It looked like the sort of kitchen that was well-used—pots hanging above the island counter, a container with stained wooden spoons and spatulas sitting below. An apron lay discarded over one of the stools bellied up to the counter.

Beyond the dining room, there was a simple living area with a flat-screen TV mounted on one wall, and two black leather couches against walls painted gray. Kitty-corner to the TV stood a low, black electric piano. A guitar leaned against it.

"Who plays piano?" Alannah asked, gesturing toward it.

Ardovinni set down the bread. "Alexei."

"Forced by my mother," Alexei said gruffly, but his deep brown eyes twinkled.

Ardovinni shook his head silently and retreated back into the kitchen.

"The guitar is Giovanni's," Alexei said as he pulled the cloth off the tray of cheeses, salami, and a dish of roasted peppers and garlic. "Giovanni is a proper musician. I just mess around on that piano."

"Amateur," Ardovinni called from the kitchen. "I'm completely amateur, I assure you." He returned to the table with a plate of calzoncini in one hand, and a bottle of wine and a corkscrew in the other. "Eat, please. Alexei, serve her food. Only five minutes ago you were starving to death."

"Geez, you sound like my mother." Alexei held out the bread for her to take. "It's true, though, I'm going to make a fool of myself and eat as much as the two of you combined. I'm still teaching Lewis's classes, the sickly little bastard. I've eaten so many kicks, and rolled with so many people, that I'm one sore muscle from head to foot."

"Oh my," Alannah laughed. The bread was warm to the touch. She smeared it with the roasted peppers and garlic and took some of the salami onto her plate.

"Wine, Alannah?" Ardovinni had the bottle already poised over her glass.

Alannah swallowed her mouthful of bread. "Oh, yes please."

Giovanni poured for Alexei, and then sat down beside him. He slung one arm over the back of Alexei's seat and proceeded to serve himself one handed. "How do you like London, so far?" he asked.

"It's good." Alannah bit her lip. It was good, now that she'd emerged from the flat. "At least I have friends here—real friends—and that is a great deal more than I can say about Winnipeg, other than Alexander, of course—when he was there."

"I understand," Ardovinni said. His dark brows drew together over his fathomless eyes. "I meant to say earlier how sorry I was when Alexei explained how we'd scared you in Winnipeg. Did you think we were there at Zoran's bidding?"

Alannah started a little.

Ardovinni held out his hand. "Forgive me. I cut to the chase very quickly sometimes."

Beside him, Alexei nodded and widened his eyes, which made Alannah smile and relax again.

"Alexei seems to agree," she giggled.

Alexei swallowed the salami he'd just put in his mouth and washed it down with a gulp of wine before he answered. "You have no idea."

Ardovinni spread his hands in a gesture that said, 'What can I say?'

"I did think you were sent by Zoran," Alannah said softly, "but that's the way I am, unfortunately. I've struggled with anxiety for years."

Ardovinni glanced at Alexei and smiled slightly, but with darkness in his eyes. His fingers rubbed gentle circles into the back of Alexei's neck. "I have never worked for Zoran," he said. "Our lives have been far more intertwined than I would ever wish, but I have never been on his side."

"I know," Alannah said.

A few minutes later, after Ardovinni had served entree of roasted chicken, vegetables, and risotto, Alannah turned to them both. "One thing I never asked you, Alexei, was where you grew up. Can I..." she was thinking of Cosima, and Alexander searching for her all these years. "Can I ask that?"

"British occupied Hong Kong." Alexei lifted his chin and smiled slightly. "I grew up there from an infant to thirty-seven years old."

"Oh." Alannah nodded. "And then?"

Alexei squinted at a point in the distance. "Where would that put us? Fifty-nine? Sixty? We spent a year in Spain, then about six months with Giovanni in Italy, and then..." he rubbed his chin.

"We moved a lot, Alannah. I didn't always live with my mother, but I never spent that long apart from her." His brow furrowed, his lips pressed tightly together.

"We moved from Los Angeles about eighteen months ago," Giovanni supplied quietly. "Cosima does not live there."

Alannah wanted to ask if Cosima would ever reappear, but she couldn't get out the words. Instead she asked, "What made you move here?" and put a bite of chicken in her mouth.

Alexei's lips quirked and his face relaxed again. "To save Giovanni on airfare. He was flying between LA and Florence every second week."

Ardovinni grimaced. "Constant jetlag. If an immortal could die of sleeplessness, I would have. Alexei found a job here and decided to move. At least it put him closer so I could live here part time."

"John Lin, you mean," Alannah said, her wine glass poised to her lips.

Alexei nodded.

"What were you doing before?"

"Fighting." Alexei's eyes glittered. "Mixed Martial Arts fighting."

"At least he only teaches now." Ardovinni muttered something under his breath in Italian. He gripped Alexei by the ear and shook his head gently. "One day you'll rebound from something and lose these... how do you call them? Cauliflower ears?"

Alexei tilted his head so Alannah could observe the slight thickening of his ears. "It's from taking hits to the ear," he said. "Stay with Jiu Jitsu and you might get them too."

Alannah drew back in alarm.

Alexei laughed.

Ardovinni chuckled. "Take better care of them than Alexei and you may not, Alannah."

"Did you meet in Los Angeles?" Alannah asked softly, "I mean like..." she felt heat bloom in her cheeks.

"Did we get together in LA?" Alexei straightened.

Ardovinni slung his arm across Alexei's chair again and gazed at him, waiting for him to speak.

"Yeah, Los Angeles," Alexei said in a low voice. His fork dangled, forgotten, from his fingers. "I'd, uh, spent about ten years away from my mom. No contact. She didn't know where I was. Giovanni tracked me down with a private investigator and scared the hell outta me by showing up at one of my fights."

Ardovinni's fingers laced into the hair at the nape of Alexei's neck, his eyes ever attentive on Alexei's face. Alannah put down her fork and knife.

"He stayed around," Alexei said huskily. "I was in such a bad place, I didn't want anything to do with him, but he stayed around."

Ardovinni smiled ruefully. "And finally I convinced you that I actually cared about you, and things"—he shrugged—"sort of went from there."

"So why...?" Alannah struggled to articulate what she wanted to say, her emotions a tumult inside her. She couldn't help but like Giovanni and Alexei together, no matter what her recent fantasies about Alexei. She couldn't help but like them as people. But what of Alexander and the effect this would have on him? "But why come to Alexander now?"

Alexei pointed to Ardovinni. "He is making me."

"I'm not making you," Ardovinni said firmly. "Do I think it for your good, yes, but I'm not making you."

"No," Alexei murmured.

"It is..." Giovanni said with a frown, "difficult to maintain a relationship between two immortals when only one is assimilated into immortal society, and furthermore it is technically illegal for me to not make Alexei's presence known to the Lords, even if Alexei is not obligated to join the Society"—he sighed—"but beyond that, I truly believe it is best for Alexei to know his father and I feel a... certain obligation of honor to give Sir Alexander a chance to know his son."

"This *is* all your idea, then," Alannah said.

Ardovinni shrugged. "Indeed."

"But," Alexei interjected gently, "there is something to be said about not"—he swallowed—"not hiding anymore."

Alannah bit her lip. Hiding from Alexander, he meant.

She'd first heard the story from Alexander, that summer in the seventies when she'd come to Dresden.

∞ ∞ ∞

Alannah was working in the library in Schwalenburg. It was nearly noon and Alexander had asked her to come get him when it was time for lunch so she headed to his office. But as she walked up to his ajar door, she heard Daniel's voice:

"He wouldn't even take a letter? Goddamn Ardovinni, you tolerate far too much from him! As if she wouldn't at least accept a letter by now."

"He said no." Alexander's voice was hollow.

"Use your authority. I tell you—"

By then Alannah was quite sure this conversation didn't concern her. She took a step back and was about to retreat, but she stumbled and, in catching herself, slapped one hand against the door. Daniel cut off mid sentence.

"That would be Alannah," Alexander said quietly. "Alannah, it's alright. Come in."

Shame-faced, Alannah pushed the door open. "I didn't mean to eavesdrop, honestly."

Alexander's face was pale. He had his chin propped heavily on his hand. "Lunch. I'd forgotten," he said.

He looked so tired.

"Alexander," Alannah said softly, "are you alright?"

Alexander pushed himself back from the desk and stood. "I'm alright. Daniel, I should go."

Daniel clearly had thoughts left unarticulated. He seemed to struggle mightily to contain them, his face finally settling on a tight smile. "Miss Krueger, I promised to teach you to drive my motorcycle. Are you busy on Saturday?"

"Oh, yes! Uh..." Alannah's eyes skittered between Daniel and Alexander. Heat suffused her cheeks. "No, I mean no. No, I'm not busy."

Daniel's face relaxed into a genuine smile. "May I pick you up at noon?"

Alannah nodded, not trusting her words to come out right.

"Excellent," Daniel said. He left without too many more words.

Alannah turned back to Alexander, who was putting on his jacket. His face was tight and serious. "Alexander, really, are you alright?"

He sat back down at his desk, rested his head in his hands, and told her the story.

∞   ∞   ∞

Initially, the evident pain in Alexander's heart had made Alannah hate the absent Cosima, and Ardovinni her co-conspirator, but over the years, hearing Alexander speak of the both of them in a favorable light had changed her mind. "Did Cosima know Alexander was looking for her?" she asked, her voice nearly a whisper with emotion.

Ardovinni's face tightened and his voice hardened, "If it had been my choice, I would have returned Cosima to Dresden as soon as we knew Alexei was for certain immortal, but she knew that to do so would wreak havoc in Alexander's life, and she cares a great deal more about bearing the consequences of Alexander's actions then she does to return to the Society. He is immortal, they cannot take him from her anymore, but they can penalize the both of them. I can only surmise that Alexander loses his position as an immortal Lord."

"But he'd do that for her!" Alannah cried. "It's not fair to him to..."

"Alannah," Ardovinni said in a taut voice, "you don't have the history with Alexander that I have. I'll grant that he's a very different man than he was a hundred years ago, but that doesn't mean he'd be willing to give up the supposed good of the many—retaining Lordship, retaining the stability of the Society—for the good of two immortals. Alexei and Cosima, I mean."

Beside him, Alexei's lips pressed in a thin line. His shoulders were bunched tight under Ardovinni's hand.

"But," Ardovinni said, much quieter, "I've spoken to him, and he wants to acknowledge his son, come what may."

The apartment fell quiet, the only sound the rumble of a bus passing.

"Pardon me," Ardovinni said with a sigh, "I did not mean to speak so roughly, Alannah. I barely know you, and Alexander is a good friend of yours. Forgive me."

"No, no," Alannah said faintly. "I did want your honest opinion. I did."

"When I see my father, I will explain," Alexei said in a husky voice. "I don't know if my mother and father will ever meet again. My mother is so accustomed to running that she may never stop. But I can tell him that she doesn't hate him, that she left him because she was afraid, and she loved him."

"That would be..." A lump formed in Alannah's throat. "That would be good," she finished lamely.

CHAPTER 21

Dresden, Present Day

Jack paused behind Daniel and Alexander as the guard signed them into Schwalenburg's jail. Jack tugged at the collar of his oxford shirt, fiddling with the top button. It seemed remarkably hot underground, in the depths of the castle.

"I will vouch for Jack. I know he is not authorized," Alexander said as he signed. His hand was bandaged, the only sign that Daniel had implanted a chip tracker in his hand. He straightened, picked up a book from the desk, and led them into the antechamber before the converted dungeon. "Jack"—he paused and turned—"I know I have already spoken at length about this, but I'd prefer if you didn't speak to Zoran at all and merely observe."

"Yes, I think I'd prefer that too," Jack muttered.

"He doesn't know you. The less he knows about you, the better. It is imperative that you don't answer the questions that I trust he will ask." Alexander's blue eyes flickered and his jaw hardened. He opened the heavy metal door into the jail and led them up one of the doors and slid a key into the lock. Alexander paused with his hand on the key, and rapped on the metal door. His knuckles thunked dully.

A voice answered in firm, soft German.

Alexander laughed under his breath and pushed the door open.

Zoran stood in the corner, his back to them. It didn't occur to Jack what he was doing until he turned and walked toward a small, pedestal sink, still zipping his fly.

Jack averted his eyes, more from discomfort than modesty.

"Excuse us," Alexander murmured.

When Jack looked up again, Zoran was gazing at him as he dried his hands in slow, deliberate movements. Zoran asked him something in German. Jack stammered and shook his head.

"I thought not." Zoran had only the softest of accents. He hung the towel on a hook over the sink and approached them. He offered his hand to Alexander. Alexander paused only the slightest instant before accepting it. "Sir Alexander." His obsidian eyes strayed to Jack again as he spoke. "I see by your entourage that this is an official visit, not a friendly one. Good day, Mr. Gunther." He held out his hand to Daniel.

Jack crossed his arms and, though Zoran turned to him, he did not offer his hand.

"Jakob Krause, I presume?" Zoran's voice was gentle, but his gaze was direct and probing. "This one is very young."

Jack flinched hard and glanced at Alexander.

Alexander ignored this statement and held out a book, a slim volume bound in auburn leather. "I brought the Chaucer you requested."

"Ah!" Zoran reached for it as a child might reach for a treat. "Marvelous. I've gone for days without something to read. I finished with your St. Augustine on Sunday. Let me fetch it for you."

"Before I begin my 'official' visit, as you divined, have you any other friendly requests of me?" Alexander asked as Zoran turned to walk away.

"I do." Zoran paused and rubbed his clean-shaven chin. "What was it?"

He paced across the room, past the pallet bed which was neatly made up, to the only other furniture in the small cell—a bookshelf crammed with every size and shape of volume, and a small desk. A slim silver laptop sat on it, beside a stack of notebooks. Zoran withdrew a thick, leather-bound book and carried it toward Alexander. "It wasn't an internet connection. For this I already know the answer." He turned to Daniel and Jack. "I apologize, gentlemen, I only have one chair and this I must offer to Lord Alexander."

"I shall stand," Alexander said.

"And I," Daniel said quickly.

"Then the youngest may sit. Please, Master Krause." Zoran pushed the wooden chair toward Jack. "Do sit."

"No, thank you," Jack crossed his arms tighter.

"Be it as you wish, then." Zoran sat down on the bed, stretched his feet out in front of him, and then leaned back against the wall. "I hear you had a rather violent initiation into our fair circle."

Jack's face flushed hot. He clenched his jaw hard and turned to Alexander. He wasn't supposed to answer questions.

"You had a request of me, Zoran," Alexander said in a quiet but firm voice. He sat on the corner of the bed and fixed Zoran with his stoic gaze.

Zoran raised his eyebrows. "So I did. Well now, I remember." He rubbed his hands together and scrunched his shoulders. "If this could be arranged I would, of course, pay whatever necessary from my private purse. There is a technological marvel I have caught wind of, which I earnestly desire—nearly as much as an internet connection." He pressed his palms together again. "They say there is an apparatus which brews a single cup of coffee from a plastic pod. You have heard of it, yes?"

"Indeed." Alexander's lips twitched in a near smile. "This seems reasonable, and can no doubt be arranged after I ask a few questions."

"Ah, it is then as I guessed." Zoran swept his eyes toward Jack again. "I have a question as well." He jutted his chin toward Jack. "This man. Is it true that they cut out his heart?"

Jack flinched.

"How the sensational rumors do filter down," Alexander said wryly. "Don't expect to hear too much from me, Zoran, I'm not here to entertain you."

Zoran laughed. "Fair enough."

"I will ask a few questions, Zoran," Alexander continued. "Daniel may interject where my questions are lacking."

Daniel nodded, short and tight.

Zoran spread his hands, shrugged, and relaxed against the white-washed wall.

"Are you in contact with your niece, Lia Brenner?"

Zoran's lips formed an amused smile. "My Lord is able to monitor all comings and goings. You know she has neither written nor visited."

"And, have you at any time bribed a guard to carry a message to her?"

"I certainly have not. Why? What has she—ahh…" Zoran held up his index finger. "You are referring to the experiments performed on young Jakob? Alexander, you know very well I need not perform any death experiments."

"No, Zoran," Alexander said quietly, "I refer to recent threats she's made online, promising to take vengeance on the Lords and to force the entirety of the Society of Immortals to take notice and resume a revolution—a revolution I can only imagine is the one you began."

A little 'oh' formed on Zoran's mouth. He squinted at Alexander. "I blame her not for seeking vengeance, for you wronged her grievously by taking her child. However, if I were orchestrating an event," he said, "I would be smart enough to know that you were watching my online movements and stop posting details for you to read." He shrugged. "Or I'd post false information, but as you know I have no internet connection."

Jack clenched his hands so tightly that his knuckles popped.

Alexander leaned across the bed toward Zoran. "Zoran, can you promise me that none of this is being done in your name?"

"Done in my name?" Zoran arched one dark brow. "Well, I cannot promise that. I didn't ask her to do them, that I can say. Why would I? As you know, I am familiar with the Oswald experiments. Surely my niece hasn't been any more creative than Joseph Oswald was." He smiled with what appeared to be genuine amusement. "Lia, you bad, bad girl. What a horrible thing to do, trying to develop a cure for our collective ailment, to once and for all rid us of this immortal prison. How terrible!" Zoran folded his hands and oscillated his gaze between Jack and Alexander. "Something which the Immortal Lords, who know full-well how to take an immortal life, will not do for us. I am sorry that master Krause had a traumatic experience—"

"Traumatic?" Jack snorted. "I'll cut your heart out, and you can tell me how traumatic it is."

Alexander gave him a dirty look.

Zoran's lips twitched in his straight face but he remained silent.

"Do you suspect she is attempting to start a revolution in harmony with the principles you espoused?" Alexander said, enunciating each word deliberately.

"Yes!" Zoran exclaimed. "I do suspect so. But can I tell you anything or help you? No, no I cannot. If I knew anything, I'd tell you none of it. Let her take her vengeance, let her start her revolution. It will do us good." Zoran turned to Jack. "Tell me, did you get quite far when she took your heart out? Could you see death?"

Jack pressed his lips tightly together. His insides were boiling with fear and confusion he couldn't place, be it from Zoran's strange mannerisms and rapid-fire rhetoric, or the black gaze that transfixed him now.

Zoran pressed his slender fingertips together. His voice grew softer as he spoke. "I know how it feels, you see. You fall. It's so black, yet so bright, and for a moment you actually believe it is going to work. Yes, we immortals are most alive when we are nearest to death—"

"No," Jack said.

"Jack," Alexander said quietly.

"—I daresay you've hit that asymptote we call rebounding more times than Alexander or Daniel might ever do in their umpteen hundred years. Perhaps you could say that Lia only tried to give you what you really wanted, what Alexander won't give you."

Jack jerked back. "Shut up."

"He won't allow us to die, and if we have children he'll take them from us," Zoran said scornfully, "and he expects us to live and be—"

"That will be all." Alexander took Jack gently by the shoulder and thrust him toward the door of the cell. "Show Jack out, Daniel. I will question Zoran alone."

In the hall, Jack leaned against the concrete walls, breathing hard. *What the hell is wrong with me?* "I, uh," he said to Daniel, who stood cracking his knuckles by the cell door, "I think I'll go home."

But Jack didn't go home. He drove the long winding road back into Dresden and ended up at a liquor store in a row of busy little shops. He walked out with a bottle of vodka and a pack of smokes. He leaned against his car and lit up. He stood there, watching the midday shoppers pass.

How the hell had Zoran managed to yank his chain like that? Was it because he felt such odd sympathy for Lia, this odd thought that maybe she was right and it was only her methods that were wrong? She'd lost her child. The child was taken. That wasn't right either.

Jack's eyes lit on a woman walking with one hand full of bags, and a little girl holding tight to the other. She was a plump little girl in a purple coat, her head a mass of frizzy blond curls, tottering along on stout legs. She must've been only two or three years old.

Jack dropped his head, blowing out a thin stream of smoke. She could almost be a little Clarissa. He could remember her so well at that age, when their family was still intact. Clarissa would ride on his shoulders, her hands clasped tight around his forehead, singing like a blond canary. Mary Rose would laugh and look up from her dishes as they passed by the kitchen door. She'd be flushed and pink from the hot dishwater.

Jack's face contorted. He tossed the cigarette butt down.

He'd never see Clarissa again except from a distance, maybe, just maybe in a quick and passing exchange. Mary Rose he would never see again at all.

Unless...

No, no, not an option.

Jack swung around and slipped back into the car. He slammed the vodka bottle onto the passenger seat.

∞

An hour later, Jack sat hunched on one of Alexander's wooden dining chairs. The sun had gone down, and the kitchen was only lit by the dim, greenish light over the stove, but Jack refused to get up to turn on the light.

He hadn't touched the alcohol yet. Every time he reached for it he felt like there was a bungee cord attached to his side that pulled his hand back.

Don't do this. You promised her.

But I want to see her. I want to see Mary Rose.

Jack shut his eyes and tried to conjure Mary Rose's face and the scent of her sweet perfume, because maybe if he could see her in his head he'd have the strength to dump the vodka down the toilet.

Why had he wanted to see Zoran anyway? What was it about that guy that had set him off like this?

He couldn't do it. He couldn't see her. He could only remember faint echoes of her, drowned out by Zoran's black eyes saying, *"Perhaps you could say that Lia only tried to give you what you really wanted."*

Jack finally sent a desperate text to Alannah: *Can you call me?*

As he sat staring at his phone waiting for her to reply, Jack's hand finally succeeded in grasping the vodka bottle. He cracked the lid and took a swig, straight from the bottle. He didn't taste it, only felt the burn slide down his throat.

What the hell was he really doing here in Germany? He was an oilman, a construction worker, a janitor, and a drunk, goddam it. Exactly what was he supposed to do in an immortal society? What was left for him with no wife to support, no daughter...

Who really cared what he did now?

Jack gripped the vodka bottle and took another swig. He just wanted to see Mary Rose again, just for a moment. He wanted to feel alright, just for a moment.

Fifteen minutes had passed. Alannah hadn't replied.

He stood up, his teeth gritted, some sort of strange resolution firing through him. Jack walked to the knife block and withdrew the largest knife from the block, a yellow-handled wide-bladed thing. He slid the sharpening steel from its slot, flicking the blade over the steel to make sure it was damn sharp.

Jack's lips pressed into a grim smile. The knife handle had warmed in his palm. He tossed the steel onto the kitchen table as he passed, holding the knife by his side and the vodka bottle in the other hand as he stalked up the stairs. He didn't know how long he had until Alexander returned. He wanted this over by then, and the mess concealed, and the knife in his drawer for when he needed it next.

Jack turned on the light in the bathroom and locked the door behind him. He stripped off his shirt and flung it aside. Then he sat down on the toilet lid and opened the bottle.

The liquor burned down his throat into his empty belly. He tipped the bottle back and let it numb his throat. His head rushed with heat. He set the bottle down on the floor and held up the winking blade before his eyes.

Right into your brand new heart.

Jack had never driven a knife into his heart. Perhaps back then he believed that might actually kill him, naive as he'd been. A knife had been his weapon when he'd wanted a prolonged death, a good long passage into the black before the 'asymptote' as Zoran had called it.

No more time to philosophize. Jack took a long gulp from the bottle and shoved it aside. He sat down in the bathtub, cross-legged, back against the wall. He pressed the tip against his chest.

Why were his hands shaking if he was about to see Mary Rose again? Who cared about the pain?

Jack gritted his teeth, shut his eyes, and gripped the knife with both hands.

Do it. Come on! Do it!

But he sat, perfectly still, his breath hissing rapidly through his clenched teeth.

Do it, you coward! Do it!

Jack drew the knife back and plunged it in with all the force he had. It glanced off the ribs, to the right and lodged tight.

For a moment he stared at the yellow plastic. He was absolutely numb. Then pain rushed in like wildfire. The wooden bathroom door and the white toilet tilted and Jack slumped forward, smiling, into blackness.

He awoke to fiery pain. He gasped and blood splattered the white bathtub.

Shit. I'm not dead.

Oh God, I can't breath.

Jack clutched at the knife protruding from his chest. The blade hadn't struck true. But he couldn't work up the strength to pull it free and end himself.

Oh God, why didn't I die? Why didn't I die?

Blood bubbled up from his chest again. Jack fought to steady himself, but his head spun like a carnival ride.

Pitch black fear overcame him. He had to end himself. If he didn't rebound, who knew how long—if ever—it would take him to recover? Jack put his shaking hands to the blade.

Yank it out and slit your throat.

Blood bubbled from the wound in his chest. Jack just stared at it, frozen.

Do it! Pull it out!

Jack yanked at the knife with both hands. It withdrew two inches from the wound. Black spots obscured his vision.

Panic welled up like the blood filling his lungs. He had to die. He had to rebound.

The ghostly whine of Lia's buzz-saw filled Jack's ears.

"Oh my god!" he cried. "I don't want to die! I want to... I want...!" Jack spat blood. Adrenaline flooded him. He didn't have a choice. He was hurt too bad to live. Jack mustered every bit of will and pulled again. Blood bubbled and spattered with every breath.

Jack held the blade to his throat. It wavered there. He couldn't move. He couldn't breathe. He couldn't die.

"Oh dear God!" He whimpered. He dropped the knife. "What am I going to do?" Where was his phone? He'd call for help.

Are you serious? You can't call Alexander. You can't let him see you like this.

Jack picked up the knife again, but in a flash his oxygen-starved mind made itself up. Fight or flight? Flight. He dropped the knife and clawed his way over the edge of the bathtub. He slithered to the floor, leaving a slippery trail of blood. He heaved himself up by grasping the sink and the door handle. As he drew upright, the blood left his head and his vision went white. Jack nearly went down, but he slumped against the door instead, whimpering with pain.

Clutching his chest, he stumbled across the hall and halfway down the stairs before his knees gave out. Jack flailed for the banister, wrenching his chest as fell. He flopped over the rail, screaming behind his clenched teeth. Blood sprayed from his chest wounds.

"Good God!" a man's voice said. Arms wrapped around Jack's chest.

"Help me," Jack whispered and his head fell against Alexander's shoulder.

∞

Jack woke up in his own bed, swathed in sheets and a light blanket. A glass of water sat on the nightstand, with a note propped up on it. "I'm just downstairs. Text me when you wake up. Alexander." His phone lay beside it.

"Oh... crap!" Jack pushed himself up, and sat holding his head in his hands. The blanket fell away from his bare chest. Jack glanced down with bleary eyes and touched his unmarked chest.

He felt fine, perfectly well. Last night's...

How long had it been, anyway?

...last night's blood and pain and panic swam in front of his eyes like a psychedelic nightmare. What had come over him?

Jack sat up against the pillows and picked up the phone. The home screen was one long list of texts and missed calls, all from Alannah, all about an hour apart.

Sorry, I was in Jiu Jitsu. Can I call now?

Hey, what's going on? Call me.

Text me then?

Jack, are you mad? Why won't you answer?

"Shit," Jack said. The whole time he'd been making a bloody ass of himself, she'd been trying to call him, and no doubt, talk him from his ledge. He set the phone down. He should text her. He should text Alexander, but he couldn't work up the courage.

Soft footfalls passed his door, paused, and returned. The door cracked open, and Doctor Kristiaan's head and shoulders poked in. He had a stethoscope around his neck.

"Ahh, you're awake. Good," he said. He walked over to the bed, and without further words drew the blanket back from Jack and pressed the cold, round stethoscope against Jack's back.

"Ah, shit!" Jack gasped and flinched away from him.

The doctor paid him no heed, just pressed the stethoscope to his back again. What the hell was he listening for? Obviously he still had a heartbeat.

"You didn't die of your injuries, in case you were wondering." Doctor Kris said. He paused, as if listening intently, then withdrew the stethoscope and pulled the earpieces away from his head. "Alexander permitted me to give you a lethal injection to expedite the inevitable. You rebounded cleanly. I see no side effects."

"Great," Jack muttered.

"Fortunately I was at the hospital, not Schwalenburg. I was close by." Kristiaan stood back and crossed his arms. "Listen, have you thought about seeing a counselor?"

Jack stiffened.

"I understand you were talking to Zoran." The doctor's pale blue eyes glinted and the vaguest hint of amusement crossed his face, probably unintentionally.

"Yeah, well, that has nothing to do with anything," Jack muttered. "Thanks for putting me out of my misery, but I'm fine. Obviously."

"Obviously," the doctor parroted, "you're a member of immortal society now, Jack. If I recommend that the Lords send you to the psychiatric home in Stuttgart, they will. But Zoran has an uncanny way of getting inside peoples' heads. You can't beat yourself up about it."

"Beat myself up?" Jack exclaimed. "That's what you call this? Fuck off, buddy!"

Kristiaan held up both hands. "Fine. I'm sorry." He backed out of the room. "I'll let Alexander know you're awake."

"Beat myself up." Jack picked up the phone again and flipped it over and over in his hands. "Beat myself up. What the heck does he know about Zoran and strange effects and shit? Beat myself up?"

"Jack?" Alexander's voice and footfalls came to the door. "I brought you food."

Jack glanced over as the door creaked open. Alexander peered in with a tentative smile. His eyes were bloodshot.

Shit. "I'm sorry, Alexander," Jack muttered.

Alexander padded in on sock feet, carrying a tray. He set it down on the bedside table. He glanced at the chair in the corner, which had a t-shirt and two pairs of pants slung over it.

"Can you pass me the shirt?" Jack said gruffly.

Alexander tossed the t-shirt his way and slung the pants aside. He pulled the chair over and dropped into it. "I'm not angry at you, Jack," he said. He blew out a breath and rubbed his eyes. "I wish that you trusted one of us enough to talk about what is making you hurt. I feel I've failed you in some way. No, no I *have* failed you. I've been so caught up in my own pain. I'm very sorry, Jack."

"Yeah." Jack felt a sudden lump in his throat. He bought himself time by turning toward the tray, where a hard-boiled egg sat in a cup next to a bowl of hot cereal. He picked up the egg, found it peeled, and sniffed at it. He set it back down and took up the oatmeal instead. It was warm, well-sweetened and seasoned with cinnamon and vanilla. He took another bite.

"Anyway," Alexander continued in a bitter tone, "I shouldn't have taken you with us when we saw Zoran. I should have known he would try to yank my chain like that."

"Yank your chain?" Jack laughed.

Alexander nodded wearily. "If he gets to you, he gets to me."

Jack shoved another spoonful of oatmeal in his mouth.

"Do you want to talk to someone?" Alexander asked in a low voice. He eyed Jack.

Immediately Jack shook his head and busied himself with his oatmeal. The truth was, there was only one person he'd ever talked feelings with... well, perhaps two. In the days after Mary Rose's death, Alannah had gotten one or two earfuls. With Mary Rose gone, who could possibly understand?

"I've done very little to earn your trust," Alexander said slowly. "It makes sense that you wouldn't confide in me. Surely you could talk to Alannah?"

"Alannah didn't reply," Jack said under his breath. "Look, Alexander, you've got all kinds of crud to deal with. It isn't your fault that I'm fucked up."

"Perhaps it is!" Alexander burst out. "It's my fault that you're immortal in the first place, Jack!"

Jack started.

Alexander stood and raked his hands through his hair, pulling some of it from its messy ponytail. "You see why I can't possibly condone immortalizing our children," he muttered.

For the first time, the idea began to come clear in Jack's mind— the idea of seeing your children, and your children's children doomed to everlasting life for better or for worse. For so many, it was worse.

"Zoran speaks the truth when he says I know how to undo immortality," Alexander continued. "I am more than seven hundred years old, Jack, and for nearly one hundred of those years I have known how to die. Do you think I've never been tempted?" One hand clenched in the air. "But I am not God! Who am I to decide if someone dies or lives?"

Alexander pressed one hand to his mouth. His shoulders heaved once, then relaxed. "When I officially acknowledge my son, I will likely be forced to give over my position as an Immortal Lord to someone else. Perhaps it is for the best."

Jack sat, dumbstruck.

Alexander gestured toward his phone. "Forgive me. You must still be tired. Call Alannah. She has texted me four times now." He left the room.

"Ah, geez," Jack groaned. He picked up the phone. He did not want to call her. He wanted to find the vodka bottle and see if there was anything left in it.

For the love of God, call her!

Jack's hands felt frozen, unable to dial. What was he supposed to say? "I was just trying to see her again?" The hell he could say that. He sounded like a loony.

Maybe he was a loony.

Jack swallowed hard. He had to face it. There would be no seeing Mary Rose again, there would be no seeing Clarissa again. Alannah was probably the best option he had for a familiar face to talk to.

He tapped on the screen and found her name in the contacts.

"Now you call me!" Alannah's smile was a bit forced when she picked up his request to video chat. The apartment around her swirled as she sat down on her couch.

"I'm fine," he said. He rubbed his bleary eyes.

"Oh sure," she sighed. "Alexander alluded to an 'episode'."

"Oh, is that what we're calling it now?" Jack growled.

Alannah rested her head against the back of the couch. "Spare me, Jack. I'm not going to scold you. What happened?"

Emotion swelled in his throat, painfully clamping his voice off. He struggled to get words out. He couldn't.

"Oh Jack," Alannah said softly.

"I just..." Jack swallowed. He couldn't meet her eyes. "I just wanted to see Mary Rose again."

Alannah didn't say anything. Her mouth hung slightly ajar.

"When Lia cut my heart out—" Jack choked. One ugly sob burst from him. He pressed his hand to his mouth, willing himself not to cry. He couldn't speak.

"Oh Jack," Alannah said, like she might say to a tearful baby. "Oh Jack."

"I saw her," Jack finished, gulping against another sob. "I saw her, and she said to me that I will be-be happy again." Oh hell, he was really going to blubber. He turned away from the camera and pressed his fingers against his eyes. His teeth clenched tight, holding in the wail of agony that wanted to come through.

"You will be happy again," Alannah said. "You will. I promise."

Jack swiped his hand over his face and forced a smile that was probably far more of a grimace. "I'm a damned mess."

"It's okay," Alannah said faintly. "We all have to be sometime."

Maybe so, but he still felt like an idiot. His chest was still heaving, throat so tight his words came out half-strangled.

"I... I met your dad, in case you were wondering what set me off. He's a piece of work." Jack looked back at the screen in time to see Alannah start.

"He's not my dad," she said. "Don't insult the good man who raised me by calling Zoran my dad."

"Sorry, sorry," Jack said. "But what is his deal? He just likes to yank people's chains?"

"Pretty much," Alannah muttered. It was now her turn to not look at the camera.

"Why can't I shake off the idea that they're right—Lia and Zoran? Why would I give anything to have an immortal kid, or death, or both? What's wrong with me?"

Alannah looked up at him with a hollow expression. "They're legitimate wants."

Jack leaned his head back against the wall. "Alexander's right, though, even if I could make Clarissa immortal now, or I could have made Mary Rose immortal, I don't think I could do it. I just..." he raised his free hand and let it drop. "I have to accept that I won't ever see them again. He said it with far more stoicism, more resignation than he felt. But true resignation was starting to creep in.

"Oh Jack." Alannah shifted on the couch, sending tinny rustling sounds through the phone speakers.

"I just have to find my niche here." Jack swiped at his nose.

"You know," Alannah said slowly, "Zoran and Lia are sort of right, Jack."

Jack blinked.

"It's not wrong to want control over your own destiny," her voice was small, hesitant. "The thing is that they'd take their freedom at the expense of other's freedoms—their children's, for instance. I don't envy you at all, Jack, but I think you're making the right decision about Clarissa."

"Even if I don't really have a choice?" Jack's voice rung wry, regretful.

"Yeah," she breathed and met his eyes. "And please don't hurt yourself, Jack. Please. Maybe see a counselor, or..."

"Well, I'll start by not visiting Zoran again," Jack muttered, "since even the good Doctor Kris seems to think he's some kind of mentalist."

"You could say that," Alannah said.

They both fell silent. Alannah's face was so still that for a moment Jack thought the phone had frozen.

"So..." Jack said after almost a minute had passed. "I guess I should... I guess I should go."

Alannah nodded, her eyes still far away. "Okay. Yeah. Text me, okay? Or call me if you're feeling bad. Call me, Jack. Okay?"

"Yeah, okay," Jack said softly.

Her finger hovered over the screen for a moment, and she hung up.

CHAPTER 22

London, Present Day

By the time Alannah hung up with Jack, she felt awful.

She would have been home, if she hadn't impulsively decided to attend the John Lin Academy's Saturday afternoon 'open mat' session. Alannah had never gone, but Alexei had texted her asking if she was coming because he was hosting, and Jules apparently was coming, and...

Truth was, she kind of wanted to see Alexei again.

Alannah had arrived just after Jules, and the two of them had done a bit of rolling in one corner of the mat before sitting against the padded wall and watching Alexei spar with a couple of the guys.

Jules imitated a few of their punches from her position on her knees. "Man, I should try Muay Thai next. That looks so cool."

Alannah watched Alexei absorb a roundhouse kick with a sharp 'thwap' to his shin and winced. "Yeah, I don't know about that. I think I'd break all my toes."

"You don't kick with your toes!" Jules' blue eyes were fixed on Alexei and his partner, a decidedly nervous-looking teenage boy.

The kid landed a jab on Alexei's ear, which he'd shielded with his glove. Alexei laughed and shook his head slightly. "Nice! My ear is ringing."

The round timer beeped, and the two guys bumped gloves.

"Good." Alexei nodded in approval. He swung his head around and grinned at Jules and Alannah. "Either of you ladies want to give it a go?"

"Yeah!" Jules jumped up. "I wanna kick you, Alexei!"

Alexei put on an expression of mock terror. "Oh gee! Oh dear!" He glanced around. "Let me get you some gloves. I'll put on some pads."

"You'll need them," Jules said.

"Alannah," Alexei said as he returned, carrying a somewhat ripped pair of boxing gloves, "you could practice Jiu Jitsu with Mike over there." He pointed to a guy in the corner who was about six feet tall, in his thirties, and heavy-set. He probably weighed at least two hundred and fifty pounds.

"I-uh..." Alannah stammered. Sure, she could get the best of Jules almost every time but Jules was a good thirty pounds lighter than she was.

Alexei waved Mike over. Mike smiled good-naturedly at her.

"It'll be good for you, 'lannah," Alexei said. "Face it, if you actually need to defend yourself it probably won't be from a little squirt like Jules."

"Hey!" Jules swung one of her newly-installed gloves at Alexei's shoulder.

He was probably right. Alannah could imagine Peter Bouwmeester, one of Zoran's former goons and probably no smaller than Mike. Martin Bertholette was a smaller man, but still sizable compared to her. Even Zoran himself was at least equal to her size.

"Okay," she said in a small voice. "Let's do it."

As it turned out, where strength failed her at least she had technique on her side. Mike seemed to be used to relying on strength. So though Alannah found herself trapped a lot of the time, she did manage finally to get the upper hand on Mike and get him into an arm bar. He laughed and tapped on the mat.

"Nice!" he said as he jumped up.

Clapping came from the side of the mat. Just Jules and Alexei were left in the room.

"All right, time's up," Alexei said. "Let's bow out."

As they exited the building, and Alexei prepared to lock up, he said to Alannah, "Hey, are you up for coffee?"

She was just fishing her phone out of her bag. The screen lit up, showing one text from Jack: *call me?*

"I better not," she said. "I need to call Jack."

"Who's Jack?" Alexei said casually as he shut the door.

"A friend in Dresden." Just a friend, she wanted to say, but that was ridiculous. A surge of annoyance at Jack's timing went through her. "I guess I'm going to have to pass this time."

"Okay." Alexei walked her across the street. As she started up the stairs to her flat she heard the motorcycle start up.

Meanwhile, in Dresden, Jack had been dying of a knife to the chest. Alannah felt so guilty, even if he was okay now. Simultaneously she felt scared because of what had occurred to her when he mentioned Dr. Kris. If the doctor was talking to Zoran, well, he also knew Louisa. Louisa, no doubt, talked about her. So by now, Zoran might know where she was. That didn't matter as long as he was in prison, but if he told Lia...

She'd always thought that as soon as Zoran left prison, he'd try to get her back. She was his, after all, in his eyes. She was his creation and his daughter.

It didn't make for a relaxing Sunday morning. That was for sure.

At about ten, while she was finishing off breakfast, Alexei texted her: *Have you heard from Alexander?*

Alannah set down her coffee and contemplated the text. Was this what Alexei wanted to talk about over coffee?

Not really. She replied. She had, but that was about Jack's 'episode' and Jack deserved a little privacy over that.

Are you free this afternoon? He returned.

Sure.

They made plans to meet up at the coffee shop across the road from Alannah's flat that afternoon.

The afternoon was clear. The sun peeked, golden, over the tops of the buildings, giving a hint of warmth on Alannah's face.

Alexei slouched under the canopy of the cafe, leaning up against the wall and texting. As she approached, he peeled himself off the wall and slipped the phone into his pocket. He was dressed casually in slim, fawn-colored pants, and a charcoal grey, long-sleeved crew neck with the sleeves pushed up.

"Hey," Alannah said as casually as she could.

"Hello." He smiled slowly and held the door for her to pass inside. She caught a whiff of sandalwood off of him.

He bought her coffee just like the last time, and brought it to her at the corner table. He was limping slightly, she noticed then.

"Did you pull something?" she asked. "You're limping."

"It's my knee," Alexei said with a grimace. He lowered his voice, "I injured it when I was young, and even though I've resurrected a few times since then, it always comes back. Is that normal?"

Alannah squinted into the distance. "I really don't know. I mean, Alexander's resurrected a few times but his depression always comes back. Maybe some people are just prone to things?"

"He has depression?" Alexei asked softly.

Alannah nodded. After a moment's hesitation she asked, "Do you get that too?"

"Not... really," Alexei said with some hesitation. He took a sip of his coffee. "Yeah, I guess so."

"How young do you mean when you say you injured yourself young?" Alannah said, hoping for a safe change of subject.

"Twenty"—Alexei smiled—"a genuine youngster. I trained in Chinese Wushu back then. It was a long time before my MMA days."

"How many martial arts do you know?" Alannah asked.

"Properly?" Alexei shrugged. "Three, I guess. Muay Thai is more my niche than Jiu Jitsu. I only started Jiu Jitsu about ten years ago. You can only acquire so much skill in ten years, whereas I've been practicing Muay Thai since the seventies. I've added a bit of Judo, but I really can't say I know that well."

Alannah wrapped her hands around the warm, ceramic mug. "How did you get started in the martial arts?"

"In our years in Hong Kong, I think my mother was afraid she wouldn't be able to teach me proper discipline on her own, so she put me under the tutelage of an older Chinese man who worked in our compound."

Alannah smiled at the thought of a tiny, blond Alexei, executing kicks and punches.

"Hey! Alexei!" a high-pitched voice cried across the coffee shop.

Alexei started visibly and twisted around toward the door.

Jules bounded toward them, toting shopping bags. "Whatcha doing? I thought you were married, Alexei!"

"We-we're not—" Alannah stammered.

Alexei gave her a wry, incredulous look. "I never said I was married," he retorted. "What, am I not allowed to have friends?"

"I dunno." Jules gave an exaggerated shrug. "You do make a pretty darn cute couple, I gotta admit."

"Geez, Jules!" Alannah said. "She had this idea when we met that you were my ex," she said to Alexei. "I'm friends with Alexei's partner too, Jules. I mean, I just had dinner with him and Giovanni on Friday night."

Jules froze for a moment. "Giovanni?" she squealed as she whirled on Alexei. "You're gay?" A couple people nearby turned to look at them.

Red splotched Alexei's neck. "Well, you don't have to yell about it."

Alannah felt suddenly sick. It had never occurred to her that Alexei might be keeping that a secret.

"Oh my god!" Jules said in a sing-song coo like this was the most adorable thing in the world. "I'd never have guessed."

"It's worse than that," Alexei said, tensely humorous. "I'm bisexual. No one is safe from me."

"Oh my god!" Jules said again.

The same thought had just crossed through Alannah's mind.

"Listen," Alexei said as he stood up and drew Jules aside. He whispered something in her ear, inaudible to Alannah. Jules's face slowly became serious. She nodded as Alexei talked.

"Okay," she said, when he was finished. She grabbed his shoulders in a little half-hug, and bounced out of the cafe.

"I am so sorry," Alannah said as Alexei returned. "I didn't think—I'm so sorry."

Alexei's face was tight. "Yeah, maybe I should've mentioned that no one at John Lin knows about Giovanni." He glanced around. "Can we get out of here?"

"Yes, of course!" Alannah jumped up, nearly spilling her coffee.

"'Geez, someone oughta tell that girl that 'You're gay' is one of those things you don't yell in cafes," Alexei muttered as they exited the cafe into the sunshine.

"Is this going to be a problem at the Academy?" Alannah asked in a small voice.

"No." Alexei grimaced. "Probably not. I explained to Jules that however tolerant society might seem, the boys might be a little reluctant to roll with 'gay Alexei' in the dojo." He gestured helplessly down the sidewalk. "Should we walk?"

Alannah fell in step with him without a word. She felt awful. She felt sick.

"You must think this is kind of pathetic," Alexei said after a minute had passed.

"No, no," Alannah said quickly. Confusing, sure. Pathetic, no. "You don't have to explain yourself to me, Alexei."

"What would Alexander think of this?" Alexei asked. He stopped below a small, twisted tree. People passed by on either side of them. He wasn't meeting her eyes. The question had rung hollow.

Alannah felt a lump well up in her throat. She turned away so Alexei couldn't see the tears welling up in her eyes as she tried to formulate an answer from her churning thoughts.

Alexei let out a breath and took a step forward.

"No, wait," Alannah cried, hurrying to follow, "what has Giovanni told you about Alexander? What did he think Alexander would say?"

"He told me Alexander was religious," Alexei said gruffly.

"But Alexander respects Giovanni," Alannah said.

"Yeah, so he ignores the fact that he's gay." Alexei's face twisted. "It might be a little different with his own... offspring."

Her thoughts finally crystalized. "Listen"—she grabbed his elbow—"Alexander's first three kids died more than six hundred years ago, but if you asked him he'd draw you sketches of all their faces." How many times had she seen those pictures, lying around in their home in Winnipeg? "He loved his children. Do you think he can't love one more?" She grasped at the thought in her mind. "Before you two scared me out of Winnipeg, I refused to leave for forty years. Alexander kept asking me to move on, and I never could. One day he told me—I'll never forget—that if I was never able to leave Winnipeg he'd still love me and take care of me. He'd hope for different, but he'd love me the way I was. And I think..." her breath shuddered, hitting up against the lump in her throat. Suddenly she missed Alexander a lot. "I think he'd do the same for you."

Alexei's face had gone slack. Deep, dark longing shone in his doe-eyes. He turned quickly away.

"I'm afraid to go to Dresden because my father is there too," Alannah said. "Maybe we should go there together. Get it over with."

"I don't know if I'm brave enough," Alexei said without looking at her. "I can eat a hundred punches, but I can't face one man."

Alannah touched his shoulder. "I know what you mean. I do. I mean, not the eating punches part, but..."

Alexei pivoted slowly and began to walk back the way they'd come. Alannah fell in step.

"I'll think about it," he said.

After she and Alexei parted ways, Alannah spent a few minutes brooding, sitting on her bed listening as Alexei's motorcycle sped away. She turned her phone over and over in her hands, trying to decide if she should call Alexander.

She wished, more than anything, that there was someone she could talk to about Alexei. About how Alexander felt about having a son, and how a devout man like that would react to his son being the partner of Giovanni Ardovinni, and how even now she was jealous of Ardovinni.

Did that make her a horrible person? To be lonely, wishing for someone to call her own? For someone who would, by their very presence, make her feel strong again?

Daniel had been like that.

∞   ∞   ∞

On the Saturday they'd set, Daniel picked Alannah up on the motorcycle at noon sharp. She'd already been waiting nervously in the entry, her hands twitching on her new blue jeans. Then he drove her out onto a remote road near Schwalenburg and parked.

"Your turn," he said.

She sat with her hands on the handlebars, trembling with nerves, yet thrilling with the rumble of the bike beneath her. "What if I crash?"

"You won't crash." He hunkered down beside the bike, his blue eyes shining up at her.

"I might!" she squeaked.

He grinned. "You're immortal, Alannah. Be brave. What's the worst that can happen?"

By evening, she was driving down the highway at top speed, with Daniel's strong hands at her waist. Fearless.

They stood on the stoop of Alexander's house as Alannah undid the catch of the helmet. Her hair tumbled down as she removed the helmet, flying in long errant strands. Daniel took the helmet from her hand and hung it on the corner of the rail behind him. A little smile played on his mouth. He brushed the hair back from her face, leaned in, and pressed his lips gently to hers.

"I enjoyed this," he said softly, millimeters from her mouth. He kissed her again. She reached for his face, but he turned. "Good night, Alannah."

"Good night," she whispered as he went. She touched her lips, where his mouth had been. It was her first kiss.

∞   ∞   ∞

How could she not miss that kind of tenderness?

CHAPTER 23
London, 1921

At about seven in the evening, Cosima was upstairs sitting beside the now alive, asleep Marie. Giovanni was in the library, dinner untouched on the little table beside him, when the front door of the house banged open.

Stevens's voice boomed in protest from the entry, followed by Zoran's strident delivery. Giovanni leapt out of his chair and arrived in the entrance in time to see Zoran attempting to shove Stevens out of the way so he could ascend the stairs, and Alexander gripping the back of his coat.

"What is the meaning of this?" Giovanni shouted.

Zoran spun around. His black eyes burned with rage. "No, you tell me what the meaning of this is! Why is *my* woman in *your* house?"

Giovanni tasted bile. "If you'd taken care of your woman, perhaps she wouldn't have come to me, searching for you! And pregnant no less!"

"Gentlemen!" Cosima's face appeared at the top of the staircase. "Do you mind?"

"Let me see her!" Zoran finally shoved Stevens aside and plunged up the staircase.

He was stopped by Cosima, blocking the head of the stairs. "You listen to me!" She put her face right up in Zoran's. "This woman, who you call yours, gave birth to your child today! She hemorrhaged to death!" Cosima glanced at Stevens and stopped. "Or nearly so, anyway. She travelled from France because you couldn't even be bothered to send her a letter."

Zoran's face went from deep red to white. Whatever he had been about to say, Zoran seemed to retract and bottle up for further use. Instead he drew a deep breath. "Miss di Gaspare, could I see Marie? Please? Can I see my child?"

Cosima's eyes went past him, to Alexander.

"Zoran," Alexander said in a hard, flat voice, "don't think that we'll allow you to keep this child."

Zoran didn't say anything, didn't look at him. "I want to see the child."

"Zoran?" Marie's voice floated weakly down the hallway. "Zoran? What's happening?"

Cosima turned and hurried back down the hall. Zoran bolted after her, with Giovanni and Alexander on his heels.

"Zoran?" Marie was upright in the bed. The room was dark, the lamp now burnt out. "Where is my baby?" Giovanni could see her hands on her deflated belly. "Why is it gone?"

Cosima shoved past him with a lit candle. "Marie," she said softly, "your baby was born. She's healthy."

Zoran pushed her aside and sat down on the bed beside Marie. He gathered her into his arms and pressed her disheveled head into his bosom. Above her head, his eyes glittered in the candlelight. Giovanni sensed him thinking at a great rate.

"Zoran," Marie murmured into his jacket, "what happened to me?"

Cosima knelt down by the bed. "Marie, you hemorrhaged. Do you remember?"

Marie's tumbled head nodded against Zoran's chest.

"She's not a strong woman," Zoran said. "Leave her be. She is alright. The child is alright."

"She was strong enough to travel from France while heavy with child!" Cosima retorted, her eyes alight with the candle flame. "And she is immortal."

Marie lifted her head so suddenly that the crown of it slammed into Zoran's chin. "No, no," she said, "I'm not part of Zoran's society; I'm not one of the immortals. I've never gone through the rituals."

"Rituals?" Alexander blurted out.

"We'll not speak of this now!" Zoran exclaimed. He pressed Marie's head against his chest again. "Marie, I'll explain everything to them. Please, can't she see the child?"

"But what do they mean?" Marie whimpered.

"They've misunderstood," Zoran said in a soothing tone. "Everything is alright now. I'm here."

"Cosima," Alexander said slowly, from the doorway, "please bring the child."

A few minutes later, the baby girl was settled in the arms of her mother, with Zoran's arms around them both. Alexander pulled Cosima and Giovanni aside.

"You said she rebounded from death after hemorrhaging?" he asked in a low voice. The lines around his eyes were tight as bowstrings. "She most certainly rebounded?"

"Yes," Cosima whispered. She leaned against Giovanni for support. "I was there when she died, and I cleaned her body for burial. The tears in her..." she swallowed, "the tears have knit back together. Even the scarring on her belly from the pregnancy is gone."

"Could Zoran know?" Alexander asked.

"He has to," Giovanni murmured, slipping his arm around Cosima's waist. "Clearly she does not." A little shiver went through him. "He's already admitted to having water from the fountain. He could have made her immortal himself."

"The thought had already come to me," Alexander said. His eyes flickered back and forth, not stopping to focus on anything. "Mr. Ardovinni, would you have a message sent to Mr. Gunther for me? Ask him to come here?"

"Certainly," Giovanni said. He departed quickly to find Burke. When Burke had been dispatched, complaining good-naturedly about the late hour, he returned.

As he ascended the top of the stairs, there was a quick flurry of movement as Alexander and Cosima stepped back from each other. Cosima's hand lingered in Alexander's, a faint flush in her cheeks. Alexander's face, on the other hand, was ashen.

"Mr. Ardovinni," he said hoarsely, "when Daniel arrives, we shall arrest Zoran. My only hope is that we can explain all things to Miss Marie without causing her too much distress."

Giovanni blinked. Too much distress? What would they tell the young woman? That she was an immortal human being, and that by law her baby must now be taken from her? Sickened, he said aloud, "What can I do?"

"Perhaps nothing," Cosima said gently, "except that it may be best to separate Zoran from the mother and child. Alexander would like to question him, and"—she licked her lips—"perhaps another woman might be the best person to make an explanation to the poor girl."

So there was, then, nothing for him to do but to stand by. Angst burgeoned into irritation. "If you suppose I can help you in separating Zoran from the woman and child," Giovanni said, "you are sorely mistaken. However, you may use Zoran's former room to detain him in." He pointed to a door, near the end of the hall. "That is the one."

Giovanni turned and hurried down the stairs, into the dark library where he poured himself a stiff drink. It turned in his stomach as he thought of the young woman upstairs, most likely about to face the idea of a life stretching into eternity. His musing very quickly carried him to Burke. Giovanni's chin fell onto his chest. Burke.

He poured another.

Half an hour passed before Burke's and Daniel's voices were heard in the entry. Giovanni jumped up. His head swirled, and Giovanni recalled that he'd had a fair amount of brandy and no food that evening.

"Sir," Burke said, squinting at him as Giovanni arrived in the entry. Daniel had already gone up the stairs. "Are you well?"

"Not as well as I ought to be," Giovanni said. "I ought to eat something if I'm going to carry on drinking." He looked up longingly into Burke's blue eyes, imagining his house clear of intruders, him and Burke alone together. Yet even that picture was somewhat tainted.

"Why are you drinking?" Burke asked in a low voice, a little smile playing about his mouth. He truly had no idea what was going on in the house.

From up the stairs, an unintelligible wail cut through the quiet house, echoed by the cries of the infant. Zoran's and Alexander's voices shouted back and forth.

"Because hell threatens to break loose in my house," Giovanni said. His chest constricted painfully. "John, the woman is... I... her child..." One hand waved helplessly in the air.

Burke gripped his shoulders and pushed him back into the library. He shut the doors and wrapped his arms around Giovanni.

"No, don't." Giovanni struggled out of Burke's grasp.

"Everyone is in bed," Burke chided, reaching for him again.

Giovanni fought his hands off.

Burke growled in frustration. "Giovanni, tell me what is wrong?"

"You can't drink the water," Giovanni said. "I should never have asked. Why would I ask that of you?"

Burke blinked.

Giovanni turned his back on Burke and wrapped his arms tightly across his chest. "In which case, every day you are that much closer to lost to me. What am I to do? I should steel myself against the inevitable."

"What?" Burke said harshly. "You shall tell me to hand in my resignation? Leave your house? Giovanni, be logical. We have many good years left."

"You don't understand."

"And you are being unjust! Do you think you are the only one who has been lonely? Do you think I cannot understand loneliness because my life has a reasonably foreseeable end?" Burke lowered his voice and softly, pleadingly said, "Giovanni, don't shut me out."

Giovanni could not bring himself to face Burke. He stood, his face resolutely turned away even as he sensed Burke near to him. Upstairs, the voices continued to clash.

"If the water is what causes death," Burke murmured, "then when the time came you could follow me into the grave, Giovanni."

Giovanni shut his eyes. "Death holds no solace for me. I fear death. I fear damnation."

Burke's snort was derisive. "I have long since given up on fearing God."

"I have not," Giovanni said, "and remember how much older I am than you."

Burke's hands touched his shoulders again, one sliding up to cup the back of his head. "Then I have no comfort for you, my love, except these two hands. Giovanni," he breathed, "I beg you. Don't shut me out. I am not dead yet."

A groan tore out of Giovanni. He turned and grasped at Burke blindly, through stinging tears. "Don't leave me," he said. "Don't leave me."

∞

245

Alexander knew Zoran wouldn't go quietly into the night. He and Daniel dragged Zoran out by the arms, shouting as to wake the household.

"You won't keep her from me forever! She'll be immortal! Mark my words. She'll be returned to me!"

A wide-eyed, dressing-gowned Stevens burst into the entry.

"Mr. Kosar is not well!" Alexander grunted as they heaved Zoran out the door. "Kindly reassure the other servants."

Upstairs he could hear Marie still sobbing, babbling in Cosima's arms, unable to comprehend the life now stretching before her.

Daniel launched Zoran into the cab so hard that Zoran's head bounced against the back window. He pinned the struggling man against the bench seat and pulled a needle from the pocket of his coat. He stabbed it into Zoran's neck. Zoran swore at him and struggled all the harder, but a moment later his body went limp.

Daniel sat up, panting. The veins in his neck stood out taught like cords. "Drive!" he gasped to the wide-eyed cabbie.

Alexander leapt into the cab as it pulled onto the road. He squeezed into the back seat and he and Daniel propped up the inert Zoran between them.

"We'll have to keep him sedated for the rest of the night," Alexander said.

"The rest of the week, perhaps," Daniel grunted, rearranging Zoran by yanking on his collar. "Good god, Alexander, what will we do with this bastard after what he's done to that girl?"

Alexander's head dropped into his hands. "I am sick, Daniel, utterly sick. There is no way we can undo the damage to the girl, and now by our laws we must take her child."

"You were right not to do it now," Daniel said in a low voice. "You were right to deny Zoran's claim that you were about to take her."

"It was a lie." Alexander paused, then corrected himself. "It *may* be a lie. Face it, Daniel, we are dealing with a case to which there can be no precedent." He shook his head. "I told Cosima I would return. I don't know where Ardovinni has gotten to. I can't leave her to deal with the woman alone."

"She is capable," Daniel said. He swallowed and tipped his head back. "Ahh, we are going to have *so* much fun hauling this son of a bitch back to Dresden."

They deposited Zoran in Daniel's bedroom, sedated him further, and tied him to the bed. Daniel stayed with him, and Alexander set off on foot to return to Ardovinni's house.

It was well past midnight, perhaps one in the morning. The night was cold and damp. The streetlights couldn't cast any light on Alexander's mind. He turned his collar up and thrust his hands into his pockets. His shoulders hunched against the chill, sure, but also against the pain in his chest. He was so tired—tired of living, tired of questions humans ought never to have to answer, and tired already of holding the power of death, the power of life. Why had God abdicated and given him these powers?

"Why?" he cried aloud. "You know I can't..."

A rattle in the alley made him reel back and stumble over his own feet. A cat skittered across the road and into the darkness.

Cosima answered the front door of Ardovinni's house and pulled him inside. "She's quiet," she said softly. The entry was the only lit room on the main floor, soft gaslight burnishing Cosima's disheveled, coffee-colored curls. "Both mother and child are asleep." Her 's' slurred slightly. "Oh dear," she sighed. "What now, dear Alexander?"

Alexander's head lolled to the side.

Cosima caught his face in her hands. "Never mind, Alexander. You should make no decisions in your state." She stretched up and kissed him lightly.

Alexander cupped her head and returned her kiss deeply, the heat of her lips on his burning off the edge of the pain in his mind. He laced his hands into her hair.

"Alexander," Cosima muttered against his mouth. "Alexander you need to go home." Her lips tugged at his, her tongue belied her words. "You-you'll do something you regret."

"I've already done so many things I regret," Alexander said into her neck. "What's one more?"

"Alex—" her hands tangled in his shirt. One of the buttons popped open. Her fingers found bare skin and slid through the opening.

Alexander swallowed hard. His hand came down on hers, arresting it in place. He could be staring death in the face, his heart was pounding so hard. Instead, he was at the bank of the Rubicon, his body bursting with desire. "Cosima," his voice trembled. His whole body was shaking, "Cosima. I can't—"

"No, no!" She pushed him away, turned around and hid her face in her hands. Her back heaved. "No."

"Cosima, I want to marry you," Alexander whispered. "I have to take Zoran to Dresden, but when I return—"

She turned slowly with her mouth slightly agape. Her eyes were infinitely tired. "Don't leave me again," she said. "Don't leave me, Alexander." She reached out one hand to him.

Alexander sucked in a breath. Then he pulled her toward himself and crushed her in his arms.

∞

In the wee morning hours, Alexander awoke in Cosima's bed. Faint morning light seeped between the drapes, illuminating her skin with an ethereal, bluish glow. She lay face down beside him, one arm across his waist. Her curls spread across her bare back.

Cosima, more magnificent than his imagination had painted her, shouldn't have inspired such a sick feeling in his belly.

Alexander sat up. "Oh God," he breathed, "what have I done?"

He had to go. If Ardovinni should see Alexander in his house, there would be no bounds to his rage.

Cosima stirred and raised her head. A little groan escaped her lips.

"I have to go," Alexander whispered, his voice shaking. He scrambled out from under the blankets, trying to cover himself. But when she sat up, he could not help but look at her.

The same shame must have overtaken her, for she pulled the sheet up to her chin. "Go," she said.

Alexander dressed with hurried, shaking hands. He did not look at her. When he opened the door, the hall was silent, dark and empty. He made it down the stairs, out the door, and onto the street. It was just light enough to see. But in his head, Alexander could feel darkness encroaching.

CHAPTER 24

Dresden, Present Day

Jack sat up in his bedroom for a few minutes after Alannah hung up. He wasn't sure how to go on with his day, to go down and face Alexander. Alexander probably still wasn't doing so hot himself. What would they do, exactly?

Jack got up, collected his breakfast dishes and made it halfway down the stairs before he realized that he was still only in his t-shirt and baggy boxers. He sighed, turned around and went back up into the bedroom and fished through the tangle of clothes on the floor for a pair of jeans. Jack rubbed his eyes and glanced in the mirror. His face was pale. There were dark smudges under his eyes.

Geez. I look like hell. No wonder Alannah was so quiet.

He was a mess. Dr. Kris was probably right. He probably needed counselling. He probably needed a stay at the goddamned Hardwin Nervenheilanstalt, or whatever.

Dr. Kris.

"Wait," Jack said aloud. Something clicked in his mind.

Dr. Kris. Dr. Kris had access to the prisoners. Dr. Kris probably visited Zoran. Had they considered him at all? He could be the blogger.

Jack bolted out of the door, breakfast dishes forgotten.

"Alexander?" Jack called as he bounded down the stairs. "Alexander?" He paused on the bottom stair, listening to the quiet house. Faintly he heard a rhythmic thudding and squeaking. Jack poked his head into the little exercise room and found Alexander running furiously on the treadmill. His teeth were bared in an almost deranged expression.

"Alexander?" Jack called over the pounding of Alexander's running shoes.

Alexander held up one finger. He ran for about another thirty seconds, then suddenly leapt up on the sides of the treadmill and punched the stop. He stood, gasping for air. Sweat was dripping out of his disheveled hair. "Yeah?" he panted. He bent over and rested both hands on the tops of his thighs and took a deep breath.

"Uh," Jack began, a little taken aback, "had you ever considered that there's someone who has access to Zoran that we've forgotten?"

Alexander wiped his forehead on the sleeve of his t-shirt. "I've thought about it, yes."

"What about Doctor Kris?"

Alexander stared at him for a moment. "Doctor Kris," he echoed. "Actually, that had never crossed my mind for a significant period of time. Despite being an immortal, the doctor went through quite a vetting process to gain access to the prisoners."

"But is there a guard with him when he visits them?" Jack squinted at Alexander.

Alexander shook his head. "No."

"So, say a guy like Zoran, who likes to get in people's heads, starts talking to Kris and Kris becomes sort of sympathetic to him...?"

Alexander's breathing had now normalized. He sat down on the weight bench, wiping his face absently with the tail of his t-shirt. "It's a valid thought," he said, "but it's also a very serious accusation against a man who has no criminal record, not even a record of sympathizing with Zoran's movement for that matter."

He paused. "Naturally, the doctor would deny it if asked. Zoran would deny it. How could we begin an inquiry?"

"There *are* cameras in the prison," Jack said. "Maybe that would give us something. What about his phone or his computer, or..."

"You need a warrant for that," Alexander said, "and despite having signing authority, it would be unethical to give Daniel a warrant because I have a hunch. We'll need a little more evidence." He got up. "Let me think about this, Jack. Do you want something more to eat?"

"Yeah, I guess," Jack muttered.

Alexander's tablet sat on the table in the kitchen. Alexander picked it up and swiped the screen as Jack plopped down into one of the chairs. "You can access the immortal digital database from here," Alexander said, handing the tablet to Jack. The search window was open. "Let's experiment. What connections between Zoran and Kris might we have missed?"

Jack propped the tablet up in its case. "Well, could he have practiced medicine somewhere where Zoran lived before?"

Alexander's eyes narrowed. "I don't think so, but look it up."

Jack tried a few different search options, based on suggestions of cities Alexander gave him as he heated soup on the stove. They didn't get anything. But he did discover that Dr. Kris had worked at the mental home in Stuttgart, the 'Hardwin Nervenheilanstalt'. "Well, Zoran was never in the mental home, was he?"

"No," Alexander said without second thought.

Jack propped his head on his hands. He was suddenly tired, and it was no surprise. He'd rebounded from death only a few hours ago. By rights he should be much weaker than he was. Jack shut his eyes, and as he did, another thought occurred.

After Clarissa's birth, Mary Rose had struggled with post-partum depression for months. But Lia's baby had been taken. That would be doubly bad, right?

Jack opened his eyes and typed 'Lia Brenner Hardwin Nervenheilanstalt' into the search box. "Geez, what a name," he muttered.

"It's because in German many of the words are combined," Alexander said toward the soup. "One day you'll speak it."

"Maybe in a century," Jack said.

Only one document showed up. As soon as he clicked on it, a password box presented itself.

"Got the password?" he said to Alexander.

Alexander circled around to his side of the table, still holding a wooden spoon. He set it down and typed in the password. The document opened, a scanned image of a paper, all in German.

"It's an admittance record," Alexander said. "Lia was admitted October 8, 1930. The admitting doctor was... Doctor Kristiaan den Hollander."

Jack whistled. "Oh gee, coincidence or conspiracy, Alexander?"

Alexander gnawed his bottom lip. "Let's talk to the good doctor about this. Are you up to a trip to Schwalenburg?"

∞

"You're certain you're up to this?" Alexander said as the outskirts of Dresden fell away behind the car. His fingers fidgeted on the steering wheel. "I feel that we haven't given you adequate time to recover from—"

"No, it's fine," Jack said into the paper cup of take out coffee. His eyes were half-shut. "Once we're there maybe I can nap... or something." He'd have some fantastic dreams, he bet. Probably wake up thinking there was still a knife sticking out of his chest.

Alexander accelerated past a little red hatchback. "You're a man of action. I understand, Jack. You find work therapeutic. But sometimes rest is better when dealing with profound loss."

"You know," Jack muttered, "if you were going to tell me to rest, maybe you shoulda done it a month ago before I drank all your liquor and bled all over your house."

Alexander sighed heavily. "I am late without fail, Jack. It's the story of my long, long life." He licked his lips. "But perhaps better late than never. Hear me out, Jack." One hand fell to the shifter and rested there, twitching. "Right now it feels like your heart has been ripped out, and no moment of happiness goes untainted. It feels like a new death every day, and so actual death is a welcome relief."

Jack shifted uncomfortably in his seat.

"But one day you will forget to grieve. You'll forget again, and again, and one day you'll realize that it's been a week without sorrow." Alexander swallowed, "You will be happy again. Don't shut out the living because of the dead."

Jack turned toward the window and watched the evergreens zip past. "My daughter is still alive. What about her?"

Alexander didn't respond.

"Is there a way to see her again? Or were you just referring to immortals when you said to not shut out the living?" Jack was surprised by the bitterness in his voice. He thought this was all settled in his mind. He'd let her go.

He heard Alexander draw a deep breath through his nose. "Jack," he said gently, "this is strictly unofficial, believe me, but perhaps you don't need to rule out seeing your daughter again. While she is still on this earth, don't give up hope."

A lump was swiftly growing in Jack's throat. He turned back toward Alexander. Alexander glanced at him from the corner of his eye, then back at the road. Jack kept his mouth shut, trying to control his emotions.

"I tell myself the same thing about Cosima," Alexander said to the windshield. "Even if I only see her long enough to tell her how sorry I am."

They drove in silence for the rest of the trip.

In the foyer of Schwalenburg, Anastasie greeted Alexander with a kiss on the cheek and Jack with a concerned look. She opened her mouth to speak.

"Ana," Alexander said, "is the doctor in today?"

Anastasie pulled her phone from the pocket of her cardigan. "He isn't here now." She scrolled down the screen. "He isn't scheduled to come in today."

"I'll call him," Alexander said. "I need to speak with him."

They'd just made it to Alexander's office when Daniel popped his head in. "Alexander, you're here. I didn't expect you."

"Daniel, we need to talk. Come in." Alexander slid in behind his desk.

Jack plunked into the other chair. Daniel leaned against the wall by the door.

Alexander leaned both elbows on the desk. "Jack theorizes that the link between the blog and Zoran, and for that matter the link between Lia and Zoran could be Doctor Kris."

Daniel's eyebrows shot up. "Kris?" He laced his fingers together and frowned down at them. "Well, if that is the case he is much smarter and more devious than I thought. Are you calling him in?"

"Yes." Alexander turned his cell phone over and over in his hands on the shiny oak desktop. "But before I do, is there anything—*anything* we can dig up on the doctor?"

"Well, let's have a look." Daniel motioned for Alexander to move aside so he could use the computer.

"We've already checked everything we can think of," Jack said. "All we know is that the doctor treated Lia at the Stuttgart Nerven... whatchamacallit."

"Did he now?" Daniel leaned over the desk, the screen reflecting in his eyes. His fingers tapped out a tattoo on the keys. "Indeed. I see. That's worth asking about. I think it's sufficient pretext to interview him." He was still typing as he spoke. "Hmm, the doctor has quite a medical history himself. His law keeper in charge noted three suicide attempts between 1890 and 1901. He became doctor in residence in 2008, which means that those attempts were not considered against him during his evaluation for the job." He continued typing. "He is currently on—" Daniel looked up. "I think it would be considered a violation of privacy to carry on, though I've found his personal medical history here in Germany."

"Will it be pertinent in an investigation?"

"It may." Daniel shrugged. "Suffice it to say, Zoran would have plenty of material to work with on our doctor. Are you going to call him in?"

"I will call him now." Alexander stood up, tapping on his phone screen as he did. He put the cell to his ear. A moment later, he greeted Kris in German.

Daniel continued to type, pausing now and then to squint at the screen and read silently.

Jack slumped down in the chair. "Does everyone have to have a sob story?" he said to Daniel. "It's exhausting."

"I know," Daniel muttered to the computer. "Not me. No sobs in my story."

"The doctor expects to arrive by six this evening," Alexander said, leaning up against the wall, behind the desk and eyeing the computer screen. "Jack, if you need a nap, you could use one of the apartments."

"No," Jack slurred. His head was incredibly fuzzy. His neck and shoulders ached, and he could imagine that a sliver of pain was lodged in his heart where the knife had been. "I mean, yes. I'll curl up in the corner. Let me know when he gets here."

Alexander and Daniel glanced at each other.

Daniel shrugged. "Okay."

Jack lay down against the wall and pillowed his head on his jacket.

"Did Cyrus call you?" Alexander asked quietly. "I received a text from him. He said the Bertholettes were gone."

"Yes," Daniel said, "None of my contacts turned up any information for us. Hardwin's guys are on the way to Verdun. It seems the most likely place they would go, but I couldn't find them on this side of the Chunnel. Cyrus and Idina will come home."

Jack's eyes drifted shut.

Alexander's phone ringing woke him up. Jack's eyes opened reluctantly and his hand groped across the Persian rug trying to figure out where he was. Finally he lifted his head.

"Hello?" Alexander said from the desk. "Who?"

A long pause, in which Jack sat up.

"I'm coming," Alexander said sharply. He stood so quickly that his rolling chair shot back against the wall.

"Who...?" Jack began, but Alexander was already gone.

A moment later, Jack thought he heard a pop. Jack scrubbed at his eyes and shook his head slightly. He picked himself off the cold floor and put the coat back on. He'd just done the top button when the whole room heaved. Jack pitched forward among falling plaster. His head bounced off the edge of the desk and he knew nothing.

He woke up, for a moment deafened by the ringing in his ears, blinding by burning eyes. "Ah!" Jack rolled face up and pressed his hands to his watering eyes. When he could finally see he sat up. He was surrounded by white plaster dust and the entire contents of Alexander's bookshelf. Jack sat for a moment, panting. Far away he could hear someone yelling in German, and a high-pitched response.

"What happened?" Jack said. He remembered: Alexander getting a phone call, a distant pop, the room shaking and the boom of an explosion.

"Oh shit!" Jack staggered to his feet. He fell against the wall but pushed himself off and lurched into the hall. "Hello?" he called. "Anyone?"

"Jack?" a voice came, weak and raw-edged from down the hall. Jack saw four Library doors instead of two, and two out of the four were hanging off their hinges at a crazy angle. They came into focus, two instead of four, as did the dust that washed out in a stationary wave onto the flagstones.

Jack walked through the doors. "Alexander!" The bookshelves nearest him had collapsed entirely, pages strewn everywhere. The parchment family tree hung in tatters from the ceiling. "Alexander?"

He turned the corner, to where the circulation desk had been. All that remained was slivers of wood, and a pit in the stone floor. Alexander lay sprawled among blood-spattered shreds of paper and dust. His hands clutched at his bloody torso. A sliver of wood protruded from his eye.

Jack dropped to his knees beside him. "What can I do? What can I—holy shit," he said as Alexander turned toward him, staring at him with his one good eye. "You... can't..." he breathed, "you can't do anything for me." His mouth worked, "Bertholette. Catch her. I'll"—his face contorted—"I'll be back." He relaxed against the flagstones, his words squeezing out from between clenched teeth. "I'll be... back."

"Which way...?"

Alexander's gaze went past him, looked surprised, and the light went out of his eyes.

Jack knelt, frozen in place.

"Jack?" a voice roared outside the library. "Jack?"

"In here!" Jack called.

Daniel skidded around the corner a moment later. He reached out and steadied himself against the wall. His hand was bloody. "Alexander," he said weakly. "Damn it."

"He said it was the Bertholettes," Jack panted. "We have to search the castle. Maybe they're—"

"I don't think so," Daniel said in a low voice, his eyes still on Alexander. He knelt down beside Jack and yanked the sliver of wood from Alexander's eye.

"Shit—" Jack pressed his hand to his mouth against sudden nausea.

"Her car is gone," Daniel said as he sat back on his heels. He was breathing hard. "One of Hardwin's guys took my motorcycle and went after her. It was Camille, and if she were not a woman"—he groaned softly—"I'd tune her up for shooting Anastasie." He leaned forward and heaved Alexander into his arms. "I'll put him in the same apartment."

"Aren't we going to—?"

"I have to see if I can get the server back up." Daniel grunted as he stood up. Alexander's head lolled against his arm. "Or I'll have to go into Dresden. I have no web access. If Giordani—that's Hardwin's law keeper—can't catch up to Camille, we'll have to track her license plate. I think the server may be more important. Jack, I need you to take your phone and start taking pictures of the library. Find any bomb fragments you can. I'll-I'll send help if I can." He hefted Alexander's body into a more secure position and carried him out of the room.

Jack stood up unsteadily and fumbled for his phone, scanning the detritus for where to start.

Ten minutes later Jack stood in the blasted out space where the circulation desk had been, holding a twisted fragment of pipe. He shut his eyes, trying to imagine what the scene could have looked like. Did Alexander pursue Camille into the Library? How had she detonated the bomb? This was the only fragment he'd found thus far. Who knew what parts had melted away?

"Jack!" Daniel's shout reached him. "Jack!"

Jack dashed toward the library door, still clutching the mangled bomb casing.

Daniel stood between the hanging library doors, white-faced. "Forget the bomb," he said through clenched teeth, "Zoran is gone."

∞

Daniel's office had been the closest to the Library with the servers in the room next door. The shock of the bomb detonating and the falling plaster had damaged them and knocked out the power to them.

Daniel had fixed them and was rebooting them about the same time that Anastasie woke up from her gunshot wound to the head.

It was about ten in the evening. Alexander lay motionless but whole on the bed in the bedroom next to hers. The guard who had been on duty at the time of the bombing and breakout lay on the couch in the main area. The three of them were the only people who knew what had happened. Giordani had called saying that Camille had disappeared into the night. A search of the entire castle had garnered them no trace of Zoran, no ideas of how he'd departed.

Jack had been left in the apartment, waiting for one of the dead to wake up.

A sharp intake of breath signaled life returning. Jack jumped up out of the flimsy metal chair. It teetered and fell over, and the crash sent him rocketing in the air.

"Shit." Jack gulped.

"Whaaaa...?" Anastasie's soft voice wafted from the other room.

"Anastasie?" Jack kicked aside the chair and hurried to the bedroom door. "Anastasie?"

She sat up in the bed, staring at him, her eyes blank in the lamplight.

Behind him a door flew open. Jack gasped and jumped again.

"I've got it back," Daniel called, his footfalls stomping heavily across the apartment. "I've got the server back up. We need to look at the security camera footage—"

Jack turned in the door as Daniel sat down at the little dining table. Daniel already had a laptop in front of him.

"Anastasie is awake," Jack said.

"Oh!" Daniel swallowed hard, his eyes going past Jack, then to the screen. His face slackened. He pushed himself back to his feet, shut the laptop, and carried it with him past Jack into the library.

Jack watched Daniel sit down on the bed and gather Anastasie into his arms.

"Mon Coeur," Daniel muttered into her hair, "I'm sorry, I wish I could stay here with you and let you rest."

She shut her eyes and leaned against him.

Daniel's face contorted for a moment, emotions flickering in his eyes. "Then, perhaps I can." He glanced up at Jack, then settled himself against the headboard and Anastasie securely against his shoulder. He dragged the laptop onto his knee and typed with one hand. As he worked, his lips pressed together tightly. Jack could hear his breath, erratic, hissing through his nose.

The guy was going to crack. Jack had just seen him working among debris and fallen plaster, frantically trying to clear the dust out of his computers and put back together broken wires while Adolf Hardwin, his wife Sophia, and any other staff that were there systematically went through the castle.

Daniel's face was white from dust. His knees were caked with it. He was shedding plaster dust on Anastasie's dark blue t-shirt and the grey bedcovers. His blue eyes skittered across the screen, his mouth formed silent words.

"Here," he said, waving Jack over. He adjusted Anastasie, now asleep, and turned the computer. "Footage of the guard at the desk in the prison at the time of the explosion. Let's do..." He tapped the mousepad, "Five minutes before."

Jack put his head next to Daniel's and watched the black and white footage. A larger man, bearded, sat at the desk watching the computer, working on something. A few minutes in, the guard looked up like someone was approaching.

Jack's breathing picked up. A slim, blond man stepped up to the desk. The guard smiled at him and said something. Suddenly, the blond man's hand whipped out. The guard slumped over. The man bent over the guard, tapped on the computer keyboard, and walked through the door to the prison.

"Son of a bitch!" Jack hissed.

"Wait," Daniel said. "If the footage continues..."

The camera shook abruptly, but kept rolling. The door of the prison opened, and two men emerged. One was Zoran. He even glanced up at the camera and smiled with a flash of white teeth. The other stared straight ahead and marched Zoran out of view of the camera.

"Doctor Kris," Jack said, "you bastard."

CHAPTER 25

London, Present Day

Alannah fumbled with her keys at the building door by streetlight. Her phone began to simultaneously ring and vibrate in her pocket. When she pulled it out, Cyrus's name was on the screen.

"Hey, Cy!" Alannah finally succeeded in jamming her key into the lock. She let herself in, pinning the phone to her ear with her shoulder.

"Hello Alannah," Cyrus said cheerfully, but with a weary drag to his voice. "Hey, Idina and I are in London as you may have heard. We're flying back to Dresden tomorrow, but we were wondering if we could spend the night at your place."

"You mean your place." Alannah laughed as she ascended the stairs. "Uh..." There was only the one bed, which she was using of course. "Sure, I can move to the couch."

"The couch is a pullout," Cyrus said. "We won't evict you from your bedroom."

"Okay, sounds like a plan."

"Okay, we'll be there in about an hour."

Alannah hung up as she opened the door to her own apartment. She plunked the phone down on the dining table and glanced around. The place was neat. Dishes washed, bed made. She'd have to rifle through the closets and see if she could find Idina's extra bedding before they got there. Alannah flipped the element on under the kettle and went to the bedroom to put on a pair of sweats.

As she pulled her curly hair back into a ponytail, a sharp rap sounded on the apartment door.

Alannah frowned at the clock on the bedside table. Cy had said an hour. She padded back into the main room, picking up her phone as she went and wishing there was a peephole in the door. Alannah undid the deadbolt and opened the door as far as the chain would let her.

Instantly a hand shoved through. She saw steely blue eyes.

Alannah gasped. She threw herself against the door. The hand crunched in the door and disappeared with a muffled yowl. Alannah threw the bolt and skidded through the dining room into the bedroom. She slammed the flimsy wooden door behind her and snatched her cell phone off the bed. She jammed her finger against Cyrus's number.

"Cy!" she gasped into the phone.

A thump and a screech came muffled through the bedroom door.

"It's Alexei," his response was just as breathless.

"Alexei! Someone is breaking into my apartment!"

His voice became deadly calm, "Where are you?" She heard rustling, and Giovanni's voice in the background.

"In the bedroom."

"Is there a closet or a bathroom?"

"Yeah!"

"Go in there and lock the door."

The apartment door thumped against the wall. "Alannah," a voice called in a low, mocking voice. It was a man's voice, deep, with a thick Dutch accent. Peter Bouwmeester.

"Go," Alexei ordered.

Alannah ran to the bathroom and tugged the sliding door shut.

"Alright, I'm coming. I'll be there in ten minutes," Alexei said. "Listen to me. Is there anything you can use as a weapon? All you have to do is keep him busy for ten minutes. I'm coming, Alannah. If he gets hold of you, you know what to do. Use your training. Ten minutes."

The phone clicked.

Alannah dropped the phone into the sink and turned around. Her mouth hung open, she gasped like a goldfish. There was the post that had the toilet paper on it, a metal dowel anchored to a pedestal. She lunged for it.

On the other side of the cardboard-thin bathroom door, the bedroom door groaned as Peter flung his weight against it.

"No!" Alannah whimpered. She gripped the metal dowel with both hands, poised like a baseball bat. If Peter was here, then Zoran was collecting her. Or Lia was, or...

Deep breaths. You're not helpless.

Alannah sucked in a slow breath as the bedroom door splintered. "Ten minutes, Alannah. Give him hell for ten minutes."

"Alannah," Peter cooed, just outside now. His fist hammered against the door. It trembled.

Alannah hiked the dowel.

His fist broke through the door. Alannah swung at his fingers.

Peter grunted as the metal met his knuckles, but his hand was undeterred. He shoved the door open.

Alannah slammed the pedestal into his face.

"Ahh!" he reached for her blindly. Alannah ducked under his arm and bolted past him. His wild hand caught her by the hair, yanking her back.

Alannah screamed and thrust the dowel at him. He deflected it, but dropped her hair. Her head fell forward.

Alannah sprang away into the bedroom. She heard his feet thudding after her as she ran through the shattered bedroom door. She could almost feel his hands grasping for her. She wouldn't be taken by surprise. She spun around. His face was almost right in hers. She got one last swing. She yelled as she swung the dowel. He anticipated it. Metal scraped against flesh as he caught it and twisted it away. But Alannah's free hand came around and smacked into his face with a meaty squish.

"I'm not... coming... with you." She threw herself to the side as he lunged.

Peter's foot connected with her shin. Alannah tumbled. Her teeth snapped shut on the tip of her tongue. She tasted blood. Before she could roll, he was on her, grabbing her ankles, grabbing for her flailing wrists. The carpet burned at her bare arms. His weight fell on top of her and knocked her breathless. Peter's hands slammed down onto her shoulders. She smelled his breath, onions mingled with coffee.

For a bare instant Alannah stared up into his face.

Too fast to think it, her hands trapped his arm and her foot trapped his leg. Alannah heaved upward, and Peter rolled off. She flung herself back and kicked herself off his knee. She dove over the sofa.

Alexei! Where are you?

She gasped for air and spun around.

Peter approached slowly. His chest heaved. Blood streamed down his lip and sputtered in his breath. "Alannah," he said in a low voice, "you don't have to get hurt."

"I'm not coming." Alannah kept backing up, trying to keep herself moving in a circle. "I'm not coming with you, Peter. Just go away before help gets here."

"Oh, help?" He grinned, and his teeth were bloody. He followed her around the couch, half crouching, ready to spring at her. "Your law keepers are far, far away, my dear."

Alannah glanced back into the kitchen, at the knives in the block. She faked to the right, then leapt to the left into the kitchen, hand outstretched for the big chef's knife. Block and knives tumbled to the ground, and Alannah fell to the floor, but one slick polymer handle remained in her grasp as Peter reached her. On her knees, she swung backward at his leg. The blade bit into his jeans and sliced skin, then Peter's knee dropped and shoved her, face first into the tiles. The knife clattered away.

Peter's breath whistled through his nostrils. With his knees controlling her back, and one of her hands pinned, Peter reached for the paring knife. "If I kill you," he grunted, "you'll be easier to transport."

Alannah saw the blade glint as it swung for her throat. She heard the apartment door slam against the wall. Peter's body jerked back, and the blade bit into her skin.

"Hey!" behind them.

Sticky, hot blood trickled into her collar. Alannah lifted her head weakly, just in time to see a leather booted foot connect with the side of Peter's head. His face butted into the back of her head, and she lost consciousness.

∞

"Augh!" Alannah's eyes and mouth opened wide.

"Shhh," a firm, calloused hand restrained her head. Another applied pressure to her neck.

In her dizzy, stupefied state, all Alannah saw was the silhouette over her. "No!" she struck out at him.

"No, Alannah, it's Alexei!" Alexei's ebony eyes came into focus above her. His brow furrowed with worry and concentration.

Alannah went limp. "Where's Peter?" She could feel hot, sticky blood between her tender skin and Alexei's warm fingers.

"In hell, I hope," Alexei growled. "He's out cold."

"Am I... Am I..." Alannah's hands scrabbled at her neck and Alexei's hand.

"Shh." Alexei's free hand stroked her damp hair out of her face. "He cut you, but not deep. It's already beginning to clot."

An ugly sob burst from Alannah's open mouth. She pressed her lips tightly together, fighting for composure.

"It's alright." Alexei stroked her hair back once again. "You fought hard. You did well."

"I hit him with the toilet... the toilet paper—" *Don't cry. Don't cry!*

"You knocked out his tooth." Alexei smiled as he shifted his hand on the cut. "Did you play baseball in Canada?"

"No."

"Come, let's sit you up." Alexei slid one hand under her back and lifted her slowly upright. Alannah's head emptied, and all she saw were pinpricks of light all around, then Alexei's face came back into focus.

"See?" he lifted his chin toward the dining room. Peter lay on his sides on the tiles, his limp arms and legs bound with a belt and an electrical cord. His mouth hung slack. The paring knife lay nearby, gleaming in the fluorescent kitchen light.

Alexei ran his teeth over his bottom lip. "Maybe I shouldn't have kicked him so hard." he glanced back at Alannah. She shivered. Then her teeth began to chatter, and her tears spilled over. Embarrassment couldn't stop them.

"Ahh," Alexei sighed. He worked one arm, then the other, out of his leather jacket and wrapped it around her shoulders. He pressed his palm to the cut on her neck again. "I've no skill in comforting a woman, I'm sorry."

"N-no, It's not... I'm not...” Alannah rubbed her eyes with trembling hands. "Alexei—" A though arrested her.

Alexei's eyes narrowed, waiting.

"Cyrus and Idina—law keepers are coming here," she said. "If you don't want to meet them, you should go!"

Alexei stared for several moments. He licked his lips. "And leave you by yourself with that?" he pointed to Peter. He sighed. "No, I'm not running this time. Let them come."

In the next twenty minutes, Alexei bandaged her neck, and then settled her into bed. She huddled under the duvet and watched him through the open bedroom door as he called Giovanni. He paced across the kitchen floor, his hand dug into his blond hair. Low

Italian conversation just reached Alannah's ears, barely enough to decipher with her limited Italian, even more limited by her jangled nerves.

"He's coming." Alexei turned to her as he pocketed his phone. "We'll see who arrives first." He rubbed his eyes. "Is it alright if I make coffee? Do you have coffee?"

Alannah burrowed deeper under the blanket, digging her icy toes into the sheet. "It's above the microwave." She watched him through the bedroom door as he took down the canister and the French press.

The door buzzer grated through the flat. The teaspoon fell from Alexei's hand and clattered on the counter.

"It's Giovanni," Alannah said. She shoved herself up on her elbow. "Cyrus would call me. The buzzer is by the door."

Alexei sprang toward it.

Alannah settled back onto the pillows and lay one cold hand over the bandage on her neck, face turned toward the door.

The door rattled as Alexei let Giovanni in.

"Alexei." Giovanni nearly pushed Alexei back into the apartment with the force of his entrance. He wrapped Alexei in a rough embrace, then turned, scanning the apartment, the prone figure of Peter, looking for Alannah.

"I'm here," Alannah called weakly.

Giovanni came into her room and knelt down beside her. "Alannah, are you alright?"

"Sore," she murmured.

"What a scare," he said gently. "That is Peter Bouwmeester, no?"

"Yes."

Giovanni's teeth ran over his bottom lip. "And two law keepers are coming, Alexei tells me."

"Well…" Alannah shifted on the pillows. "Cyrus and Idina were coming to stay the night. Do you guys need to go?"

Giovanni glanced over his shoulder at Alexei, who was prodding the still inert Peter with his toe.

"I'm rather surprised that they aren't here yet," she added softly.

"We'll stay." Giovanni took her hand and squeezed it gently. "Alexei wants to stay. We'll stay."

"Where's my phone?" Alannah struggled upright. "Maybe I should call Cy and Idina?" Her head swirled. She gripped Giovanni's hand to stay upright.

"I'll call." Giovanni pressed her hand.

"Check this out." Alexei padded into the bedroom carrying an envelope. He handed it to Alannah.

"Maybe you shouldn't—" Giovanni began.

But Alannah had already opened the envelope and unfolded the paper inside, revealing a photo of a little blond girl in a blue dress. She shook out the paper. It said, simply, "Dear Alexander: one daughter for another."

∞

"Hey."

Alannah stirred.

"Alannah." Fingers gripped her own.

Alannah lifted her head. The wound on her neck sent a jab through her. "Oh!" her vision swirled.

"Holy shit, I'll kill him." Idina's face, framed by her wild red hair, came into view as she bent over her. The bedside lamp lit up her face.

"Idina!" Alannah succeeded in sitting up. She was kneeling on the bed beside her, long legs dangling off the edge of the mattress.

"Alannah, I'm so sorry." Idina's face was a mix of fatigue and righteous anger. "I'd kill him, but it seems that Baby Alexander already did a good job on him." Her hands twitched on her knees, her body taut. "I'm so sorry."

"Baby Alexander?" A hysterical giggle welled up in Alannah's throat.

Idina's face slacked just a bit. She grinned. "You've been keeping him under your hat, Alannah? He's just been around?" She shook her head and her face became serious again. "Never mind that. He's already explained everything."

"Is everything alright, then?" Alannah asked softly. She nodded toward the door. She could hear low conversation coming from the other side.

"No." Idina rubbed her eyes. She glanced at the bed. "Hey, can I lie down? I am beat."

"Yeah, sure." Alannah skooched over, and Idina lay down on the other side of the queen bed. Alannah leaned back against the pillows again.

A deep sigh wracked Idina's body. She stared straight up at the ceiling. "Alannah, something happened at Schwalenburg this evening. That's why we were late."

"What?" Alannah gasped.

"Camille Bertholette blew up a pipe bomb in the library."

"Oh my god!" Alannah cried. "Is everyone—what happened?"

"Alexander was killed," Idina said quietly. "Jack texted about fifteen minutes ago that he has started breathing again. Anastasie was also killed, and she is now awake as well."

Tears welled up in Alannah's eyes—confusion, anger, and terror milled around inside her.

"There's one more thing," Idina said. She took Alannah's hand, gripping it tightly. "Alannah, Zoran was broken out of prison. He's gone."

CHAPTER 26
Dresden, 1921

"You're going to house me in a jail cell?" Zoran scoffed as Daniel pushed him down the stairs toward Schwalenburg's prison. "What, is there no 'innocent until proven guilty'?"

"There is no need to prove guilt anymore," Alexander said wearily, "there is only to decide how long you get to stay in said jail cell."

"In other words," Daniel said as he marched Zoran before him into the prison, where a guard held the door of the jail cell open, "you may as well get comfortable, sir."

"Will you be prosecuting Ardovinni for withholding information?" Zoran turned back as he entered the cell. His dark eyes snapped. "Or am I to be the sole focus of your so-called trial?"

"Ardovinni will do his part," Alexander said. He swung the door nearly shut.

"But I'm sure you haven't prepared a cell for his lodging," Zoran said through the window, "because he'll pay his fines and walk free."

Alexander turned his back on Zoran. "None of us shall ever walk free, Zoran. We're immortals."

"Coward!" Zoran shouted after him.

∞

Nothing in the trial went differently than Giovanni expected, not the packed counsel room, nor Zoran's verbal jabs at him throughout. He knew Zoran considered him entirely at fault for the trial in the first place. Zoran probably considered insults to be Giovanni's due.

Giovanni didn't mind that Marie had been taken from Zoran. The poor woman had never recovered from the revelation that she was immortal. He minded a great deal that her child was taken away, even after Alexander had said the baby would not be taken. The baby girl was gone, already in the arms of a fine German family as he understood, and Marie was a broken woman.

"Zoran says the child is immortal," Giovanni confronted Alexander and the other two Lords in the antechamber off the counsel room. He'd just received word that Daniel had handed the child over to adoptive parents that morning. "We're not going to keep her long enough to find out?"

"Who would raise her?" Frederick von Schwalenburg said, looking up from his notes with steely grey eyes. "You?"

"Her mother cannot give her a proper life," Adolf Hardwin said gently. "Marie is not well."

Giovanni glanced over at Alexander, but Alexander didn't meet his eyes. "I understand that, Sir, but she may be well again and if the girl is immortal then why should they be separated?"

"The law is in place," von Schwalenburg said.

"But this is an odd case," Giovanni said flatly. "You've not half finished Zoran's trial. Do you think he's lying when he says the baby is immortal?"

"Of course we'll watch her," Alexander finally spoke up. "If she is immortal, her mother will eventually get her back. But if she is not immortal, then her best chance at a normal life is to give her to a mortal home."

Giovanni clenched his hands behind his back. Alexander would feel a great deal different if he could divine the contents of the letter Giovanni had received that morning from London.

A letter frantic in tone, spotted with tears. Cosima was pregnant by Alexander.

His own letter still sat half-written on his desk in his borrowed Schwalenburg chambers and his breakfast dishes were left shattered on the floor.

He knew, now, why Alexander had avoided him at every turn even before they'd left England.

Alexander turned away from him again. His jacket bunched up as he planted his hands on the windowsill.

Giovanni swallowed and said, "So she is gone and Marie is in Stuttgart. Will Marie be informed where she is?"

"Marie isn't of sound mind," Hardwin said. "I'm sorry, Mr. Ardovinni. It is a terrible scenario at every angle. Truly, I am very, very sorry." His blue eyes were sincerely sorry, and Giovanni remembered that the Hardwins had lost a child many years ago, though it had been to a miscarriage.

Giovanni's shoulders dropped. "Mr. Hardwin, I realize that I have no experience with loss of children. I only request"—he pressed his lips together a moment—"I request that this trial be used to reflect on how we deal with our future children."

"The idea," Frederick von Schwalenburg said while eyeing him, "is that there be no more."

Giovanni fixed his eyes on Alexander's back. "There will be more."

He did not return to the council room, instead trudged back up to his chambers. The shattered dishes were gone, his clothes gone from where he'd thrown them. For a moment he could imagine that Burke was there with him.

Burke. Giovanni shut his eyes and let out a slow breath. He sat down at the desk and withdrew a new sheet of paper.

Dear John, he wrote. *There is something I must ask you to do for me. I know I can trust you with my sister and closest friend.*

∞

"Sir!" Burke stood in the doorway of Zoran's French house, the rain fell down in a curtain off the overhang before him.

The driver shoved Giovanni's mud-splattered trunk in the door, and as soon as he was gone Giovanni embraced Burke, pushing him back into the house.

Burke kissed him roughly. "I missed you."

From the dim interior of the house came a squeaky, insistent cry of a newborn. It came again, and again, unanswered. Burke turned his head, with Giovanni still clutched close, listening. A moment later, soft footfalls travelled unseen across the hall.

Giovanni and Burke met each other's eyes.

"She hasn't named the baby yet," Burke said in his ear. He stepped back and turned around, facing the dark hall, clearly straining to listen.

Giovanni also stopped to listen. He could hear a raspy woman's voice singing in French.

"The housekeeper is a decent woman," Burke muttered. "She liked Miss Marie and Mr. Kosar better than Miss Cosima and I, but best of all she likes the baby." He raised an eyebrow. "If Miss Cosima persists in wanting to get rid of the child, I am sure she would take him."

"And have him be raised French?" Giovanni said.

Burke turned back and smiled.

"I'll greet Cosima," Giovanni said quietly, "then I will change out of these travelling clothes. Where can I find her?"

Burke led him down the dark hall and pushed open a door that was already ajar. The shutters were open inside, admitting gray, stormy light. Thunder crackled outside.

"Cosima," Giovanni said. He could see her sitting up in bed, her eyes dark hollows beneath her disheveled curls.

Her head lifted slowly. "Giovanni," she said. Her voice was strangely hoarse. "You've come." She stirred in the bed. "You'll take care of finding him a family, then, so I can go back to England before Alexander returns."

Giovanni swallowed hard. Burke turned to go but Giovanni reached back and grabbed his hand. "Stay," he whispered. He wasn't sure why.

Burke seemed to understand. He pressed his hand to Giovanni's back for a moment, then leaned against the doorframe.

Giovanni approached the bed and sat down beside her. He took her cool, clammy hand in his and pressed it to his cheek.

"I'm sorry," she said softly, "of course, you're tired. I shouldn't bother you just yet." She paused and glanced down. "Was the result of the trial satisfactory? Mr. Burke has only told me the barest details."

Giovanni glanced over at Burke. "Only so much immortal law can be contained in one letter. I..." he swallowed, "...Zoran shall be incarcerated for fifty years, as well as paying a considerable fine. I too paid a considerable fine, but this house is now mine." He squeezed her hand and laid it back in her lap. "Marie's child was taken away."

Cosima's eyes filled. She blinked away her tears and looked away quickly. "What will I do?" she whispered. "Alexander will have to give away our child also."

Giovanni gathered her up and leaned her cheek against his shoulder.

"It would destroy him," she said into his coat. "How could I face him?"

"If you don't tell him," Giovanni said gruffly, "how will you face him then?"

"I don't know." Her voice was small, childlike.

Giovanni turned and met Burke's blue eyes. *What do I do?*

276

Distantly the baby began to cry again.

"It needs to eat." Cosima lifted her head.

"I'll get the child," Burke said behind them. His footsteps thunked softly away on the wood plank floor.

I have to fix this. Somehow.

God, I know you don't listen to me, but...

Burke returned before long with a bundle of blankets in his arms. He gazed down at the little face among them as he seated himself beside Giovanni and Cosima on the bed. The baby gurgled.

"A false alarm?" Burke laughed softly and stroked the baby's pink cheek.

Giovanni eased Cosima away from him and leaned over Burke. The newborn's murky eyes gazed past him. He had one wrinkled, red fist pressed against his puffy cheek. There was just the finest skim of blond hair on his head.

"Ohh," Giovanni said with a sigh, despite himself, "let me hold him, John."

Cosima shifted beside him. "Just let me feed him and take him away."

"No," Giovanni said. He slid one hand between the infant's little head and Burke's arm, the other underneath the baby's bottom. The baby's face screwed up as he was lifted out of his safe haven, and he emitted a croaking cry. "Shhhh," Giovanni murmured against the child's downy head, "shhh, baby. I'll give you to your mother in a moment."

Cosima's breath hitched. Her head fell against his shoulder and trembled with her shaking body. "Oh Giovanni, I..."

The warmth of the baby in his arms, the gentle pressure of Burke pressed against his side, Cosima on the other, sent up such a pang of longing in Giovanni that he wanted to weep. He swallowed again and again against the painful block in his throat. Not since childhood had he had so much family in one room, as patchwork and illegitimate of a family as it was.

"What would you name him, if you could?" Giovanni turned his head toward Cosima. His breath blew in her uncombed curls.

"I'd name him for his father," she said in a low voice.

Giovanni shut his eyes and nuzzled the baby's hair again. "Very well."

Burke and Giovanni left Cosima to nurse her child. Giovanni put on dry, clean clothes and lay down in his bedroom, on top of the blankets. Arms stretched out, he stared up at the moving shadows on the ceiling, made as the trees outside blew in the storm. Rain drove against the window.

Burke entered the room and set a cup of tea on the bedside table. He knelt down at the hearth and prodded the embers of the dying fire. He placed a log on top, and they crackled to life. He lay down, then, beside Giovanni.

"You are quite free in Cosima's presence," Giovanni observed hoarsely. "You've become friends."

"We are," Burke said. He took Giovanni's hand in his and rested them on top of his stomach.

They lay in silence for a few minutes. The fire blazed now, adding another dimension of shadows across their forms.

"Giovanni," Burke said in a low voice, "do you still have the water?"

"Yes," he whispered.

A long pause. "If you gave it to the child..."

Giovanni jerked his head up.

"I know," Burke said, "but if his mother had the option... If she could raise him, and have him forever, perhaps she would keep him. Wouldn't it be best to keep him with his mother?"

"It would," Giovanni said with a sigh, "but at what cost? She wouldn't agree to it." His mind had caught the notion, though, and whirled it around at a tremendous speed, gathering more and more ideas as it turned.

If he immortalized the child he would have to send the both of them away, at the very least until they knew the baby was immortal for certain, otherwise it would be for naught. The child would be taken by the Lords and given away.

"I am thinking," Burke said slowly, toward the ceiling, "of when I am gone." He gripped Giovanni's hand tightly. "And of who will care for you then. If you had a family..."

Giovanni squeezed his eyes tightly shut.

God save me. I am condemned already. What is one more sin to repent of?

"She must make that decision," Giovanni said, "not I." He licked his lips, already trying to find the words to explain to Cosima the power he had in his hands. "God help me," he breathed. "No man should answer questions like this."

Burke's laugh was bitter as he rolled onto his side to face him. "Sometimes we must make up our own answers, Giovanni."

∞

"Cosima?" she was awake, Giovanni could see. Her eyes were open, staring blankly out the window at the pale dawn. He sighed, and slipped into the room. He lay down on the bed beside her and took her hand. His pulse pounded in his temples, like it had all night.

Cosima didn't look at him, but her warm fingers squeezed his. Giovanni opened her hand and pressed the little brown vial into it.

Her head lifted. "What's this?"

"Water," Giovanni rasped. "Water from the fountain."

Cosima drew in a breath. "I don't want to die," she whispered, "why are you giving me this?"

"I want..." he pressed his lips together for a moment. "I want you to think about what you might do if the child were immortal."

She twisted around in the bed to face him, backlit by the grey light. "If the child were..." Her face contorted in the shadows.

"You would have to go away," Giovanni whispered. "You would have to hide for a time. I would ask Burke to take you away."

Her tongue darted across her lips.

"Think about it." Giovanni got up. As he reentered his room, where Burke still slept, he heard the weak cry of the baby. Giovanni stood in the doorway, his eyes oscillating between his bed, Burke, and the door of the nursery to his left. Before he could make a move, he heard footfalls come from Cosima's room and pass him by. The nursery door opened, and soon Cosima's voice came softly from within. He could hear her cooing in Italian to the baby.

Heartsick, confused, Giovanni lay down again beside Burke.

Several hours later he returned to Cosima's room. The baby slept beside her. On the bedside table sat the jar. It was empty.

CHAPTER 27

London, Present Day

When Alannah awoke, she was alone in bed. She'd gone to sleep with Idina asleep beside her and Cyrus leaning against the bathroom door, guarding the inert Peter within. He was gone now. The bathroom door stood ajar. The flat was silent.

Alannah sat up, blinking. Her entire body ached. The cut on her neck stung beneath the bandage. The whole debacle had really happened, and Zoran had really escaped from Schwalenburg.

Was she alone? She swung her legs off the bed and grabbed an oversized sweater out of the closet. A few moments later she padded into the main area of the flat, her arms wrapped tightly across her chest. As she did, Alannah heard the faint sound of rhythmic breathing. Giovanni and Alexei were curled up together on the pullout bed. She wasn't alone after all.

She stood looking at them for a moment.

Move.

Alannah tiptoed into the kitchen, filled the kettle, and set it on the element. She leaned against the counter and wondered exactly what she'd do with herself.

"Good morning," came a soft voice. Giovanni had sat up and peered at her over the back of the sofa.

"Did I wake you?" Alannah whispered. "I'm sorry!"

"I'm a light sleeper," he said. "It's okay." He glanced down, she imagined, at Alexei. "How do you feel?"

"Fine—" Alannah's smile was wobbly. She felt a sudden rush of emotion and couldn't finish. She turned away, swallowing hard.

"Alexei and I will stay with you as long as you need."

She heard Giovanni shifting on the creaky little mattress. Alexei grunted. A moment later, Giovanni stood beside her, surveying her cabinets. He picked up the French press from the kitchen sink and put it under the faucet. He swirled the residual grinds around and dumped them down the sink. "Would you drink coffee if I made it?"

"Most definitely," Alannah said in a shaky voice, "but you'll wake—"

"Alexei would sleep if I fired a gun off beside his head," Giovanni said calmly. He picked up her grinder and examined the beans in the hopper. Whatever he was looking for, they seemed to pass muster, for he nodded, set it down and set it to a coarser grind than she'd had it on. He twisted the nob, and the whine of it filled the flat.

True to Giovanni's word, Alexei remained sleeping. Giovanni dumped the grinds into the press. The kettle sputtered and hissed, near a boil, on the stove. "Idina asked me," he said, "to ask you if you would consider going to Dresden now. She is concerned that we—they, that is, should keep a closer eye on you."

Alannah's shoulders sagged. "I was just beginning to like life here. Why does this have to happen now?"

Giovanni pressed his lips together and picked up the kettle. He didn't reply until he'd set a cup of coffee in front of her. "How fleeting our moments of happiness seem," he said. "I know my time must be passing also." He eyed her with a sort of weary sadness. "Alexei and I will go to Dresden soon, so Alexei can meet his father. Alexei cannot live with this dread forever, and I have faith in Sir Alexander. He will welcome his son."

Alannah nodded. Suddenly a longing to see Dresden came to her, to see Alexander, to see Jack, to wander through Schwalenburg again. If Zoran wasn't in Schwalenburg, then perhaps it was as safe or unsafe as any other place. Perhaps it would be as homelike as London had become, if the people she loved were there.

"I'll go with you," she said, looking up at Ardovinni. Suddenly she couldn't bear the thought of staying behind. "Alexei—Alexei is going? Willingly?"

"Yes." Ardovinni nodded. His face twisted ruefully. "I am, perhaps, the more unwilling party now that it comes to it."

Alannah licked her lips, afraid to ask for an explanation.

"But"—Ardovinni sighed—"now that we've opened the closet we must deal with the skeletons, no? I must set my face toward Jerusalem, so to speak."

Zoran's face came to mind, quickly replaced by Daniel's. She smiled.

What would he say when he saw the bruises she'd inflicted on Peter? She could imagine his slow, approving grin.

I don't want to be afraid any more, she thought.

Aloud she said, "Then I will set my face also, come what may."

ABOUT THE AUTHOR

Geralyn Wichers writes from the Canadian prairies, where she moonlights as a manufacturing operator at a large factory. When she's not wearing a respirator and handling hazardous chemicals, Geralyn is either writing about the impending zombie apocalypse, or training to survive it by running long distances.

Geralyn is a marathoner, a foodie, and a coffee addict. She is the author of *We are the Living*, an apocalyptic story of love and hope in the midst of destruction, and *Sons of Earth*, the story of a clone finding his humanity in a dystopian near-future.

Follow her on Instagram: @geralynwichers
Visit her Facebook page: @geralynwichersauthor
Check out her website: geralynwichers.com